MORE ADVENTURES FROM BLACK PONY INN

MORE ADVENTURES FROM BLACK PONY INN

by Christine Pullein-Thompson

illustrated by Glenn Steward

AWARD PUBLICATIONS LIMITED

ISBN 0-86163-908-1

Text copyright © Christine Pullein-Thompson 1978, 1989
Illustrations copyright © Award Publications Limited 1999

Prince at Black Pony Inn first published 1976
Catastrophe at Black Pony Inn and *Good Deeds at Black Pony Inn*
first published 1989

This omnibus edition first published 1999 by
Award Publications Limited,
27 Longford Street, London NW1 3DZ

Printed in India

CONTENTS

Prince at
Black Pony Inn

CONTENTS

One
A bucking bronco

It was December and the first day of the holidays. We were all in the stable-yard staring at our newest arrival, a liver chestnut gelding of fifteen hands called Hillingdon Prince, nicknamed Bronco. Usually we take human guests at our Black Pony Inn, but he was decidedly equine and our greatest challenge yet. My brother Ben was there, tall, fair-haired, with broad shoulders and brown eyes. He is older than me, but younger than my elder brother James. Lisa, my younger sister, was also there. She is small for her age with a thin face and a determined chin and she never takes no for an answer. Bronco's owner, Mrs Nuttal, was small and wispy, with the lined look of a woman who has given her life to horses.

"Are you putting him in tonight?" she asked.

"We would rather he went out," replied Ben.

"You won't catch him, then. It took three of us five hours to catch him yesterday," she replied.

"Thanks for telling us," I replied, without meaning to sound sarcastic.

"We'll manage somehow," said Ben.

Bronco's owner was going now, starting up her horse box, looking ageless and fearless and completely without vanity.

Ben was holding Bronco. He was a beautiful horse

with breeding written all over him, with an eye which had fire, superiority, fearlessness and pure devilment in it, evenly mixed. His head had an Arab look about it, and his legs were fine with short cannon bones, which looked as strong as steel. His shoulder sloped, his chest was wide, his girth deep, his quarters strong and muscular, his back short and straight. He was the sort of horse you dream about, and he had come to us as unrideable – we were the last hope, all that stood between him and the humane killer.

I touched his shoulder and he flinched. I touched his neck and he tossed his head. He was as tense as a balloon about to burst.

"Don't touch him. Leave him alone," said Ben.

"He's mad," cried Mummy. "I forbid you to get on him, absolutely, and that's final." But she knew her words were empty words, without meaning for us. We had accepted the challenge weeks ago when we had written back to his owner saying that we would have him. There was no going back.

"Let's put him out," Ben said. "We'll catch him somehow. If we leave him in, he'll go mad."

"Your necks are more important than money," said Mummy. "Why did you take him on?"

"Because we like to be tried and tested," answered my brother. "And because we are going to succeed and earn the bonus Mrs Nuttal offered us . . ."

"That's right," I cried. "We need the money."

We always needed money. It was like a disease in our family, which we all suffered from – a chronic incurable shortage of money. And we had expensive tastes. We liked hunting, and going to shows, and Pony Club camp and keeping a horse each, and one to spare. And Mummy and Dad liked good food and dinner by candlelight and living in the large house, which Dad

12

had bought in our better-off days.

"He's lovely," said Lisa, speaking for the first time. "But he looks so wild, as though he'll never be tamed, as though he doesn't want to be, as though he despises us all, and is greater than any of us. I wish he had never come."

"Don't be stupid," I snapped, though half of me felt the same, while the other half was full of hope, and a fantastic dream of success.

We turned him into the smallest of our paddocks and he galloped round it like a wild mustang, his tail arched above his back.

Then he stood on his hind legs, before reeling round to give a display of bucking which made us all gasp.

"You'll never stay on that," cried Mummy.

"Not in a month of Sundays," said Lisa.

I began to feel weak at the knees, but Ben said, "Of course we will. Don't be silly. Sitting on that little display is no more difficult than riding across country over a testing course. Anyway, we'll lunge him tomorrow and get the bucks out of him. We're not crazy, not yet, anyway."

It was nearly dark now with a raw, biting feeling in the air, and a crispness which meant frost. Ben and I fetched hay for our new horse while everyone else disappeared indoors to get tea. He wouldn't come near us. He looked like a horse in a Western, fresh off the prairie; he smelled the air and stamped with his hoofs and I said, "I think we're going to be defeated, Ben. I feel it in my bones."

Welcoming lights shone out from the house. Mrs Mills, our oldest lodger, opened the back door to call "Tea!"

Our own horses were already settled in their loose boxes for the night, their teeth munching hay steadily, their eyes quiet and contented.

"We're going to have a fight," said Ben, walking towards the house. "And I love a fight."

"Either we win and he's broken, or we're broken," I answered.

"We'll take it slowly, make friends, win his confidence," Ben said.

"If he had come from a bad home, it might be easy. But Mrs Nuttal knows about horses, she loves them. Why should we succeed when she didn't?" I asked.

And Ben gave no answer.

We walked into the house, comfortable in our ordinary

clothes after a week of school uniform.

"We've got to succeed," said my brother, "because our reputation is at stake. If we win, more horses will follow. We will be considered experts and experts have a habit of growing rich, and I want to be rich. I want to wear breeches made by the Queen's tailor, and boots made to measure."

"You're mad," I answered. "Clothes don't matter. It's what you *are* that counts."

We poured ourselves mugs of tea in our old-fashioned kitchen which I love. Mummy still looked worried. Mrs Mills was knitting socks for us, sitting on a chair by the Aga cooker. Twinkle, our cat, was waiting for somebody to put food down for her, while Lisa was playing Monopoly by herself on the floor. There were Christmas cards hanging from the ceiling.

"We'll make friends with him tomorrow," said Ben. "We'll make him love us, Harriet, trust us. We won't ride him until he does. It's the only way."

Ben was walking up and down the kitchen, his eyes alight with excitement. I saw myself on Bronco, cantering a perfect circle. It'll take time, I thought. But the best things in life take time and, when we've finished, we'll be famous. And it seemed quite easy then, just a short, hard struggle and then victory, like embarking on a long walk and knowing you can make it with a bit of an extra effort – that it's possible. I never imagined at that moment the heartache, frenzy and anxiety which lay ahead; the tears I would shed, the sleepless nights I would endure, all for one beautiful horse, and because of a letter we had recklessly answered at the end of the summer.

Lisa continued playing Monopoly with great concentration. She is clever, obstinate, brave and infuriating in almost equal parts. Ben ate five fairy cakes in quick

15

succession without noticing what he was eating.

Mummy said, "If you break your necks I shall commit suicide."

Then Dad came in, fresh from the job he hated, to complain about the telephone bill. The moon was lighting up the stables, making everything look like fairyland outside. The ground will be rock hard tomorrow, I thought, so we won't be able to ride, and if it continues cold for a month the holidays will be over, and we won't have ridden Bronco at all. What then?

"Why do you all always collect in here?" asked Mummy. "There's three sitting-rooms. How can I get dinner with you all in here?"

"It's because of you. We love you," replied Lisa. "We want to be near you."

"I don't care. Scram!" cried Mummy. "Clear off! Play your game on a table like a human being. And stop eating cakes, Ben. You won't want any dinner."

It was like any other day and yet it was a beginning of a part of our lives we would never forget. The next few weeks were to change us, leave us harder but more wary. They were going to test us as we had never been tested before. But we didn't know that then. Ben was full of jokes and bravado and went whistling upstairs, while I sat down to read a book called *Breaking and Schooling from A-Z* by George Hammerson, late instructor at the World's Equitation Centre, New England. Outside the ground froze harder and harder and Bronco stood alone in his paddock, aloof and untamed, beautiful beyond words.

Two

A horse in a thousand

The ground was white with frost in the morning, the water troughs covered with ice thicker than the thickest glass.

"If only we had an indoor school," grumbled Ben, thawing out the yard tap with the house kettle.

"Or even an outdoor one," I replied.

"We had better spread the midden in the smallest paddock and lunge him on that."

I didn't need to ask who "him" was for Bronco seemed to dominate everything. He was like one of those people who changes the atmosphere of a room when he enters, who makes heads turn automatically, who dominates a party.

We could sense his presence as we went about our chores, watching us, measuring us up. And it wasn't a nice feeling. It was rather frightening, in a strange, uncanny way.

"I think he's lived before," I said to Ben. "I think he really was a prince."

"More likely a dictator," Ben replied.

We couldn't get near him. We simply broke the ice and threw him a wad of hay while he watched us from a distance, ears upright, eyes wary.

"We'll be stronger after breakfast," said Ben. "Let's eat lots and then tackle him. We can drive him into a corner. There's enough of us . . ."

"And we're stronger than poor Jean Nuttal," I added. We ate eggs for breakfast, and huge helpings of cereal.

"How is he?" asked Mummy.

"Still alive," replied Ben.

"Have you caught him yet?"

"We haven't tried."

"Do be careful."

"We will. I promise," I said.

"I'll wear the cross-country helmet when I ride him for the first time," announced Ben.

"Why should you ride him first?" I asked.

"Because I'm bigger and stronger," he answered.

"Yes, let him," said Mummy.

"We have to catch him first," I muttered.

Ten minutes later we approached him with a bowl of oats and halters hidden behind our backs. He wasn't interested. He looked rather bored and simply walked away.

"He's summed us up," said Ben after a time. "We had better get James and Lisa."

"And do what?" I asked.

"Drive him into a corner."

"Supposing he goes mad when he's been cornered. What then?" I asked.

"Oh don't be stupid," snapped Ben. "What's the matter with you?"

"I don't know. I just wish he was like Lorraine," I answered. Lorraine is my own grey mare and in my eyes entirely perfect.

"If he was like Lorraine, he wouldn't be here," replied Ben. Then he started to call, "Lisa, James. Come here, we need you."

"They won't hear," I said; but presently they came, pulling on boots and gloves.

19

"What is it now?" James had a half-drunk mug of coffee in one hand.

"You won't need that," said Ben, pointing at the coffee mug. "We're going to corner him."

"Corner what?"

"Bronco, of course."

"You know I hate horses," said James.

"We'll give you a rake-off when we're paid," I replied.

"If you are paid," answered James, putting his coffee mug on an upturned bucket.

We walked slowly towards Bronco, our arms outstretched. He watched us calmly, as though he had seen it all before. Then he started to walk towards the corner of the paddock nearest the stables with a knowing look in his eye.

"He's going to give in," said Ben. "I can see it on his face. He knows he's beaten."

But as he neared his corner, he started to trot. "He's going to make a break. Stand firm," cried Ben.

Lisa began running. Cassie neighed from her loose box, her eyes alight with admiration. Bronco lengthened his stride and sailed over the rail fence as though it was a mere two foot high instead of four feet six. "Run for the yard gate!" screamed Ben.

Lisa slammed the yard gate shut, while Bronco's hoofs pounded across the frozen lawn and Ben ran towards the front gates. Then Bronco's hoofs churned up the frozen strawberries and pounded across the last of the leeks. Our paying guest, Colonel Hunter, appeared, clutching *The Times*.

"He's ruining the garden," he shouted, as though we didn't know!

"He's on my strawberries," cried Mrs Mills, tiny in woolly cap, checked coat and bedroom slippers.

We'll never catch him now, I thought. He'll have to live in the garden and Dad will be furious.

Ben had closed the front gates which are wrought iron and rather majestic. "What a devil," he shouted, rubbing his hands together. "Let's drive him into the yard."

"Supposing he jumps the yard gate and disappears?" I asked.

"He can't. It's far too high," replied Ben. "But Lisa, you'll guard it, won't you? Just in case."

"Supposing he jumps Lisa too?" I asked.

"Do shut up," said Ben.

"And hurry up," cried James. "It's freezing and I need more coffee."

Bronco pounded round the garden three times before he eventually entered the yard, his head high, his nostrils snorting, while Cassie went wild with delight in her box. We tried to corner him, but he defeated us every time, brooms went flying, the bucket with James's coffee on it was kicked and the mug ended in smithereens, while James stood crying, "My coffee, my coffee!" in mock dismay.

"It was *my* mug," cried Lisa. "It had an Easter egg in it last Easter, don't you remember? Mrs Mills gave it to me. Why do you always take my things? I hate you, James."

"Shut up," yelled Ben.

Bronco was on the lawn again now, watching us with glee in his eyes.

"He's enjoying himself," Lisa said bitterly. "I can see it on his miserable face."

"We'll chase him into the paddock," shouted Ben. "Come on."

We opened the gate. Snow was now falling like soap powder from a leaden sky. It will grow thicker soon, I thought. We're in for a white Christmas.

He went into the paddock quite easily and turned round to snort at us in triumph.

"We'll have to starve him out," said Ben. "It's the only way."

"He'll jump the fence again," James cried over his

shoulder, already running towards the house. "He'll keep going round and round the garden. You had better send him back."

"He'll ruin Christmas. I hate him. He looks so superior. Look at his face now. He knows he's beaten us," said Lisa, her nose running. "My hands are freezing."

"No more food until you're caught. Do you understand?" shouted Ben. "It's being cruel to be kind. You've got to give in; otherwise it's the abattoir for you."

"Why couldn't he be ugly?" I asked. "He doesn't even look mean. He looks brave – he really is a horse in a thousand."

"That's why we must succeed," replied Ben.

"But it's cruel not to feed him," I answered.

"He's clever," said Ben, "he'll know when he's beaten. He won't starve."

"If only it was summer," I said.

The snow was falling faster and thicker now. Ben's fair hair was coated with it, and the woolly gloves I was wearing were soaked through.

"If only there wasn't a time limit. If only we had months instead of weeks to break him," I continued.

"If only, if only. Why can't you forget 'if only'?" snapped Ben.

It snowed all afternoon. Bronco looked miserable but unbeaten. We offered him food from a bucket but he refused to come near. And now he wouldn't look at us. He stared into the distance as though there lay a happier land over the horizon with green pastures and no humans to bother him; or maybe he wouldn't look for fear of being tempted. We couldn't tell. I had never left a horse without food before. It made me sad inside and I knew that I would lie awake half the night worrying about him.

We shut all the gates before we went indoors. Bronco

23

was standing, resting a leg, in the far corner of the field, still staring into the distance, his mane soaked through with melted snow. We walked in slowly.

"It's our only hope," said Ben. "Perhaps tomorrow he'll give in."

"We can give him a warm mash then and a great pile of hay," I suggested.

"Not too much. He must stay hungry if we're to catch him again," Ben replied quickly.

"I feel cruel," I said. "If it wasn't snowing, I wouldn't mind so much."

"He'll give in all the sooner because of the snow," replied Ben.

"Have you caught him?" shouted Mrs Mills, who is deaf, the minute we entered the kitchen.

"Not yet," replied Ben.

"Is he still in the garden?"

"No," I said.

I was miserable all evening because of Bronco. Later the snow stopped falling and there was a pale moon in a dreamy night sky, and I could see Bronco standing in the same corner as he had been most of the day, resting a leg, his mane all frosted, but his eyes still alert. What is he thinking? I wondered. Is he making plans? Or dreaming of his youth? What do horses think about when they stand up all night long, hungry and alone in an empty paddock?

I went to bed early and dreamed that Bronco was galloping round London, dodging the traffic until at last he met a bus full on and lay with broken legs, while a crowd collected and two strong policemen took me away in a police car.

When I got up, Bronco was standing in the same corner of the paddock, his belly line run up like a greyhound's.

The landscape was sprinkled with snow, with the ground rock hard underneath. The sky was a cold grey with no promise of sunshine in it. I dressed quickly and put some oats in my pocket and approached Bronco, talking to him all the time, saying, "Come on, I'm not going to hurt you. I'm your friend. You needn't be afraid."

But I knew that he wasn't afraid. He never had been. He just didn't want to be a slave for the rest of his life. I knew how he felt. He was too clever to be a horse, to accept a horse's life without question. He had broken the ice in his trough with a hoof, but it was nearly empty, so soon he would be thirsty too.

I looked at his proud head and wondered how long it would take him to give in. I imagined him starving to death. I said, "Please give in, Bronco, please." But he simply looked away like someone who doesn't want to know you.

"All right, have it your own way," I said then. "Starve to death. Don't you know we all have to work? You can't have oats and hay and not work. It's the same for all of us. We would all like life to be one long holiday. But it can't be. Can't you accept that?"

Hearing the anger in my voice, he started to trot in a small circle, snorting and blowing, as though trying to say, "I'm not giving in."

"Have it your own way then," I shouted. "Starve to death."

I left the paddock, slamming the yard gate after me, and the snow started to fall again. From the kitchen came the sound of Lisa and Ben shouting at one another. We've made another mistake, I thought, and all for the sake of money. There won't be any riding these holidays anyway, the weather isn't good enough.

Then Ben appeared, crying, "Any luck?"

I answered rudely, "Of course not, you fool. He's far too clever for us."

Ben asked, "Did you really expect to succeed in twenty-four hours? You must be mad."

And I knew he was right, that we couldn't expect breaking Bronco to be easy, that it had to be long and hard.

"It will take time but we'll win," said Ben. "He's looking less confident already. He's a tough nut and you can only crack them with tough nutcrackers; there's no other way."

"And we're the nutcrackers?" I said. Ben nodded. "And supposing we break?" I asked.

"Nutcrackers don't break," replied Ben.

Three

I'll wear the crash-helmet

The next day was the same, only worse, because now I couldn't look at Bronco without feeling cruel. He had hardly any stomach on him now, and it went right in where the hair parted on his flank. Poverty marks had appeared, and his neck looked thin and droopy and his hoofs were full of snow. A lump rose in my throat when I looked at him. I said, "Can't we give in? Supposing he gets colic or gets really ill standing out in the cold with nothing inside him?" There was only solid ice in his trough now.

"Just another twenty-four hours," pleaded Ben, "and then we can telephone Jean Nuttal and admit defeat, and Roy can come with his humane killer, and *bang, bang*, it will be all over."

"He looks so pitiful," I said.

"It's no worse than war. Ask Colonel Hunter about wars. He'll tell you about the trenches in the 1918 war; the mud and the horses lying half dead with their quarters shot away. And the rats gnawing at – "

"Shut up," I screamed, my hands over my ears.

"We are being cruel to be kind," bellowed Ben.

"Two wrongs don't make a right," I yelled.

"It's always darkest before dawn," quoted Ben. "He's looking at us. Look, Harriet." It was true. He wasn't looking into the distance any more but staring at us with clear, courageous eyes, which I thought held respect in them.

"Let's give him some water," said Ben. "We can stand by the trough while he drinks." We fetched a bucketful and poured it in.

He approached gingerly, and drank with his nose outstretched. Ben touched his mane and he moved away, but calmly and quietly, as though the human hand simply annoyed him a little.

"We're winning," said Ben.

"We hope," I added.

Our own horses needed exercising. We rode them out, riding one, leading another, across the frozen landscape, our hands and feet freezing, while they slipped and slid and the snow blew in our faces.

"We had better cut their oats altogether," said Ben. "We don't want any azatoria."

"They're not very fit," I answered.

"But it's still possible," said Ben.

Bronco was looking over the fence when we returned. "I think he's come to a decision," said Ben. "I think he's changed his mind."

I had the same feeling. He was looking at everything with interest now; as though he might yet take part in it. He was no longer staring at us from the outside, he was coming inside our lives to join us.

"We'll catch him after lunch," said Ben. "I knew he was clever. He's worked it out, he understands. We must treat him as though he's clever. It's no good treating him as though he's a normal horse."

We were excited. It was as though we were suddenly capable of clearing the first obstacle in a long line of jumps, each one growing higher. We thought we had found the key to Bronco's character. That one step would lead to another. Ben started to whistle and I said,

29

"He will be marvellous to ride. He'll learn everything so quickly with his sort of brain."

"And just think of riding him across country," exclaimed Ben. "Wow!"

"I wish it was tomorrow already. That he was already caught and tamed," I said.

We stayed indoors for a long time after lunch watching the snow falling. Ben fell asleep with a book in his hand, while James paced the kitchen, saying, "I can't stand college for another term. I can't stay there another two years . . ." And Mummy looked distracted while Lisa sat next door watching television.

At three o'clock I wakened Ben and we wrapped ourselves up in thick mufflers and our warmest coats and fed our own horses, because we wanted Bronco to see that "good" horses have lots of food while "bad" horses

have nothing. He watched us over the fence with snow-crusted mane and hoofs washed pale by the snow. His blaze looked off-white on his forehead against the whiteness of the snow; the trees were bowed under the weight of it and the flowers were buried. The house looked smaller thatched by snow, and everything seemed much stiller and somehow muted, and older – far, far older.

When we had fed our own horses, we approached Bronco with oats in a bucket and he walked up to us and gave Ben a familiar nudge, as if to say, "All right, you win."

I gave Ben a rope to attach to the headcollar we had left on him, and he followed us into a loose box. We fetched him water and hay and then, very slowly, we put a rug on him with straw underneath. We hardly dared to breathe for fear of upsetting him. Then we bolted his door top and bottom and rushed into the house screaming, "He's caught. He's in a box, he's given in."

Ben started to dance round the kitchen crying, "Think of all that lovely money – and a bonus if we succeed. What shall we spend it on?"

"Don't count your chickens before they are hatched," said Mummy from behind the washing-machine.

But Ben wouldn't stop. "A black hunting coat for you, Harriet," he cried. "And mahogany-topped hunting boots for me. Or a dinner jacket. How about a dinner jacket? How would I look in a dinner jacket?"

"What about a saddle each?" I asked. "A jumping saddle; a plastic one for you because it won't need much cleaning, and a leather one for me?"

After a time I went upstairs and stared out of the passage window. Bronco was looking out of his box, his eyes shining, and he didn't look as though he had suffered a defeat; he looked pleased with himself, confident. Cassie was leaning out of her box trying to touch

31

his nose, and it wasn't snowing any more. Everything looked clean and peaceful and I suddenly remembered that there were only a few days left until Christmas, and I hadn't bought Mummy a present.

The next day we put a saddle on Bronco and he shook all over like a leaf in a wind and cowered in one corner of his box. I gave him bits of bread and talked to him, but he went on trembling, and Ben said, "We had better leave it on him, let's tie him up. He's got to get used to it."

So we tied him to the ring on the manger and left him trembling, his quarters hunched under him, his eyes wild. And we both knew it was a setback to our hopes, though we didn't say so.

"He really is afraid now," said Ben.

"Exactly," I agreed. "He's terrified. I wonder why?"

"Your guess is as good as mine," replied Ben.

We spent the rest of the morning carting the midden to the smallest of the paddocks, so that we could ride on it. After a time our arms started to ache, and we were so hot we took off our coats.

"Where's Lisa? Why doesn't she help?" cried Ben. "She'll ride on it as soon as it's finished, for certain."

"There's only two wheelbarrows, and she's much slower than us," I answered.

We kept slipping on frozen snow and our clothes started to smell and then, at last, it was lunch-time. Bronco was still shaking, so we took off his saddle, talking to him all the time.

"There must be some reason for his fear," I said.

"I think he's pretending," answered Ben, walking towards the house.

"I don't agree," I said. Dad was home and made us change our trousers before lunch.

James had been tobogganing with friends and was ruddy-faced and cheerful and Lisa was warm from reading all morning with Twinkle on her lap. Mrs Mills had been for a walk and kept shouting about the snow and how deep it was on the common.

Afterwards we decided to exercise Lorraine and Ben's Welsh cob, Solitaire, and we turned the others out to exercise themselves, all except Bronco who rushed round and round his box like a lunatic.

"He's getting exercise, anyway," said Ben as we set off across the common.

Our mounts made hoofmarks in the untouched snow and the sky was now an endless blue. We walked and

jogged, but there was a wind which stung our faces and soon we turned homewards again.

"Let's lunge Bronco tomorrow in a full set of tack," suggested Ben. "He can buck to his heart's content then."

"And he needs exercise," I agreed.

"We'll lunge him for ages," said Ben. "And the next day we'll lead him out off a horse for miles and miles. And the next day we'll ride him."

"If the weather allows," I answered.

"The roads are clear now," replied Ben.

"And we must have a target. One never gets anywhere without a deadline."

"I think we should take our time," I answered.

But Ben wouldn't listen. Like Lisa, he hated waiting for anything. He wanted money and success and fame, all at once before he was any older. We were all tired of being poor, of watching other pupils at school boasting of computers and new bicycles, of holidays in exotic places and TVs in their bedrooms. They gave the teachers end-of-term presents which cost a fortune, and went to the cinema every week, and bought make-up and had their hair cut at the most expensive shop in the area. And Ben wanted all those things too. So we hurried home and settled the horses for the night, and Bronco nudged us over his box door like an old friend, his liver chestnut coat gleaming, his eyes sparkling.

"We've won one battle already, can't you see?" said Ben. "He trusts us!"

"Touch wood," I cried, grabbing the loose box door.

"It's all in his mind. He's accepted us now as superior beings," Ben said with frightening self-confidence.

"I wish the weather would change. If we fall on this ground, it will really hurt," I said.

"We're not going to fall," replied Ben.

When Lorraine was rugged up for the night, I joined
Bronco in his box. "We're your friends," I told him.
"Really, truly."

He smelled my hair and pushed me with his nose. He
was calm and friendly, but I had the feeling that he was
keeping his options open, that he was fully independent
with a mind of his own, because he was himself a leader
who wouldn't want to be led.

"Be nice to us," I pleaded. "Please."

I followed Ben into the house, thinking: He's making
it sound too easy, nothing in life is that easy.

And I dreamed that night that Bronco was galloping with Ben along a long, long road, while I followed on Lorraine, calling, "Stop, please, stop."

Next morning everything was dripping and the air was warm. We tacked up Bronco and lunged him and he looked at us with confidence and did everything he was told. We lunged him at the walk and trot, first on one rein and then on another, and it was obvious that he had been lunged many times before.

"Let's ride him after an early lunch," said Ben.

"Isn't it a bit soon?"

"I'm not scared, and he isn't, just look at him!" cried Ben. "After all, he's been here four days. It's ridiculous how little we've done."

"I think we should wait."

"Well, I don't," answered Ben. And as usual he won. I was filled with misgivings all through lunch. Ben had sworn me to secrecy. "You know how Mummy is – nothing but nerves. I'll wear the crash-helmet. We can lead him for a few miles first, exhaust him, then I'll get on," he said. "You lead him to begin with and I'll follow on my bike."

"The weather's changed," shouted Mrs Mills. "You would never think there was a drought back in the summer, would you?"

"No," I shouted back.

"When can I have a motor-bike?" asked James. "I'm seventeen, and all my friends have motor-bikes."

"You'll kill yourself on a motor-bike," replied Mummy.

"My friends haven't. Why can't I have a motor-bike for Christmas?" asked James, sounding like a three-year-old.

And I realised that tomorrow was Christmas Eve and

I still hadn't bought Mummy's present.

"Let's leave Bronco in today. I need to go shopping," I said.

"We can't. He needs exercising. We can't leave him cooped up in his box day after day. He'll go mad," replied Ben.

"How is he?" asked Mummy.

"Marvellous, super, a reformed character," said Ben.

"I shall be dashing in to shop tomorrow, Harriet," said Mummy. "So you can come with me; and will you make the brandy butter again this year?"

"Yes," I answered quickly, because I adore brandy butter.

"And James, you'll do the tree again, won't you?" asked Mummy.

It didn't feel like Christmas. Bronco had set our minds elsewhere and now I wasn't ready.

Lunch was over by now. "Let's put it off," I whispered to Ben. But he shook his head. "You can shop when we get back, we won't be late," he said. "And do stop fussing. You won't be hurt. I'm not asking you to ride him."

"It's not that," I answered. "It's just that I don't want anything to go wrong before Christmas."

"It won't. I promise," said Ben with a wide grin. "I'm looking forward to this afternoon. I love challenges."

"Well, I don't," I answered, following him towards the stables, filled with trepidation.

Four

Stop him, for heaven's sake!

I tacked up Lorraine. The yard was full of slush, but outside, on the common, the snow was still white and thick, only wet at the edges like melting ice cream.

Ben fetched his bicycle and leaned it against the wall. He tacked up Bronco, while I mounted Lorraine. He tucked the reins under the stirrup irons and attached a headcollar rope to the bit.

"Are you ready?" he asked. I pulled up my girth, Lorraine was anxious to be off. I looked at my watch and it said two o'clock. Ben was putting on the cross-country helmet we share, pressing the fasteners together. He was wearing his rubber riding-boots, two jerseys, jeans and an anorak. He handed me the headcollar rope and I thought: This is it, and pushed Lorraine on with my legs.

At that moment, Lisa came running, crying, "Where are you going? What are you doing?"

Ben said, "Mind your own business. Go away," and mounted his bike. And somewhere, deep within myself, I knew that what we were doing was wrong, that we should have told Mummy, and warned someone that there could be trouble ahead.

"I'm coming," shouted Lisa. "Where's my bike?"

"Punctured," said Ben.

The common was deserted. Bronco and Lorraine

went well together. He was larger and his stride was longer, but she lengthened hers and they kept pace with one another. The trees were emerging from the snow, and the grass, pushing its head through the whiteness, looked green and new. But underneath the snow and the slush, the ground was still hard. Ben was having a tough time on his bike. "Make for the woods," he called. "I'll meet you on the far side, okay?"

"Okay," I shouted.

It was peaceful in the woods and strangely silent because everything was muffled by the snow. The paths looked narrower because of it and were hard to find and the trees were still bowed by the weight they had carried and looked tired, like people who have walked a long way.

Lorraine insisted on trotting and Bronco seemed to be enjoying himself. I could have been happy too if I could

have rid myself of the anxiety gnawing at my mind. I tried to sing, but the words died in my throat. I said to myself, "Cheer up, Harriet," but nothing would kill the awful sense of foreboding which hung over me.

I could see beyond the woods now, to the lane where Ben would be waiting. And I could feel the sun trying to push through the clouds and the air growing lighter. I remembered the times I had ridden through the woods before, good and bad times.

"How is he going?" yelled Ben when I reached the lane. "Has he settled yet?"

"If you mean is he tired, the answer is no," I answered.

"We had better go on then," he said.

I don't know how many miles we covered. I simply let Lorraine trot on and on, while Ben pedalled behind and the minutes turned into hours. Then, when we had reached the old disused railway track, I drew rein, and said, "He's tired now."

The old railway track held memories for me too, good and bad. Ben leaned his bike against a tree, "I'll come back for it later," he said.

"Supposing it's stolen?" I asked.

"It won't be," he said. And suddenly I knew that we were both talking to cover up our fear.

"You don't have to ride him," I said, dismounting.

"What do you mean?" cried Ben.

"He's had a good exercise. We can go back now," I answered.

"Thank you very much," replied Ben. "And I've ridden all this way on my bike – very nice, I must say."

He was checking the fastening on his helmet now, adjusting his anorak, making sure everything was well arranged before he mounted.

"Am I to hold him?" I asked.

"Of course. What do you think?" said Ben.

He was being aggressive because he was scared. I'm scared sometimes; I know what it's like. I'm scared when I'm called to see the headmaster at school; or when I walk home across the common in the dark.

"You can walk with me, lead both horses," said Ben.

Everything seemed very still. There wasn't a soul to be seen, not even a rabbit. I pulled up Bronco's girth. He had got his second wind by this time and was staring into the distance as though searching for something.

"I think we should postpone it," I said. But Ben had his foot in a stirrup.

"Hold on, for heaven's sake," he said.

The hair was standing up on the back of my neck as Ben swung his leg across the saddle. I could feel Bronco growing tense, and silently I started to pray, "Please, God, make it all right."

Ben sat down as though he was landing on a row of pins. He started to talk to Bronco and the air was suddenly full of electricity as before a storm. And then we were moving on and Ben was saying in a relieved voice, "I knew it would be all right."

"Touch wood," I said, but there was no wood to touch.

We had to go on because we were afraid to turn round. Weeds and grass grew on the track which had been a single-track railway until a few years ago. I could see cows in the distance, clustered close together, and a tractor on a hill moving slowly and dramatically. Lorraine was reluctant to go on, but Bronco hurried, his eyes rolling backwards, his ears straight upwards with anxiety. I could smell the sweat rising from his body, sending steam into the air. Ben was sitting very still, not daring to move a muscle. He wasn't smiling. It was nearly half past three now. In half an hour it would be

41

dark. I felt full of apprehension.

"We should be turning back," I said.

"In a minute," answered Ben in little more than a whisper. "He's too nervous to turn at the moment."

I thought of Mummy or Mrs Mills putting on the kettle for tea. I thought of Limpet and Jigsaw waiting for their hay, and Cassie with her foal Windfall waiting to come in. The sky was growing darker already. It seemed to promise something – snow or rain? I didn't know which.

"We must go back," I said again.

"Have patience," replied Ben.

"It will soon be dark," I said.

"Try and stop," Ben said after a time. "Try and turn round."

"Whoa, walk," I said, as though I was lunging Bronco. "Whoa . . ."

There wasn't much room to turn two horses. Bronco was still very tense, while Lorraine was in a hurry to go home to her warm box and evening feed, and somehow their stirrups caught together. Bronco leaped high into the air. "Hold on," shouted Ben.

Bronco was on the wrong side of Lorraine now, her shoulder between us.

"I'm trying to," I shouted. Suddenly Bronco was on his hind legs and Lorraine was swinging into him with her quarters. Then one of them knocked me sideways and the next moment I was lying in the snow watching Bronco bucking and then galloping, with my brother still on top, crying "Whoa! Do something, Harriet! Stop him, for heaven's sake!" And I was scared, more scared than I had ever been before and I saw dreadful tragedy in my mind.

Then I was running, shouting, "Stop! Whoa!" But there was nothing anywhere, no help, no house, just the

track going on mile after mile, like a miniature race-track. And no hope either. The horses were small in the distance already. We didn't tell anyone where we were going, I thought. They won't know where to look. And I blamed myself for giving in to Ben, for not being strong enough to say No.

Soon snow and mud hung heavy on my boots, but nothing could be as heavy as my heart. It was almost dark and sleet or snow brushed my face, cold and wet.

The track was suddenly hell on earth. I wished I was someone else altogether – a neat town child living in an apartment, a little girl still at playgroup, anyone but Harriet Pemberton. And then I started to pray, "God, make Ben all right. It's all that matters, just Ben. Kill the horses if you must, but make Ben all right."

I could feel tears running down my face, stupid, childish tears. The track felt the loneliest place on earth and I saw myself never reaching home, and Mummy sending out search parties and Dad in a rage, Mrs Mills shouting, "Why didn't they say where they were going?" And Lisa would be crying, and James drinking more and more coffee. At intervals I stumbled on great clods of snow and mud thrown out of the horses' hoofs as they galloped.

Then, at last, I saw Ben approaching through the falling sleet, holding an arm, saying, "I couldn't stop them." And, for a minute, the fact that he was alive was all that mattered. Then I saw that his arm was hanging in a peculiar way and his face was very white in the gathering darkness. "Your arm's smashed, isn't it?" I said.

And he said, "Yes, I don't know how it happened." I started to cry again and Ben, seeing me crying, tried to laugh. "I always was a reckless fool," he said.

"What are we going to do?" I asked next.

"I'll make for the road and get help," he said. "Look down there, there are lights moving on a road. The lights are cars. It's only two fields away as the crow flies, and I reckon there's only a gate to climb and I can manage that, if you'll just help me through this fence."

"What about me? What am I to do?" I asked. And then I saw my own dear Lorraine coming back and I knew the answer. "I'll go on and find Bronco," I said.

"I hoped you'd say that," replied Ben.

Five

Are you all right?

I helped Ben through the fence. I couldn't bear to look
at his arm.

"How did it happen?" I asked, pointing.

"I don't know. I think my foot caught in the stirrup
and Bronco jumped on my arm. I'm a bit hazy – sorry,"
he answered.

"You had the little stirrups. Why didn't we change
them? Why are we such fools?" I asked.

Ben gave a twisted kind of smile. "Does it hurt?" I
asked.

"Not much. It's kind of numb now."

I watched Ben walk away into the dusk towards the
cars which looked like shooting stars on the road below.
Then I mounted Lorraine and rode on. She didn't want
to go, but eventually we were cantering on with sleet in
our faces in the last dwindling light of day. And as I
rode I started to wonder what we would do with Bronco
now. Would he have to be killed? Was there no more
hope? And I knew we had failed. We had rushed instead
of taking our time. And I knew that with horses the saying More haste, less speed is true a hundred times over.
And because of that Bronco's last chance was gone.

Lorraine felt tired, the mud and snow were heavy in
her hoofs and the sleet was turning into hail which hit
our faces like bullets until we could hardly see anything

any more; my feet were freezing in my boots, and my gloves were wet and flabby on my freezing hands.

Then, after a time, I realised that the hail had become snow and was falling like confetti from the night sky. I had been riding in a sort of dream for an hour or more and had reached the old station with the signal box before it. Lorraine's mane was heavy with snow and my hands were numb. It's time to go back, I thought. I shall never make it if I stay out any longer. And then I heard a whinny and saw Bronco standing beyond the signal box, with his reins broken and his saddle hanging over one side. He looked very tired. I dismounted and called him and he stood shaking like a leaf, as though he expected a beating. I waited and he came to me and stood waiting to be taken home. I knew that this was a victory, though a hollow one. I put his saddle straight with numb fingers and then I remounted and turned Lorraine's head for home. The snow was growing thicker, it wasn't falling like confetti any more but in the biggest flakes I had ever seen.

Suddenly I was frightened. It was six o'clock and we were a long way from home. The snow was balling in the horses' hoofs now, so at times Lorraine felt as though she was on stilts and, because of that, we couldn't hurry. Everything was silent, so that I had the feeling that we were the only things left alive in the whole world.

When we came to the end of the track, I turned the horses' heads for the road below. The snow was much deeper and we slid down a long hill and low branches smothered me with snow. The snow in the horses' hoofs made them clumsy. I thought about Ben. Where was he? Had he been given a lift home? Was he in hospital having his arm mended? Or had he fainted somewhere and was now dying from exposure? Because I was tired, everything started to seem very bad and I began to cry again. I left everything to Lorraine and she found her way down a track which led to the road, through snow and branches and over the ruts underneath.

Cars were moving very slowly along the road in single file. They were revving up and skidding and it looked like some crazy game down below. I wondered how we would survive on the road, but I couldn't turn back because the snow was too deep and we were too tired.

I halted the horses, and we stood and stared, and I swear that all our hearts sank when we looked at the traffic. There were men pushing cars and men digging with shovels, and women screaming at no one in particular. There were cars in a ditch and cars across the road and a beautiful new Renault upside down. The horses raised tired heads and looked, and I felt some of the spirit go out of Lorraine. And I said, "We must go on."

It was very slippery on the road. People looked at us as though we were mad and several people shouted unprintable words at us. One jolly man called, "Give us a tow." Lorraine slipped on to her knees, while Bronco's hind legs slipped under him so that he was sitting on the road. Somehow they struggled into standing positions again and I thought help must come soon – gritting lorries, snowploughs, something. I dismounted on to numb feet and pulled snow-wet reins over Lorraine's head and suddenly I didn't know which way to turn for home. I stood and stared at the road and I knew we couldn't travel along it; and I looked back to the track we had come down and it was black as night. The horses recognised my despair and hung their heads. Then a young man came across the road towards me. He had long hair and tattered jeans, and he was very thin and there was a gap in his teeth.

He asked, "Are you all right? You're not going to faint, are you?"

I said, "No, I'm not, thank you. Do I look like it? because actually I'm quite all right, thank you; it's just the road . . ." and I knew my voice sounded as though I was on the verge of tears.

"Is there anyone you can phone?" he asked. "There's a phone box just twenty yards on and I can hold your nags if you like."

"I haven't any money," I said.

"Well, I have. I can't move my old bus anyway, so I don't mind waiting," he said. "Walk on the verge and you'll be all right."

He gave me some money and took the reins from me.

When I reached the box there was a man inside shouting at the AA. He was wearing a suit and carrying

an umbrella and a small case, and he was very angry. Finally he came out swearing under his breath and said, "Don't be long. I want to telephone the council, this is disgraceful. Where are the gritting lorries?"

My numb fingers dropped the receiver twice, but then I was talking to James, saying, "I'm stuck on a road and I can't move, the horses can't stand up. Has Ben come home?"

"Ben's gone to hospital," he said. "Where are you?"

"I don't know."

"Look on the phone, it says somewhere. Don't be a fool," replied James.

"It says The Ridgeway," I answered.

"Okay," replied James. "We'll pick you up."

"I've got two horses," I shouted. But he had rung off. I wondered how they would manage without Ben. He knows how to manage the Land Rover, when to push down the yellow knob, or when to put it in four-wheel drive. Mummy is not mechanical and Dad would still be at work. I found the young man still holding the horses.

"All right?" he asked. "Everything in order?"

"Yes, thank you very much," I said.

Some of the cars had gone but more kept arriving, and then grinding to a halt. Three men were turning the Renault over.

"You look a bit pale. How about some coffee?"

"Yes, please."

His car was old and battered; the sort the police stop to demand an MOT certificate, insurance, licence. One of its bumpers was tied on with string. The coffee was lukewarm and the cup I drank it from had sugar encrusted on the edge, but it didn't matter.

"Have you had an accident?" he asked when I had finished drinking and handed back the cup.

"Not me, my brother."

50

"Bad?"

"Yes, smashed-up arm." I didn't want to talk about it, because thinking of it made me feel sick.

"He's not up there, is he?" he asked, pointing at the hills.

"No, he's in hospital."

"Do you want another coffee?"

"No thank you."

"I'll stay with you until someone comes."

"I'll be all right," I answered.

A breakdown lorry had appeared and two AA vans and a police car. The snow wasn't falling any more.

"Who's coming for you?"

"I don't know, just someone," I answered.

"If you could put your horses somewhere, I could take you home," he said.

"I'm all right. You had better go," I said. "You've been marvellous."

He looked at the police car and said, "Okay, if you're sure you're all right."

I said, "Yes. And thanks a million for saving me."

"Don't mention it," he answered.

Then I saw the bright lights of a Land Rover and trailer, and the horses pricked their ears. I felt hope come back. I waved to my rescuer and shouted, "I'm all right now. Look!"

And he shouted, "Good! Bye for now."

The Land Rover slithered to a halt and James was yelling at me, "Hurry up. Get the ramp down. There's only me. Why didn't you tell me the police were here?"

"Where's Mummy, then?" I shouted back.

"In hospital with Ben. What do you think?" yelled James, leaping out. "And a lot of new guests have arrived and it's utter chaos at home – hell on earth."

We had the ramp down now. James had forgotten

51

headcollars. "They'll have to travel loose," he said. "Hurry up, will you."

The police were questioning my rescuer now, and a young officer with a moustache was writing in a notebook.

Luckily the horses boxed without any fuss. I threw up the ramp. "We'll turn at the next crossroads," said James.

He drove too fast. I could feel the trailer rocking behind us. The Land Rover was in four-wheel drive and
made a lot of noise. "Why did you do it?" he shouted.

"Do what?"

"Go all that way without telling anyone where you
were going," shouted James.

I didn't answer for a bit; then I said, "Because we
didn't want to be stopped."

"Fools! You knew you were wrong, then, and look at
the trouble you've caused. I'm breaking the law because
of you. And the house is full of demented guests – all because of you."

He turned down a side road and the Land Rover
skidded and he pushed down the yellow knob and suddenly the day seemed to have lasted for ever and I
started to long for bed, for peace and warmth and a
great mug of hot soup.

"I suppose the guests are having my room," I said.

"No, they all crammed together in the attic – five
kids and one incapable mother. Mummy had to take
them in. She said it was almost Christmas and she
couldn't turn them away, because it would be like Mary
and Jesus and no room at the inn."

"Are they going to be with us for Christmas, then?" I
asked.

"Yes, and the food will run out and they've brought
two frightful dogs. They were evicted, if you know what
that means."

"Of course I do – turned out. But who's paying?" I
asked.

"Social services, of course," replied James, nearly hit-
ting a car coming the other way. "You know how
Mummy is, she believes every hard-luck story she hears.
I don't know what Dad will say when he comes home."

"They sound nice," I said through chattering teeth.

We were nearly home now. I could see the common still white with snow, the pond romantic in the moonlight, familiar trees suddenly strangers in their coats of snow.

At that moment I loved home more than ever before. It was all I wanted – the warm kitchen, the smell of supper and my bed waiting for me.

Lisa was toiling in the stable-yard. "At last," she shouted. "Everything's ready. Just put the horses in and go away. I can manage."

James stopped the Land Rover with a jerk.

Inside the trailer the horses were soaked with sweat. They fell out on trembling legs and looked round the familiar yard with pleased eyes. Their boxes were ready, thick with straw, with bulging haynets and water buckets full to the brim.

"Go away," shouted Lisa. "I can manage. Go in and get warm."

"What about Bronco?" I asked.

"I can manage," shouted Lisa. "I'm not six years old."

James was unhitching the trailer. I was shaking all over with cold and exhaustion and I could hear dogs yapping and a strange voice yelling, "Shut up, will you. I said Shut up. Do you want a thrashing?" And somewhere a baby was crying.

Then Mrs Mills opened the door to call, "Is that you, Harriet? Come in, dear, at once. You must be half dead!"

And I told my shaking legs to walk and they walked, while behind me I could hear Lisa shouting, "Stand up, Bronco, will you. Get over," as though she handled him every day of the week, and James putting the Land Rover away.

Six
Christmas Eve

Our new guest was called Mrs Cutting and she had five children of various ages, a scruffy dog called Trixie and another larger, smooth-coated one called Spot. Mrs Mills introduced me, but my mind went blank and I could think of nothing to say. Mrs Cutting said, "Pleased to meet you." She was hardly taller than Lisa and her hair was turning grey and her face was a mass of wrinkles. She can't have been more than forty but she looked much older. She kept calling to the dogs, "Sit down, Spot," and, "Off that chair, Trixie, you're not at home." And when she wasn't shouting at the dogs she was screaming at her children.

I wondered how long Colonel Hunter and Dad would stand her. Mrs Mills pushed a mug of steaming tea into my hand and my feet started to come back to life.

James had started to decorate the Christmas tree and a heap of new Christmas cards had arrived, including one from a previous guest of ours called Commander Cooley. It came from one of Her Majesty's prisons. I couldn't believe that Christmas had almost arrived – another Christmas. My mind kept returning to Bronco. They can't shoot him on Christmas Day, I thought.

Then Mummy returned, calling, "Where's Harriet? Isn't she back yet?"

I called, "Yes, I'm here. I'm all right."

"They are keeping Ben in overnight," she said, looking me up and down. "Are you all right?"

"Yes."

"However did you get the horses home?" she asked.

"It's a long story," I answered, not wishing to get James into trouble. "How is Ben? Is he unconscious?"

"They are setting his arm now. They had to wait for the consultant to come. It's a bit complicated," replied Mummy. "But he'll be all right. Whatever made you do it, Harriet?"

"Do what?" I asked to gain time.

"Go out so late without telling us where you were going," replied Mummy.

"It's a long story," I said again.

"He'll have to go," Mummy answered.

"Who?"

"Bronco. You can't keep him. He isn't safe. He's bad," replied Mummy. "There must be bad horses, just as there are bad people, and he's one."

"But it was our fault," I said. "We rushed him. We tried to move too quickly. We didn't give him time. It wasn't his fault at all. He's all right. He's super, honestly, Mummy."

"You can't manage him on your own," answered Mummy. "And Ben can't help you now, so he must go."

"Not until after Christmas," I answered desperately.

"Why?"

"Because it isn't Christian to kill a horse at Christmas," I said.

"You'll have to telephone Mrs Nuttal," said Mummy, as though I hadn't spoken. "You can ask her to take him away. You needn't ask to be paid anything, just let her take him away and let her vet put him down. Now don't argue, do it . . ."

"I can't," I said. "My lips won't speak the words, my

feet won't take me to the telephone. I can't anyway without asking Ben. He's in it too, Mummy. He's broken his arm but he won't want to give in. Please."

"Leave it until the morning, then," replied Mummy after a short silence. "You'll be stronger then."

"I'll wait until Ben is home," I said. "He'll know what to say."

It was late by now and no one had had any dinner. Colonel Hunter was sitting in the dining-room, coughing at intervals to draw attention to himself.

Mummy grilled chops while Mrs Mills cooked potatoes, and Mrs Cutting said, "I'd rather eat in the kitchen if you don't mind, and the kids can have bread and jam upstairs."

She had brought tins of dog food, a potty, baby clothes and nappies, and not much else.

I said, "What are your children called?"

"Millie, Pete, Jimmy, George and the baby is Saman-
tha, that's a lovely name, isn't it?" she replied.

"Super," I said. I went upstairs and changed into dry
jeans and a polo-necked jumper and felt warm for the
first time in hours. I was beginning to feel more opti-
mistic. The afternoon and evening seemed like a nightmare now. Outside there was a proud, pale moon riding
high in the sky.

"The horses are all right," said Lisa, coming into my
room. "And guess what – I've been sitting on Bronco's
back."

"You haven't!" I cried.

"I have. Do you want to see? He's as quiet as a lamb."

"No, thank you – just don't tell Mummy, that's all," I
said.

"I got on off the partition. He didn't mind at all. He
smelled my foot, if you want to know," continued Lisa.
"It was dead easy."

"He's tired, dead tired," I said. "He won't be the
same tomorrow."

"He's not going to be shot, is he?" asked Lisa.

"Not if I can help it."

"He's so beautiful. We must call him Prince when he's
schooled. We can't go on calling him Bronco when he's
perfect," said Lisa.

"That's a long way away," I answered.

"But he will be one day, won't he?" asked Lisa,
staring at me with worried brown eyes.

"I hope so . . .!"

Dinner seemed to last for ever. Mrs Cutting wouldn't
stop talking and Colonel Hunter kept ringing the little
bell on the dining-room table and wanting things like
mustard. And I missed Ben.

Dad came in late and I left Mummy to talk to him. But later he sat on my bed and said, "Harriet, you must try to be more responsible or we'll have to give up keeping horses. You broke the golden rule, didn't you? You didn't tell us where you were going. You must always say – mountaineers have to do it, so do yachtsmen if they've got any sense. It's not fair on the people left behind. If things had worked out differently, we could still be looking for you. Now tell me exactly what happened to you both."

So I told him, beginning at the beginning and ending with telephoning home. But he said, "Go on, how did you get home? You haven't finished, have you?"

And I answered, "I'm not saying unless you promise not to be cross."

"Who with?"

"Any of us."

"All right."

So I told him how James had come and rescued me and he said, "I can't blame him, given his age and the situation. I would have done the same but it mustn't happen again, Harriet, you see that, don't you? Because he isn't covered by insurance and if there had been an accident we could be paying damages for the rest of our lives. And what if he'd been hurt as well – perhaps even crippled for life? That would be terrible, wouldn't it?"

"Yes, but I didn't ask him to come," I answered. "And now, what about Bronco?"

"Let's leave that until after Christmas. I can't face any more difficulties just now. Just forget him until Boxing Day," said Dad, who isn't horsy so doesn't know that you can't just forget horses.

So he kissed me goodnight and Mummy came in too and said, "Sleep well, Harriet darling, and don't bother to get up early. I've just telephoned the hospital and Ben is all right, there's nothing to worry about, and it's nearly Christmas . . . so don't do anything silly tomorrow, will you, because we don't want Christmas spoilt."

"What about the Cuttings?" I asked.

"They'll be all right. I'm just organising their stockings," she answered, kissing me goodnight. I fell asleep instantly into that heavy dreamless sleep which comes with complete exhaustion.

I overslept the next morning and when I rushed down to the stables, I found Lorraine and Bronco standing at the back of their boxes, looking very tired. They both whinnied a welcome and I looked them over for cuts and scratches but found none. Presently Mike, one of our lodgers, appeared and helped me muck out. He has red hair and freckles and is immensely strong. He isn't clever, but he's kind and likes horses, and though his father is in and out of prison the whole time he's as honest as the day is long. He is nearly sixteen and has a girlfriend called Karen who lives in the village, so we don't see much of him. Soon he'll leave school and work permanently at the near-by farm where he's been helping out for more than a year. But today, at any rate, he decided to help me.

"Seeing that Ben isn't 'ere," he said with a grin. "And Christmas is just round the corner. I hear you had a bit of a to-do yesterday one way and another. What happened?"

So I told him as we mucked out, and slowly the sun came out and everything started to drip with melting snow.

Later Mummy took me shopping and I bought her a lipstick and a book of cartoons for Christmas, and Dad a packet of cigars, and Mrs Mills two embroidered handkerchiefs, and Mike a penknife. I had already bought my brothers and Lisa books, and Colonel Hunter a calendar. Mummy bought the Cuttings presents as well as things for their stockings and she looked exhausted. When we had finished shopping, we collected Ben from the hospital. He was waiting for us, looking very clean and smelling of antiseptic, with a large plaster cast on his arm.

'Thank goodness you've come," he cried. "I've been waiting for ages. Bronco's not dead, is he?"

So on the way home I told what had happened for the third time. I couldn't believe that tomorrow would be Christmas Day.

"How will we manage now?" asked Ben when I had stopped talking.

"How do you mean?"

"Without me," he answered.

"I shall ride him," I said.

"No, you won't, he's going back," replied Mummy quickly. "He's going back directly Christmas is over."

"It's not over until Boxing Day," I said, to give myself more time.

"You'll never ride him," said Ben. "You couldn't stay on the sort of bucks he gave yesterday, nobody could."

"He was scared," I answered. "If he isn't scared, he won't buck."

"He's going back," repeated Mummy.

"We can't always win," added Ben. "And you'll have enough to do looking after the other horses without my help."

"Mike and Lisa are helping," I answered.

"We're back at school in two weeks."

"A lot can happen in two weeks," I replied.

"And you know they'll grow tired of helping after two days, they always do," said Ben.

We were home by now and I could see Bronco looking over his box door. Lisa was showing the Cutting children Limpet and Jigsaw, saying, "I'll teach you to ride after Christmas, I promise."

The sky was a dazzling blue. I gave Lorraine and Bronco oats from my pocket, while Ben watched, saying, "He's beautiful, isn't he? A dream of a horse. It's a pity he's going to end up as dogs'-meat."

"He isn't going to," I answered. "Lisa sat on him last night and he didn't do anything – "

"What, in the box? She could have been killed!" cried Ben. "Supposing she had been thrown against one of the walls? I bet she wasn't wearing a hat either."

"Mummy doesn't know," I said. "Don't make it public, Ben. Just tell me what happened to you yesterday."

"I thumbed a lift. I chose a Land Rover so it didn't skid and the bloke drove me straight home. He was a very nice bloke, and he took me right to the front door. He was worried about you, though, but I said you were like a bad penny, you always turned up again."

"Thank you very much," I said.

It was lunch-time now. I had my lunch in the kitchen with the Cuttings, because I didn't want to do my hair, and Mummy won't let you eat in the dining-room unless you're what she calls "respectable". Ben had his lunch there for a change and so did James, because he couldn't bear the Cuttings' chatter.

After lunch I made the brandy butter. Then Lisa and I wandered down to the stables and I put the cross-country helmet on and said, "Come on, we'll lunge Bronco for a bit and then I want you to hold him while I get on."

Poor Lisa turned pale and said, "What will Mummy say?"

I replied, "This is his last chance. Do you want him shot? He knows us now."

The cross-country helmet was covered with dried slush and so was Bronco. We tacked him up and then lunged him, first with the stirrups up and then dangling against his sides. Then we filled up sacks of straw and hung them over the saddle and lunged him with them on, and we talked to him all the time. He still looked proud and his stride was long and low and tireless but he looked relaxed too. Lisa said again, "He really should be called Prince . . ."

Then the moment had come to mount and I tried to keep very calm, because horses are supposed to be able to smell fear. The stirrups were already down and Lisa

63

fed Bronco pony nuts while I mounted, and though he moved slightly as I sat down in the saddle he didn't tremble. He had a marvellous sloping shoulder and his ears seemed miles away and my legs didn't reach as far as the line of his stomach.

"Do you want to move yet?" asked Lisa in a small scared voice.

"Not yet," I said, and sat stroking his neck and talking to him. Then I said, "Just three steps and then more pony nuts, please." We moved on and I saw how small Lisa was to hold a horse of fifteen hands and knew that, if he decided to take off, she would never hang on. But he didn't take off. We walked round the front paddock three times and I could feel him relaxing underneath me.

"Let's stop. Supposing someone sees us," said Lisa.

I answered, "They won't. They're far too busy getting ready for Christmas." We walked round once more and then I dismounted very slowly and patted Bronco until my arm ached.

"He won't be shot now, will he?" asked Lisa, relaxing at last.

"I don't think so. I think he's going to be all right," I said, leading him back to the stable.

We untacked him and fetched him a feed. "Why did he buck Ben off?" Lisa asked.

"Because we rushed him and the stirrups banged together and he was scared," I said. "And Lorraine got in a state too and they started galloping. He probably thought he had a tiger on his back."

We settled the horses for the night and twilight came. I felt full of hope and saw myself riding Bronco through the wintry countryside.

"Don't tell the others. Don't tell them anything. We'll give a display on Boxing Day," I told Lisa. "And won't they be surprised!" I held on to the gate as I spoke because I believe in touching wood.

James was calling "Tea!" and Dad was home, and it was less than twenty-four hours to Christmas Day.

"Listen – carol singers," said Lisa as we walked towards the house. "Next year I'm going to sing carols."

Seven

A telephone call

Christmas was fantastic. My stocking was full of useful things like Sellotape, pens, hair shampoo, chocolate and a tiepin with a horse on it. Mrs Cutting rose very early and brought us all tea in bed, while Mrs Mills made coffee and laid the tables for breakfast. Later we all went to church. I was out of practice and lost my way in the service and Mike sang very loudly, while Colonel Hunter knew everyone and enjoyed being social. Then we opened our presents and I had a new riding-coat from my parents and lots of super things from everyone else.

We had Christmas dinner at lunch-time because of the Cuttings, and after we had digested it Lisa and I slipped outside and I rode Bronco. Lisa led me at first but after ten minutes she unclipped the leading-rein and I rode him alone. I only walked and I concentrated on stopping and starting, saying "Whoa" when I wanted him to stop and "Walk on" when I wanted him to move off, just as when we had lunged him, and he understood. Finally I trotted a few steps and then we decided he had done enough. We tried not to feel too triumphant, knowing that pride comes before a fall, but we couldn't help feeling hopeful.

"We've won!" cried Lisa. "He won't have to be shot now; we've saved him."

"Don't speak too soon," I cried.

"Why was he so crazy?" asked Lisa. "What had happened to him before he came? What made him like he was?"

"I don't know; perhaps one day we'll find out," I answered.

"Won't Mrs Nuttal be surprised?" asked Lisa next. "When will you tell her?"

"Not yet, not until we're sure," I answered.

"Why hasn't she rung up? If she loved him she would have rung up," cried Lisa.

"Perhaps she heard about Ben – news travels fast – and she was afraid our parents would be angry," I answered.

"Poor Ben. He's out of it now, isn't he?" asked Lisa.

"He can still advise," I answered. "But it's been a most peculiar Christmas, hasn't it? Quite different from any other."

"And now it's almost over," said Lisa. "And Mummy says there's new guests coming; a married couple who like rambling – and they're tweedy, she says, and slightly peculiar – called Mr and Mrs Trippet."

The sun shone on Boxing Day. Mike and Lisa helped me with the mucking out and feeding while the older Cutting children followed us around, getting in the way. Lisa and I tacked up Bronco and lunged him, and then I rode him on my own while Lisa disappeared indoors to fetch our parents. He was rather fresh and ready to shy at anything and Spot ran in and out of the paddock yapping, which didn't help.

I wondered how Ben would feel when he saw me riding Bronco. He might be angry or jealous or pleased. He had spent most of Christmas asleep. Mummy said that he was still suffering from shock. But now Lisa was running towards me calling, "They're coming," and Bronco had his ears pricked and was prancing.

"Oh, Harriet, I told you not to ride him," called Mummy. "You are naughty!"

"Absolutely disgraceful!" shouted Dad.

"But he's all right," I called. "Look."

I trotted him round the paddock and Dad called, "How did you do it?"

"I don't know; trust, I suppose," I replied, and all the time I could feel a sense of triumph running through me. We've done it, I thought, we've succeeded. He won't be shot now.

"It's most extraordinary," continued Dad. "I didn't think you had it in you, Harriet."

Ben was standing behind him now, saying nothing, and I didn't know what to say either.

"Well done! When are you going to ring up Mrs Nuttal and tell her the good news?" asked Mummy.

"Not until we're certain," I answered. "I want to hack him first."

And still Ben said nothing.

"Don't go alone then, and tell us where you are going this time," pleaded Mummy.

"You bet I will," I answered.

"He's certainly a beautiful horse," said Dad, "and very valuable, I should say." They were turning to go indoors now. I slid to the ground.

"We'll take him out tomorrow," I told Lisa.

"I can't believe it's true," she said. "That all this is really happening."

"By the way, Mrs Mills is leaving tomorrow, her daughter has come back to England. She's going to live in a granny flat. We'll miss her, won't we?" asked Mummy.

"I shall," said Lisa, wiping her eyes. "Who will mend my socks when she's gone, or play Memory with me?

Does she really have to go, Mummy?"

"She wants to be with her grandchildren," replied Mummy. "It's only natural."

"I wish she was unnatural, then," said Lisa.

"Well done, Harriet," said Ben, suddenly smiling. "How did you manage it?"

"I don't know, I think he wants to be good, really. He doesn't like being a rogue," I answered.

"I don't think he likes men," suggested Lisa.

"Anyway, he won't have to be shot now," said Ben.

"Does your arm hurt? I'm just sorry it wasn't you riding him just now," I replied. "It seems so unfair, somehow."

"No, it doesn't hurt, and perhaps you're better for him," answered Ben. "You seem to suit him, you go together. I like a more solid horse, something which never hots up. I like a horse which will go through anything, face anything. I haven't got much patience, have I?"

"I wouldn't know," I answered. "But you're better at staying on than me, and braver by far."

The next few days rushed by. I rode Bronco every day while we turned the others out to exercise themselves, except for Lorraine whom Lisa rode with me, sitting up very straight and looking like an expert.

Mrs Mills left and Lisa cried but we all missed her; then the Cuttings were found a house to live in by the council and the Trippets came. Mr Trippet had a small, neat moustache and glasses and Mrs Trippet had dark hair which fell like a curtain on each side of her face. Mummy said that Mr Trippet wrote, and Dad said they were something to do with films, but no one seemed quite sure. Lisa said that they looked like spies and James thought that Mr Trippet was an arsonist and would set fire to the house one night when the moon

was high. Ben said that he was certain they smoked pot in their room at night and Colonel Hunter said that Mr Trippet wasn't quite a gentleman.

After a few days they became interested in the horses and were always hanging round the stables asking tiresome questions like, "Why don't you bed on sawdust?" and, "Are you going to clip the horses out before the spring?" Then Mr Trippet began to talk about Bronco.

"He's just the sort of horse that does well in films," he said. "They like that chestnut colour, or ones with a pale mane, and he carries himself so well. How about it? Would you sell him? I'm sure I could get at least a couple of thousand for you."

Finally I had to admit he wasn't ours and then, of course, the inevitable questions followed. I had sent a postcard to Mrs Nuttal after Boxing Day, saying: *All going well, I am riding Hillingdon Prince, hope you will come and see him soon.*

I had received a postcard back saying: *Well done! Will telephone.* Nothing more. So I said to Mr Trippet, "He belongs to a Mrs Nuttal but she doesn't want to sell."

"Where does she live?" he said.

I had to say, "Middlesex." And I looked at Mr Trippet and I didn't trust him. I didn't know what to do.

I took my anxiety to Dad, but he only said, "Look, Harriet darling, the horse does belong to Mrs Nuttal and if Mr Trippet wants to make an offer for him we can't interfere, can we? And how do you know Mrs Nuttal doesn't want two thousand pounds? Do be reasonable."

"But he's not ready for a change of homes," I answered. "He needs time to settle. He's at a very crucial time in his education."

"Well, I don't suppose Mr Trippet will do anything – he's just interested, that's all," replied Dad. "He's interested in everything. He wants to buy the Turkish mat in the sitting-room and Mummy's china ornaments. He wants to make a quick buck. He's after someone's oak chest as well, I'm told."

"China ornaments and oak chests don't have hearts and minds," I replied, more worried than ever. "Why do we have such peculiar guests?"

"They aren't peculiar, everyone likes making a quick buck," answered Dad. "He's been down to the farm and offered three hundred pounds for an old horse bus they've got there. He's a collector of sorts."

"Of all sorts," I said. "But tell him to keep his grubby hands off Bronco, please."

But Mr Trippet was always hanging round Bronco, saying, "Can I see him gallop?" and "What's he like over fences?" Questions I refused to answer.

The New Year had come and it seemed time to ring up Mrs Nuttal and ask her over. I started to feel mixed up over Bronco and Ben said, "You're a fool, Harriet. If we're going to take horses to train, we can't be sentimental over them; they'll have to come and go; you can't keep track of all of them."

"But Bronco's special."

"They'll all be special to you," answered Ben.

But I knew it wasn't true. There was an affinity between us, something indescribable, which only a horseman would understand. To hit Bronco would have been an insult. He wasn't like a normal horse. I never carried a stick on him. We hadn't broken him; we had come to an agreement. And I couldn't bear the thought of anyone riding him without understanding him first.

The Trippets were constantly disappearing, and then returning with things which they sorted in their bedroom – one day it was a wooden rocking-horse, another day a pewter tankard. James called them their foraging expeditions and compared them to hounds foraging for food.

Then one evening at the end of the holidays when we were in the kitchen talking about our guests, Dad said, "You know, some people can't resist a bargain when they see one. It's a compulsive thing; almost a mania. Finally they live for nothing else. I think the Trippets

are like that, they are always searching, their room is full of *Exchange and Mart* and local papers with bargain pages."

"I heard Mr Trippet talking to a film company yesterday on the telephone," said Lisa. "I didn't hear all the conversation – just the beginning really because I didn't want to eavesdrop."

My heart had given a jump and I felt sick suddenly. "Did he mention a horse?" I asked.

"Yes," replied Lisa, beginning to sniff. "I was afraid to tell you. I kept putting it off. He said he had found a beauty, just right for the part, he said. But aren't you pleased? Don't you want Bronco to be famous?"

"It could be marvellous. You could have your name on telly, you know, trained by . . ." said Ben.

"How much money did he mention?" I asked slowly.

"Two thousand five hundred pounds."

I used a word we're not allowed to use.

"I heard him say, 'Of course, when you've finished with him, he'll be worth twice that . . .'" continued Lisa.

"In fact, you listened to the whole conversation," said Dad.

"Yes," replied Lisa, turning crimson.

But now Mummy was calling, "Telephone. It's for you, Harriet."

"Who on earth?" I said. But going to the telephone I thought I knew. I picked up the receiver with a shaky hand and the voice at the other end said:

"Mrs Nuttal here – "

This is it! I thought. This is Bronco's Waterloo.

" – I thought I should tell you that I've sold Hillingdon Prince," continued Mrs Nuttal. "A film company have bought him. They made a very good offer, so good I couldn't refuse it. Now I know it's all due to you, because you've had some sort of film scout staying with you and you've done wonders with Prince, haven't you? So I want you to have something too. Will £250 do? The film company are sending a box tomorrow. Is that all right, dear?"

I wanted to scream, "No!" Instead I said, "I don't know whether he'll behave; he's still quite nervous."

"Not to worry, dear. I've explained all that and they've got some expert riders just waiting to train him on. Who shall I make the cheque out to? And be ready for the box at ten o'clock, won't you, dear?" finished Mrs Nuttal.

Lisa was breathing down my neck, listening to every word. Ben was standing in the kitchen doorway straining his ears. "Make it out to Black Pony Inn," I said.

"Thank you, dear," she said and put down her receiver, and suddenly money didn't matter any more, nothing mattered except that Hillingdon Prince was going and he wasn't ready to go . . .

"Why couldn't Mrs Nuttal simply hire him to them?" I asked.

"He isn't yours to keep," said Mummy, suddenly beside me. "He never was yours. He'll have a lovely home now."

"You're just being selfish," said James. "Why shouldn't poor old Bronco be famous?"

"He's not Bronco any more. He's Hillingdon Prince now," replied Lisa.

"You'll be able to watch him being a wonder horse on telly," said James. "He'll be immortal."

At that moment the Trippets came into the hall and, looking at us gathered together, Mr Trippet said, "Ah, you've heard about the horse! Are you pleased? Quite a rags to riches story, isn't it?"

And Dad replied. "It's tremendous. How are you? Have you accomplished a lot today?"

Mr Trippet's small moustache twitched and he said, "Not too badly, thank you, just a few knick-knacks and a copper coal scuttle. Not a fortune by any means but passable, I would say. But Mrs Nuttal's giving you something, isn't she?" he added smiling at me. "I said you deserved something . . . after all, you've put a lot of work into the horse, haven't you?"

"So has Ben," I answered. "I don't need money anyway, thank you all the same."

"Oh dear, aren't we high and mighty this evening?" asked Mrs Trippet, nudging her husband while I, unable to bear another minute of the conversation, rushed upstairs to my room.

Eight
Goodbye to a horse

I couldn't sleep that night. The moon was high in the sky and every time I looked out of the window I could see Bronco's head staring into the moonlit night over his box door.

I lay in bed imagining him uncontrollable again, bucking and rearing like a Wild West rodeo horse. I thought: If only they could have given me a few weeks more to make him safe for anyone to ride. I'm not proud of my riding, I am no better than most people; but I had built up a fragile relationship with Bronco which could easily be broken.

In the end I overslept and was woken by Lisa shouting at my door, "Harriet, wake up! It's half past nine. The horse box will be here in a moment."

She was still in her pyjamas. I pulled on my clothes and raced to the stables where I found the horses banging on their doors and neighing, and they needed everything – hay, water, feeds, grooming, mucking out. Lisa fed while I fetched water from the kitchen because the yard tap was frozen. Then I started to groom Bronco, working at a frantic speed, while Lisa fetched travelling bandages for his legs, a tail bandage and a rug.

"Why did you oversleep? I was relying on you to wake me," she said.

"Never rely on anyone but yourself," I answered.

"Remember the saying: Love many, trust a few, learn to paddle your own canoe."

"You're cross, aren't you?" she asked.

"No, only a bit frantic." And now the horse box was turning through the gates and I knew it was goodbye to Bronco, or Hillingdon Prince – whatever you called him – and he was the best horse I had ever ridden.

I turned towards the house and could see the Trippets watching us through a window, no doubt congratulating themselves on the money they had made.

And I hated them.

The horse box was large and smart and two girls jumped out and called, "Are you Harriet Pemberton? We've come to collect Hillingdon Prince," as though I didn't know.

"I'm just putting on some travelling bandages," I said. "They are ours, so I would like them back, please."

The girls were in their twenties. They wandered round the yard looking at our dirty boxes and the hay Lisa had spilt everywhere and I felt ashamed. They wore headscarves, and tweed jackets and jeans with high heeled boots underneath.

I led Bronco out into the winter sunshine and one of them said, "We've brought a rug."

"He's nervous," I said. "He needs time to get used to people."

"Don't worry, we know all about horses. I'm Janet, by the way," said the taller.

Bronco didn't like the rug. In the end I sent the girls away and Lisa held him while I put it on.

"He is a handful, isn't he?" said Janet. "Never mind, he'll soon settle down with us. We've got a super trainer, a real smasher."

Bronco wouldn't box, he kept looking back at the stables and then standing on his hind legs and swinging

round. Finally I suggested that the others should go
away, and I talked to him, telling him that it was like
school and he had to go, and that we all had to earn our
living in the end. He nuzzled my hair and finally he
seemed to say, "If you are coming too." So I patted his

neck and he followed me up and suddenly I was crying. The girls rushed from behind and shut the partition doors while I tied him up and then climbed through a little door at the front, and Bronco started to neigh, knowing he had been betrayed.

"Well done!" said Janet in tones of relief. "We'll be off, then, and we won't forget to send the bandages back."

They both smiled at us before they climbed into the cab and started up the engine. Bronco neighed again and I could hear his hoofs pounding on the box door. Lisa said, "He doesn't want to go. Poor Bronco," and started to cry.

I could see the Trippets moving away from the window. The box was through the gate and I said, "We must get on, we've got all the mucking out to do. Where's Mike?"

"He's gone out for the day with his girlfriend. Mummy says he was gone by seven," replied Lisa.

"Charming," I said.

We turned out Lorraine, Cassie and Windfall, and Solitaire. The ponies, Limpet and Jigsaw, slept out all the year round. I couldn't bear to look at Bronco's empty loose box. Presently Ben appeared and said, "I wish I could help. Let me do some forking anyway."

"He's gone," I said.

"Yes, I saw," answered Ben. "And for goodness sake stop crying. You've still got Lorraine, so what's the matter?"

"I didn't want him to go like that. I wanted him to go somewhere near. It was as though he was being taken away to prison. He didn't want to go . . ." I cried.

"He'll have everything," replied Ben. "Food, shelter, experts to sort out his problems – he's so lucky, can't you see?"

But I couldn't. I could only see him leaving us, betrayed by me whom he had trusted and it was almost more than I could bear.

"And think of the money we're getting," continued Ben. "We can halve it. I've asked Mummy and she says it's ours; she and Dad don't want any part of it because we've earned it, me with my broken arm and you with your courageous perseverance."

"I don't think I want it. You can have it all," I answered. "I feel as though I've sold a friend. I can't explain it."

"You'll feel better tomorrow," Ben replied after a short silence. "No one but a nutcase can refuse a hundred and twenty five pounds fairly earned."

Later we went indoors and ate bread and cheese because it was too late for breakfast and too early for lunch. Mummy looked at my tear-stained face and said, "You are a fool, Harriet. You'll never make a horse dealer. You make a fantastic success of something and then you cry. You're completely crazy."

"You'll be famous now as a horse-breaker and trainer," said Lisa.

"It's for the best, anyway. You start school tomorrow and you could never have coped with all the mucking out; you know you couldn't. And when would you have found time for exercising Bronco?" asked Mummy.

"I had worked it all out," I answered. "I was going to get up at six and muck out by electric light and then lunge Bronco before going to school and ride him when I got home. I was going to buy a stirrup light and a fluorescent jacket so I could ride him in the dark."

"It sounds highly dangerous to me," said James, coming into the kitchen. "Has anyone seen my football socks?"

"Not again!" replied Mummy. "You can't lose your

football socks twice in less than a week."

"James can," said Ben.

I could see the Trippets driving away in their estate car, no doubt looking for more bargains, their faces eager with anticipation, like dogs looking forward to a walk.

"He's wearing plus-fours," said Ben, following my glance, "and smoking a curly pipe, you know the sort."

"Colonel Hunter has asked to have breakfast in his room. He can't stand them either. Can't we get rid of them, Mum?" asked James.

"They've paid in advance and they're no trouble," replied Mummy. "They're out to lunch today and they won't have anything taken off the bill."

"I wonder when Bronco will arrive," I said. "I wish we knew exactly where he's going. Why didn't I ask? I never ask the right questions."

"Do go and get ready for school," replied Mummy. "I can't bear you all in the kitchen."

I went upstairs and collected my things for school – my overall for science, my blouse and blazer and boring pleated skirt.

Outside, the ground was rock hard again; the mud frozen into shapes as hard as metal; the bare trees decorated with frost – like white icing sugar. On the common, boys were sliding on the pond. So, slowly, the day passed. Lisa spent the afternoon playing Memory with Twinkle our cat, though how a cat plays Memory I've never understood. She was missing Mrs Mills who had been an ever-willing card player. Ben read *Horse and Hound* from cover to cover; James made countless cups of coffee and searched for books he had lost since last term. Mummy prepared supper. I wandered about trying to think about school but thinking of Bronco instead. Lisa and I mucked out in the evening together. Mike was

still away and there was a cold wind now which scur-
ried round the yard, blowing straw off the wheelbarrow
and hay out of our arms. Ben hung about talking about
what he was going to buy with his earnings and slowly
the day turned into dusk and then into night.

We put our things ready for school before we went to
bed; Mummy gave us our lunch money and Dad gave us
a lecture on working hard. The Trippets returned in time
for dinner, smelling of whisky, and Ben said that their
car had a heap of valuable glass in it, so obviously they
had had a good day.

"We'll stay another day or two if that's all right with
you," Mr Trippet told Mummy, his moustache twitching. "We've had a most marvellous stay and you've
made us most comfortable. We will certainly recommend you to our friends."

I dreamed that night that I was hunting on Bronco.
We jumped fence after fence until suddenly we were
alone in front of hounds in a moonlit countryside. We
seemed to be painted with silver and Bronco's ears were
made of glass and then the moon started to come towards us, enormous and terrifying, and whichever way

we galloped we couldn't escape because it was larger than the world. I wakened crying, "Stop, please stop," and heard the post van come into the drive and Mr Trippet opening his window to call something to the postman.

Later, Lisa and I rushed round the horses at top speed, helped by Mike who is very strong but a bit slow on the uptake.

There wasn't time for a proper breakfast so I ran for the school bus clutching a piece of toast and marmalade in my hand.

"It's going to snow some more," said Ben, looking at the sky.

"And then we can toboggan," cried Lisa. "And make a snowman and throw snowballs at each other. How lovely."

School passed slowly. I couldn't concentrate and I didn't seem to have a single friend when breaktime came, which was hardly surprising since I had ignored them the whole holidays. Ben wandered about with his arm in plaster telling everyone of his disaster.

"But all's well that ends well, because Harriet conquered the brute and now he's going on telly," he said. I wondered why he always talked differently at school, because he would never have used the word "brute" to describe a horse at home.

The playing fields were too frozen for games so we spent the afternoon in the gym and then at last it was time to go home.

Ben and I never talk to one another on the bus. He sits with his cronies and I sit in the front usually on my own. The bus wanders all over the place before it finally drops us on the common. Lisa is still at Primary so she reaches home before us. Today she met us in the yard shouting, "Harriet, Mrs Nuttal's rung. I don't know what about. You've got to ring her back."

"It's probably about the money," said Ben.

"She sounded in a stew," said Lisa.

But now I was running to the house, my heart pounding against my ribs, thinking: It's Bronco, something's happened to Bronco.

"She's rung twice," said Mummy as I rushed into the kitchen.

"What can she want?" I yelled. "Where's her phone number? I don't know what it is."

"I've written it down. Look on the front of the directory. It's in red chalk," said Lisa.

"And calm down," said Ben. "It can't possibly be that important."

"Why wouldn't she leave me a message?" I asked, dialling.

"I don't know," replied Lisa. "She didn't say."

Then I could hear her voice at the other end and I said, "This is Harriet Pemberton, you rang," and I could feel my heart pounding inside me.

"Yes, I did. I have some bad news – Bronco's gone."

"Gone!" I cried. "Do you mean dead, or stolen? What do you mean?"

"He's escaped. They put side reins on him this morning and he seemed to go mad. He got away with a lunge rein trailing behind him. He jumped a six-foot boundary fence, and he hasn't been seen since."

"With the side reins still on?" I said after a moment, seeing it all in my mind's eye.

"I suppose so. They've told the police, of course. They say he went mad," continued Mrs Nuttal.

"I suppose he'll collide with a lorry," I said.

"He hasn't so far. He's simply disappeared," replied Mrs Nuttal.

"Ask where he was," hissed Lisa.

"Where was he?" I said.

"In the Midlands, near Coventry, I believe."

"But that's miles away," I answered.

"There's nothing we can do. I don't know why I rang you really. I just had to tell someone. I'm so upset," said Mrs Nuttal.

"If only we could search," I answered. "I feel so help-less. And how can he rest with side reins on?"

I looked at my hand and saw that it was shaking. Lisa was crying and Ben was looking out of the window as though the answer to everything lay somewhere in the garden. And I could hear the old clock ticking in the hall and it seemed to be Bronco's heart ticking its strength away. And I didn't know what to say. Suddenly I was lost for words. So I said, "I'm sorry. Goodbye," and put down the receiver and thought of Bronco somewhere with side reins running from his bit to a roller and a lunge rein trailing behind him and I thought the sight of him must be the saddest sight in all the world. I imag-ined him rolling in desperation trying to detach the reins and I prayed that they weren't too tight. I was right, I thought, he shouldn't have gone, not for all the money in the world – he wasn't ready.

Then Mummy was beside me saying, "Don't pine, darling, he'll turn up somewhere. He can't get far like that, can he?"

And I said, "He's jumped a six-foot fence." I didn't want any tea. I went outside and fed our horses and Bronco's empty box reproached me. I looked at it for a bit and then bedded it down, and now it looked like a bedroom waiting for someone's homecoming. I thought: Perhaps the police will find him and bring him home to die. But I knew they wouldn't because he had never be-longed to us and he didn't belong to Mrs Nuttal any more either, he belonged to the film company. If he's hurt they'll shoot him, I thought, and he'll be just a £2,500 loss on a balance sheet, nothing more.

Cassie looked over her box into the twilight, whinny-ing, and I thought: She's missing him too. But Lorraine was quiet and dreamy and Solitaire his usual self. Lisa wandered about the yard without speaking and Ben filled water buckets, carrying them with his good arm, and none of us felt like talking. Finally Lisa said, "Poor, poor Bronco. Do you think we'll ever hear what hap-pens to him? They don't have to tell us, do they? I mean, he belongs to them."

And I said, "That's right," and suddenly it was the worst thing of all.

Nine

Funny joke?

A cheque for £250 arrived the next day from Mrs Nuttal. I handed it to Mummy, "I don't want it," I said. "It's like blood money."

I couldn't concentrate at school. Maths seemed to last for ever and I broke a test tube in science. I missed lunch altogether and my eyes strayed to the window all through the cookery class. But, at last, school was over and we were in the bus once more, trundling round the villages, taking hours to get home. Lisa was waiting for us in the yard again when we eventually arrived.

"No news," she shouted, "no telephone calls, nothing at all!"

There was a cold wind and flurries of sleet and a sky colder than the coldest sea.

"It's going to snow again," said Ben, turning up his coat collar. Immediately I saw Bronco dying in a snowdrift, his proud head slowly sinking to rest in a white grave, his hoofs protruding, slowly to be covered too by falling snow.

The kitchen was warm and welcoming.

"We've got some new guests coming next week," said Mummy. "Isn't that lovely? They're quite young, with a baby, and they want us to babysit for them."

"Super," said Ben without much enthusiasm.

"Any news? Any news at all?" I asked.

"You mean about Bronco?" replied Mummy. "You must be reasonable, Harriet darling. We can't expect news because he isn't ours, so please stop hoping for it, and forget the horse. He isn't our responsibility any more."

"I can't," I answered. "It was so wonderful saving him from the knackers – and now this. I can't bear it."

"Oh, Harriet," cried Mummy. "Do be sensible; he's only an animal after all."

I didn't mention him again but all the time my heart was aching for news and I kept imagining hoofs coming down the road but when I looked there was nothing. I'm going mad, I thought. Soon I shall start talking to myself.

I dreamed he was swimming in the sea. I kept putting out my hand to touch him but he sank every time before I could stroke his chestnut mane. I went to get help but when I came back in a boat he was gone altogether.

I was wakened by Lisa shaking me, "It's time to get up," she cried. "You've overslept again."

I felt ill all day and snow started to fall again. At twelve o'clock the headmaster, fearing drifts, shut the school and the buses arrived. People threw snowballs at the staff, but Ben couldn't join in because of his broken arm and I felt too ill, so we sat in the bus and talked.

"He can't have disappeared," said Ben. "Horses don't just disappear."

"Couldn't we ring up the film company and ask after him?" I suggested.

"Let's try Mrs Nuttal first," replied Ben.

"He doesn't belong to her either," I answered.

"But he did," said Ben as if it made a difference.

The journey home took even longer than usual. Lisa was waiting for us. "The Trippets are leaving," she said. "Isn't it super?"

"Any news?" I asked.

"No nothing."

We'll forget him in the end, I thought. He'll be nothing but a memory in a few years' time. But I didn't want to. I wanted to know whether he was alive or dead.

The Trippets were loading up their estate car in front of the house.

"Any news of the horse?" asked Ben.

"How should I know?" snapped Mr Trippet. "He's not my responsibility."

They looked as though they had had a bad day; his moustache wasn't twitching any more and she looked defeated.

"Good riddance to bad rubbish," muttered Lisa.

I telephoned Jean Nuttal. "Any news?" I asked.

"No, nothing. I don't expect any," she replied.

"Won't they let you know if they find him?" I asked.

"They don't have to." She sounded despondent. I hung up.

"Any news?" asked Lisa.

I shook my head. "There may never be any news as far as we're concerned," I replied. "You see, it's none of our business."

"You mean we may never know whether he's alive or dead?" asked Lisa.

"That's right," I answered. Tears were pricking behind my eyes because now there seemed no hope of anything – news good or bad.

The Trippets were settling their account in the hall. The young married couple had arrived with their baby, so I showed them their room. They admired everything – the staircase, the pictures, the view. Their baby was sweet and called Emma.

"We've just made it and now we're going to be snowed in," said the wife and then, "By the way, call me

Janet, and my husband's Steve. I'm so looking forward to being here . . ."

"I'm Harriet," I said, holding out my hand.

"I hope there's a big log fire downstairs," said Janet, who had long dark hair and a marvellous retroussé nose.

"It's just been lit," I answered. "And you must come and meet Colonel Hunter, he's our longest-staying guest. He talks about India all the time, and now if you'll excuse me, I'll go and do the horses."

Lisa helped me feed the horses; it was a long job because everything was weighted with snow. Gates were heavier than usual; buckets were lined with it and our backs became coated with it. But at last everything was done. It was six o'clock now and the snow was stopping and the sky suddenly full of stars.

Janet was breast-feeding her baby in the kitchen when we went indoors again which made Lisa feel shy, for neither of us had ever seen a baby being fed before. Mummy was making soup, Mike was tobogganing with his girlfriend and Ben was talking to Steve about motorbikes.

"For goodness sake dry your hair, Harriet," Mummy said. "It's dripping on everything."

"No news, no telephone calls?" I asked.

"No, and stop asking, there's no point," replied Mummy, and started to tell Janet about Bronco.

And then James appeared, his hair on end, a mug of tea in his hand. "Bronco's alive," he said.

"What do you mean?" I asked. "How do you know? You're just pretending, aren't you?"

"It was on the news," he said.

"Ha, ha," I cried, "funny joke."

"He was really," said James. "He was seen trotting through Banbury. They showed him on telly and he hadn't any reins on or anything much. Honest . . ."

I felt sick with hope. "You're not being funny, are you?" I asked.

"He's heading this way," said James.

"Did they say so?"

"No. It wasn't our usual local news. I was fiddling about and it wasn't very clear but it looked like him."

"Was he covered with snow?" asked Lisa.

"Yes, and the traffic was held up and then he vanished across fields. I'll get a map."

He returned with Ben. "He's travelled miles already," he said. "Look how far Banbury is from Coventry."

"He could yet be killed," said Ben.

"But he's coming this way," I cried. "And he may be all right. Oh, I'm so happy. We know he isn't dead yet anyway. There's still hope."

"He's still over a hundred miles away," said James.

"About three days," said Ben.

"I'll ring up Jean Nuttal. I must. She'll be so pleased," I said, running to the telephone. She answered at once. "He's on his way back," I cried. "He's been on telly. He went through Banbury."

"Is that you, Harriet dear?" she said.

"Yes, it's about Bronco."

"But are you sure it's him? Did they say so, dear?" she asked.

"No, but it must be," I answered.

"I don't think so. I don't think he could have got from Coventry to Banbury in that time, dear. It's a long way and then there's the traffic. Don't be too hopeful, dear."

I could feel a battle going on inside me between hope and despair. Hope won. "It must be," I said and hung up.

"Well?" asked Ben.

"Crushing. Disbelieving," I said. "But I don't care."

"Was it really Bronco? Are you absolutely sure?" I asked James later. "Could you have made a mistake?"

"I've told you it looked like him but the reception was bad because it wasn't in our area," he replied.

We listened to the news on radio all that evening and Lisa stayed glued to the television set until Mummy chased her to bed. But no one mentioned a runaway horse again. I listened for the telephone to ring. I was certain that news would come from somewhere somehow, but it didn't. We were all on edge and there was nothing we could do about it and that was the worst thing of all.

In the morning there was another foot of snow and none of the school buses were running. The snow came to the tops of our boots now and the whole countryside seemed suddenly silent and remote. The post arrived two hours late and the papers didn't arrive at all. And I could only think of Bronco. Was he struggling through drifts to reach us? Or was he dying somewhere of hunger and exposure? I no longer noticed what I ate. I did everything automatically; and then wondered whether I had done it at all.

Janet seemed to be forever in the kitchen washing clothes or bathing Emma. Dad was at home complaining about dirty fingermarks on the walls and the state of our bedrooms. The house was thatched with snow, the windows edged with it. We cut the horses' oats to nil. Later James, Steve and Janet disappeared with toboggans, while Mummy and I watched over Emma.

"You must be tougher, Harriet," said Mummy. "You can't go into the horse business if you're going to become so attached to a single horse. It just won't work. Can't you see?"

"Yes, of course I can," I answered. "But Bronco is special."

"But won't they all be?" asked Mummy.

"No."

I peeled the potatoes for lunch and swept the stairs.
But I didn't really see the potatoes and I missed most of
the dust on the stairs, because I could see nothing but
Bronco – Bronco jumping fences, Bronco trotting on and
on with the snow balling in his hoofs, Bronco being
caught and taken back to the film company, Bronco dying. I thought I was going mad. I kept hearing hoofbeats
which weren't there and imagining distant neighing, and
the telephone ringing.

"You look as though you're in a trance," said Ben,
waving a hand in front of my eyes.

"Can't we ring the police?" I asked.

"But he isn't ours," replied Mummy. "Forget him,
Harriet. That's my advice."

"Oh, not that again," cried Dad coming into the
kitchen. "If anyone mentions that wretched horse again,
I'll go barmy."

"Go barmy, then," said Lisa and was sent to her
room for being rude.

The snow kept falling. Lunch was eaten and eventually teatime came. Lisa and I spent the afternoon cleaning tack, while Ben stood about doing what he could
with one arm, but mostly getting in the way.

Dinner lasted a long time, because Dad opened some
wine and we all talked our heads off, because the Trippets had left and our new guests were great fun and always laughing. Colonel Hunter became very merry and
chatted up Janet and Dad liked Steve. At ten o'clock I
went to bed and, looking at the snow outside, I thought:
There's really no hope now, no hope at all. He must be
dead by now.

I wakened early and listened to the news. A whole family had died in snowdrifts and more snow was forecast.

There was fighting in Africa and the Conservatives had won a by-election and the dustmen had come out on strike. There was no mention of a horse trotting down a high street or appearing like a ghost on a motorway.

I found Mummy downstairs already laying the table for breakfast.

"Can't we start looking?" I asked. "The Land Rover would be all right in drifts."

"Looking? Oh, Harriet, you're not still worrying about that horse, are you? But darling, we're cut off, look outside. And the deep freeze will soon be empty; I really can't worry about a naughty horse at this period in time."

The snow was well over our boots now. We had to dig a path to the stables. In fact we had to dig out the whole yard. Luckily Dad and Steve came to our rescue.

Instead of helping, Lisa made a snowman and Mike threw snowballs at her. I shouted, "Come and help." Then I heard a voice calling me and I went to the yard gate and saw our nearest farmer, Mr Rawlings, sitting on his tractor, coated with snow.

"I thought I ought to tell you there's a horse back yonder trying to get up the lane. He's covered with snow and very weak. Is he one of yours?" he asked.

I started to say, "Yes, it's Bronco," and then I was shouting, "He's come home. Lisa, Ben, he's in the lane!"

"I don't know how you'll get him up here," Mr Rawlings said doubtfully. "The snow is three foot deep and he's very weak."

He's come home to die, I thought. But I said, "Thank you, Mr Rawlings. Thank you very much." It was only half of me talking because the other half was already making plans, crying, "We'll need ropes. Hurry."

Ten

Snowdrifts

Mr Rawlings didn't go away. He said, "You may need the tractor. I'll stay." Dad tried to start the Land Rover but it would only groan.

Lisa cried, "I knew he would come home. I never gave up hope."

Ben said, "We'll need the toboggans, we can lay him across them and drag him behind the tractor."

"Get all the spades and shovels together," ordered Dad.

"Could we get a snowplough from anywhere?" asked Steve.

"Let's see how he is first," answered Dad.

"I'll meet you there," said Mr Rawlings, starting up his tractor.

I filled a bucket with oats. Lisa fetched a headcollar. We loaded everything on to the two toboggans and set off. The snow came over our knees on the common. We tried to make a path but it was hard, cold work; Lisa started to cry after a time and had to be sent home. Then we saw that Mr Rawlings was making some sort of path with an ordinary plough and Dad said, "Thank God for Mr Rawlings."

I wanted to run, to throw my arms round Bronco's neck. But running was out of the question because in places the snow was now waist-high.

"Nobody else would do this for a mere horse," said Dad. "Talk about mad dogs and Englishmen."

"We're never ready for anything in this country, are we?" asked Steve.

"You're dead right," agreed Ben.

"I shall hate snow for ever after this," I said.

"It's like the sea; it's all right until you start drowning," laughed Steve.

Dad and Steve went first because they were the tallest but we didn't seem to be making much progress and there was no one to be seen besides ourselves and Mr Rawlings, not even a dog.

"Why haven't we got snowshoes?" asked Ben, who was hardly moving with his broken arm.

"Don't ask silly questions," snapped Dad.

We could see the woods now and the lane which led to them, usually a mere five minutes walk away. Mr Rawlings was in the snow trying to unclog the wheels of his tractor. I could see Lisa, a tiny figure, turning into the stable-yard. Mike was going back too, muttering, "I'll never make it and I'm not going to risk my life for a horse."

I was soaked through, my legs were aching from struggling and my feet were numb. So near and yet so far, I thought, God give us strength, please God, he's come so far, he can't die on the last lap.

Mr Rawlings was waving now, calling, "The tractor's broken down. I'll have to go home."

"But how?" yelled Dad.

"I don't know," shouted Mr Rawlings.

Dad turned on me and yelled, "It's all your fault, Harriet. It's because of you and your stupid, worthless horse. We're all going to die of exposure because of you."

I felt too small and frightened to say anything.

"You're wrong, Mr Pemberton," said Steve. "We came of our own free will. Don't blame your daughter."

The snow was falling faster and faster now and we weren't even halfway to the lane.

"He'll have to die," said Dad at last. "We'll have to go back."

"What about Mr Rawlings?" asked Ben.

"We'll send the police to rescue him. They'll send a snowplough. And don't cry, Harriet. We've done our best; we've risked our lives for your damned horse."

"He's come so far," I said.

"That's life," replied Dad.

"You can't reproach yourself for anything," said Steve.

"He was doomed from the beginning. We gave him a few more weeks of life," said Ben.

Dad cupped his hands round his mouth and shouted, "We'll send help to you, Mr Rawlings, don't worry."

Snow blew into our faces and blinded us. "There's going to be a blizzard," said Steve.

"He's probably dead by now, anyway," said Ben. "Frozen stiff; it's a peaceful death, Harriet, you just grow sleepy."

"But he's come so far," I said again. "Couldn't we get the Land Rover started?"

"And drive in this? You must be dotty," replied Dad. "It would be over the wheels . . ."

Our earlier footprints had already vanished. The snow stung our eyes. Suddenly Steve cried, "Look, look over there. There's a snowplough; it's clearing the road."

Then we were all shouting, "Help, we need you. Help!" Mr Rawlings was waving and pointing too.

"They won't hear," said Ben. "The snow is muffling our voices."

"They'll hear me," said Steve, holding his breath and

then yelling, "Over here. Come over here."

"Make for the road, they're clearing it," said Dad.

The two men on the snowplough were wearing goggles. We reached the road following the path we had made, and waved like people on a desert island waiting for a ship to rescue them.

I said, "Will they help with Bronco?"

Dad replied, "Forget that horse for five minutes, will you?" We were all shivering and my teeth were chattering too, so I seemed to be shaking all over.

"Here it comes," said Steve, whose brown hair was coated with snow.

The men on the snowplough turned off the engine. "What are you doing? Do you want to die out here?" they shouted. "Why didn't you stay at home? Don't you listen to your radio?"

"There is a horse over there," I yelled. "And he's dying. We were trying to rescue him. Is that a crime?"

"What's he doing there?"

"He's come from Coventry," I answered.

"If you can just clear the road, we can manage the rest. We've got a trailer. Could you clear the piece to our yard gate, please? It's just there," said Dad, pointing.

"Then we can get home," added Steve.

They started the engine and we followed the path they made.

Lisa was waiting in different clothes by the gate. "Have you seen him?" she asked.

"No, but they're clearing the road. The snowplough is here."

"We've got to start the Land Rover," cried Ben, running towards it.

Mummy and Janet and Lisa had dug out the yard for the second time. Steve threw up the bonnet of the Land Rover. "I expect it's the distributor," he said.

"He could be dying now," I said.

"Shut up," replied Ben.

James brought tea. "I'll dig out the trailer," he said. Lisa fetched me dry clothes because I couldn't stop shivering.

"I can hear Emma yelling, I'd better go," said Janet.

Steve had the Land Rover going now. Dad backed it out. We hitched up the trailer. "Bring the spades," said Dad. "We'll have to dig him out."

"If he's still alive," said Ben.

We threw the spades into the trailer. Another minute and we were driving away along the road which leads round the common to the woods.

"Feeling better?" asked Steve, smiling.

"Yes, but still afraid," I said.

The snowplough was waiting by the lane. "We'll go

ahead," shouted the men. "We shouldn't but we will."

Mr Rawlings was there too. "I can always pull him out with the old tractor," he said.

It all seemed a little unreal. I suppose it was the snow. I had never seen so much snow before.

I didn't want to look when we reached the lane. The snowplough had cleared a path and I could see Bronco lying on his side. "He's breathing," said Ben.

"He's alive," screamed Lisa.

"Don't frighten him," said Mr Rawlings. "Keep your voices down."

Dad started to dig his legs out of the snow. I kneeled down beside him. He looked exhausted; he smelled my coat and I said, "It's all right, Bronco, you're home." And then, "Give me the oats, Lisa." But he wouldn't eat.

"Careful, don't chop his legs, Dad," said Ben.

"We can get him up now," said James. ·

"Don't rush him, let him take his time," replied Mr Rawlings, bending down to massage Bronco's legs.

I started to scrape the snow off his sides.

"Poor, poor Bronco," said Lisa.

We pulled his forelegs out and I saw that he had lost a shoe. He was shivering uncontrollably now. I put his headcollar on.

"Gently does it," said Mr Rawlings. "Someone help me with his quarters. Steady now."

I pulled on the headcollar rope but Bronco wouldn't move.

"Give him time," said Mr Rawlings, rubbing his legs again.

"Perhaps he's been blinded by the snow," cried Lisa. "Test his eyes."

"Don't be silly," said Ben.

"Why doesn't he get up, then?"

"Because he's exhausted," said Steve.

"If we don't hurry, the road will be under snow again," said Ben.

"The snowplough is still here," replied Dad, glancing over his shoulder.

"Come on, Bronco, make the effort," I said, my face against his. "You're nearly home and you're never going away again. You're home for good now." And then slowly he began to move, to tense his stiff muscles, to stretch a little.

"Leave him alone," said Mr Rawlings. "Let him do it in his own way." Bronco looked at me and nickered and then very slowly he lurched into a sitting position and the next moment he was up, a thin, exhausted horse but still alive.

"Take it slowly," beseeched Mr Rawlings. "Let him look about him."

The men on the snowplough were drinking from a Thermos flask. They shouted, "Well done, mate. He's still alive, then?"

Dad shouted, "Yes, mostly thanks to you, because a little longer and he would have been dead for certain."

"We'll be going then."

Lisa ran ahead to put down the ramp of the trailer and we loaded him slowly and carefully, inch by inch.

The snow was still falling. Steve cleaned it off the windscreen and then at last we were moving slowly, gently towards home. But first we called our thanks to Mr Rawlings who called back, "It was nothing. I'm glad he's saved. I was afraid he would be dead."

And Dad said, "What a wonderful man."

And I said, "We'll never be able to thank him enough, will we?" But no one answered.

Mummy and Janet were waiting for us. "We've arranged his box and made him a mash," said Mummy.

"Everything's ready." They were wet to the skin and covered with hay.

"What about lunch?" asked Dad.

"Colonel Hunter's watching the potatoes," said Mummy. Bronco raised his head and gave a great sigh when he saw his box waiting for him and Lisa and I dried him while the others put the Land Rover and trailer away. He drank a little and after a time he ate his mash, so we knew now that he would live.

"It's a miracle, isn't it?" asked Lisa as we put a jute night rug on him with a blanket underneath.

"I shall have to ring Jean Nuttal and tell her," I said. "I must put her out of her agony."

"Not yet, not until after lunch," pleaded Lisa.

"Why?" I asked.

"I don't know. I'm just afraid," she said.

Eleven
He's half dead

I was afraid too when I dialled Mrs Nuttal's number.

"It's Harriet Pemberton here. Bronco's home."

She gave a gasp. "Are you sure?" she asked.

"He's in the stable," I replied. "He's eating a mash. He's exhausted."

"But how?"

"Under his own steam."

"I can't believe it. I'll have to let the film company know, of course," she said.

"Will they want him back?"

"I expect so."

"Tell her they can't have him," shrieked Lisa in my ear, nearly piercing the eardrum.

"He's not well enough to travel. He's really quite ill. He'll need a vet's certificate. He's half dead. Anyway, we're snowed up. It's impossible to get in and out. The snowplough cleared the road this morning but it's blocked again already," I cried desperately.

"They can't take him away now," cried Lisa.

"I'll tell them what you say. But they have paid for him and I've cashed the cheque. And you've had your money too, haven't you?"

"Yes, but we haven't cashed the cheque yet," I answered.

"Well, I should," she said. "I'll be in touch. Thank

you for ringing, dear. It really is amazing, isn't it? What about the bridle and roller?"

"All gone," I said.

"I'll tell them, dear. Goodbye." She hung up.

"So?" demanded Lisa, hands on hips.

"The film company still own him," I cried, tears blinding my eyes, "and we can't even offer to buy him back, because we haven't got two thousand pounds."

"We can hide him, then," said Lisa. "Every time they come, we can pretend he's disappeared. Or we can make him unrideable again."

"Legally he's theirs," I answered.

"Who cares about that? He loves us. We can't let them drag him away again."

"They can't do anything while we're snowed up," said Ben, who had been listening in on the extension upstairs.

"He may be ill," I said. "I'm going to look at him, anyway."

The snow had stopped falling. A robin perched on a gate looking like a bird on a Christmas card, reminding me that it was only a short time since Christmas, though it seemed like years. Bronco was lying down. He looked very tired and his sides seemed to be going in and out too fast for normal. "He's probably getting bronchitis," I said.

"He isn't coughing," replied Ben. "If you have bronchitis you cough."

"It's something else, then. We'll have to have Roy." Then I looked at Jigsaw who had been brought in because of the snow and he looked peculiar too. He didn't want to move and, when he did, his quarters didn't move properly. And suddenly Ben and I were both looking at Lisa, who turned scarlet.

"You've been giving him oats, haven't you?" cried Ben.

"He kept asking, whinnying and nudging me. He was so sweet," replied Lisa.

"So now he has Monday morning disease, better known as azoturia," cried Ben. "Too much protein, in fact, for no exercise. Oh, Lisa!"

And Lisa buried her head in her hands, and screamed, "I didn't mean to. I didn't know."

"Well, you know now and why do you think we cut their oats to nil? Didn't you notice?" said Ben.

"No one told me," cried Lisa.

"We'll have to have Roy now," said Ben.

"If he can get here."

"I'll make Jigsaw a very wet bran mash with salts in it; that may help," I suggested.

"How many oats has he been having and for how long?" asked Ben.

"Half a bucket, twice a day," said Lisa.

"Oh . . ." shouted Ben and used words we are definitely not allowed to use. "No wonder he's sweating and in agony. You're a horrid little fiend, Lisa."

"Even when he's working, he doesn't need that amount," I cried. "You must be crazy."

"We had better not give Bronco too much either," said Ben. "Let's pick him out some good hay."

At three o'clock we rang up Roy, our vet, and he arrived at four, walking from the crossroads, carrying his bag.

"So he really did come from Coventry," he said, looking at Bronco. "I thought you were joking when you telephoned."

"He's ill, isn't he?" I asked. "He must be. Do you think he will ever be well again? Look at his breathing for a start."

"Actually, considering everything, he appears to be in remarkably good condition," said Roy, shaking his stethoscope.

"He's not fit to travel, anyway," I suggested.

"Obviously not for a day or two," answered Roy, listening to Bronco's breathing while I held his head. "But his chest is clear and in a few days he'll be almost his old self," he finished.

My heart was in my boots now. "Let's look at Jigsaw, then," I said.

He gave Jigsaw an injection while Lisa watched him, tense and distraught. "Nothing but meadow hay, no

clover, please," he said, shutting his bag, "and as soon
as possible quiet walking exercise. I'll call again the day
after tomorrow unless you ring me. And don't worry
about the liver chestnut, he's going to be all right."

We said, "Thank you very much," and watched him
go.

"So that is that," exclaimed Ben. "It's back to Coventry for Hillingdon Prince and there's not a thing we can
do."

"Have you noticed a warm airstream?" asked James,
appearing from the direction of the house. "Look at
the weathercock on the stable. The wind is changing,
it's moving to the southwest, and listen – things are
dripping."

"It's the gutters," said Ben.

"Just at the wrong time," I answered.

"Why are you so glum?" asked James.

"Because it means Bronco can go," I said.

Then at six o'clock Jean Nuttal rang. "The film company want him back," she said. "So I'll send a box for him as soon as the weather clears. It's not fair that you should have all of the expense, and really he isn't your responsibility, dear."

"He won't box," I said.

"Perhaps you can ride over. I'll pay you for it, dear," she said. And there was no answer to that.

"It's thawing," she continued, "and the roads are clear here; thanks to the snowploughs and salt. Could you bring him over in three days' time?"

"If the roads are clear," I said.

"You are a dear. Thank you. It's so lovely that he's safe and sound, isn't it? You must tell me all about it when you come. Goodbye for now, dear . . ."

"That's that, then. She wants him back in three days," I said.

I prayed for rain, but the weather forecast announced a thaw right across the country. The fields and yard became a sea of sludge. The roads ran with melting snow. The sun shone. Suddenly we had spring in January. "Just our luck," I said.

Bronco improved every hour. I listened hopefully for breathing difficulties and looked for swollen joints, for anything which would delay his going, but without success. Jigsaw made good progress too. Roy came again and marvelled at Bronco and announced Jigsaw cured, subject to sensible feeding, and slow exercise. "We caught it in good time," he said.

The sun shone. Snowdrops forced their way through the last of the snow.

And then the day came to take Bronco to Mrs Nuttal's, a distance of some eight miles. "I'll come with you," said Lisa. "I'll ride Lorraine and lead Jigsaw. He'll be better with company."

112

Mummy packed us sandwiches, though we had been promised lunch by Jean Nuttal. "Ring up when you get there," she said. "Otherwise I shall worry the whole day long."

"I wish I was coming with you," said Ben, seeing us off in the stable-yard.

There was still snow on the hills, so we had to ride all the way by road. Bronco felt bouncy and alert, Lorraine jogged. It was a lovely day for a ride – an April day in January.

Yet, as I rode, it was as though my heart was breaking. I am betraying Bronco again, I thought, and he's been through so much to come home. But as Dad said, one must keep to the law of the land and that law made it possible for people to own animals, and the film company owned Bronco.

As for him, he walked with a swinging walk, little knowing what awaited him, and that made it worse. If he could have talked I could have told him, explained. As it was, there was nothing I could say which could make him understand. The sunshine made it worse, for the day was too lovely for sorrow. Mummy called the weather a gift straight from heaven, and it was in a way, after the snow.

Every time I looked at Lisa she was crying, and that didn't help at all! The roads were full of cars and lorries travelling too fast, as though trying to make up for the time when they couldn't travel at all.

We rode for two hours and then we could see Mrs Nuttal's place, which was called Badger's End. Bronco raised his head and sniffed the air and we could see a stable-yard of modern loose boxes, and two plump dogs lying in the sun. We had eaten our sandwiches at eleven o'clock but we were hungry again.

Jean Nuttal appeared from the house and waved. The

dogs came to life and barked. Horses raised their heads and neighed, foals pushed their noses upwards, desperately trying to see over loose-box doors.

We dismounted and Jean Nuttal, patting Bronco said, "Yes, he does look a bit poorly, doesn't he? But all to

the good, he won't be able to put up such a fight when he gets back."

"When are they coming for him?" I asked.

"Not for a few days. Put him in the loose box over there and shut the top door; we don't want to lose him again, do we?" she said. Lisa put Lorraine and Jigsaw into empty loose boxes, which had hay and water ready, and then we wandered indoors and told Jean Nuttal about Bronco's rescue, as she cooked us omelettes. The house was full of sporting prints and photographs of Bronco's relations, with champion rosettes pinned to their bridles.

When I had finished Mrs Nuttal said, "Well, I think you've all been marvellous, dear. Now sit down and eat before it's cold."

I thought: She'll never understand how awful it was, nobody will.

Then Lisa asked a very sensible question. "Can you tell us why Bronco has been so difficult? I mean all his relations look all right. What happened?"

Mrs Nuttal said, "It's a long story but simple too. It all began with my back, it gave out on me. Usually I break my young horses myself, all by kindness, but my back was agony and Hillingdon Prince was a strong young horse and I just hadn't the strength to cope. So I did something I had never done before, I sent him away to be broken."

"Before you sent him to us?" I asked.

"Yes, that's right. I sent him to a man called Jim Chapman for three weeks."

"And what happened?" cried Lisa.

"He put a dumb jockey on him. Do you know what that is?"

"I think so."

"A terrible contraption which runs from the bit to the

back and puts the horse's head in an overbent position and keeps it there. Of course, if I had known he had one, nothing on earth would have persuaded me to let him touch Bronco," she said.

"And how long did he leave it on?" I asked, seeing it all in my mind's eye. Bronco's back aching, his hocks, his neck.

"This is the worst part of it," replied Jean Nuttal. "He put it on meaning to come back in half an hour and remove it, but he crashed his car and didn't get back until next day . . ."

"Didn't he have any help?" I asked.

"No, he lives alone."

"Couldn't he have sent anyone?" asked Lisa, beginning to sniff.

"He was unconscious."

"So Bronco stood all night with his head strapped in one position?" I asked, just to be sure.

"Yes. And after that he wouldn't let anyone touch his back, not until you had him," said Jean Nuttal.

"Which explains why he went mad when the trainer at the film place put side reins on him – he thought they were going to be on all night," I cried.

"I expect so, dear." Jean Nuttal was opening a tin of fruit now.

"It's so sad," said Lisa.

"It's worse than that," I answered. "It explains everything. Poor little horse. I never thought he was a rogue. It must have been agony – torture. Think how his neck must have ached, and his back. I can't bear to think about it."

"But he was always strong," said Mrs Nuttal, handing me a bowl of tinned peaches. "Even as a foal, he knew where he was going. His dam was the same. Whatever happened, he would have been a handful."

"Have you told the film company about his background?" I asked. "Because it is important, isn't it? He's got to trust them and I have a feeling he doesn't trust men after what happened to him."

"I will," replied Mrs Nuttal.

"He knew I wasn't a dumb jockey," said Lisa.

"He may have felt safer without having a bridle," I answered.

Now everything seemed over. We understood Bronco, too late, of course, but at least we now knew the reason for his fear.

After lunch I said goodbye to Bronco and then I locked him back in his prison and rode away with the sound of his despairing neighs in my ears.

I felt very cold and very sad, as though someone I had loved was dead, and Lisa's small face looked pinched with despair. We didn't talk on the way home because we knew that words were now incapable of altering anything. We rode very fast; but it was still dusk when we eventually reached home. There was a crowd waiting for us in the stable-yard.

"What happened?" cried Mummy.

"Nothing."

"You promised to telephone."

"We forgot," I answered. "Why didn't you ring Mrs Nuttal?"

"We did but she didn't answer," replied Mummy. "We were about to send out a search party."

"I'm sorry." I slid to the ground, realising for the first time how small and ponyish Lorraine was after Hillingdon Prince.

"It's back to school again tomorrow," said Mummy. "The roads are quite clear now."

And so, I thought, the chapter's ended. Bronco, Hillingdon Prince, whatever you call him, goes back to his owners and this time they will be more careful. And I go back to school.

Mike had cleaned out the boxes for us and put everything ready. The lights from the house glimmered in the dusk.

"We've got a granny and three children coming at Easter," said Mummy. And so, I thought, in spite of everything, life goes on. We are back to the old routine. But I was wrong.

Twelve

Proper contracts

I dreamed that Bronco was in the yard and that I was locked in my room, unable to get out. I could hear the clatter of buckets and Cassie's welcoming neigh but my door was bolted and the window barred. And then suddenly I realised that it wasn't a dream, but real. I leaped out of bed and rushed to my window. The yard was full of moonlight and Bronco really was wandering about, pushing his nose into buckets. I pulled on a sweater and trousers and rushed downstairs and found my boots. I bumped into Lisa in the kitchen.

"Bronco's back," she cried.

"Yes, I know," I shouted.

I fell on the garden path because the slush had frozen. When I reached the yard, Bronco raised a bedraggled head and whinnied. I opened his box door and he went inside.

"You don't belong here," I said. "You're not ours any more. Can't you understand?" He looked in the manger and nuzzled my pockets. He looked pleased with himself, and then I saw that one of his legs was soaked in blood. "You are a fool," I said. "What have you done now?" I leaned down to look and he nuzzled my hair.

Lisa was staring over the box door.

"We need antiseptic and cotton wool. He must have broken his loose-box door down," I said.

His chest was covered with scratches and one of his
eyes was half closed, but it didn't seem to worry him; he
was obviously delighted to be home. We bathed his leg
and fetched him hay and water and Mummy appeared
inquiring, "What's happening?"

"Bronco's back," I replied.

"He seems wedded to this place. How far has he travelled this time?" she asked.

"Only eight miles," I answered, sponging his injured
eye with cold water.

"He really trusts you, Harriet," Mummy said.

"He's like a faithful hound, he always comes home,"
I answered.

When he was settled, we drank mugs of tea in the
kitchen, gathered round the Aga because the central
heating was off.

"I wonder what Jean Nuttal will say this time," said
Lisa.

"I'm not taking him back again," I replied.

"She needs a cage with a mesh roof to keep him in,"
said Mummy, laughing.

It was nearly morning now, so we didn't go back to
bed. Later Ben came down and at seven o'clock we telephoned Jean Nuttal. She sounded sleepy and rather
cross. "I never heard a thing. Are you sure it's Prince?"
she asked when I told her my news.

"Yes, without a doubt. He's pretty cut up. Has he had
a tetanus injection, or will he need one?"

"No. He had a combined one – tetanus and equine
flu vaccine – six months ago. What are we going to do
now?" she asked.

"I don't know," I said.

"I had better ring the film company. They can collect
him from you this time. I don't want all my boxes
smashed up. I can see his box now; the whole front is

down, not just the door. It will cost a mint of money to repair. Drat the horse," she said.

"When will they come for him?" I asked.

"I'll tell them to ring you. They can pay you for keeping him in the meantime, it's only fair," replied Jean Nuttal. A second later she rang off.

"The film company will telephone. Can't we miss school today, Mummy, please?" I cried. "Because they won't be able to box him."

"Certainly not, it's Saturday tomorrow. They can come then. Now get ready, your shoes need cleaning and your blazer's covered with horse hair."

In spite of getting up early, we all missed the bus and Mummy had to take us to school in the car, complaining loudly.

"It's not every day Bronco, sorry, Hillingdon Prince, comes back," I said.

"It seems like it, though," replied Mummy.

I couldn't concentrate at school and fell asleep in maths. Finally I was sent to see the headmaster, Mr

Chivers, who is bald with an egg-shaped head and gog-
gly eyes behind glasses. He made a great many tut-tut-
ting noises, while I explained that I had been wakened
early by a horse returning home. He was not amused,
because nothing ever amuses Mr Chivers. He told me
that I would never pass my GCSEs and that frivolity
wouldn't find me a job in life and did I know that there
were scores of unemployed school-leavers?

I said, "Sure, but I have a job already. I school
horses."

He looked furious and answered, "Now go back to
your classroom and behave in future or I shall have to
see your parents and you wouldn't like that, would
you?"

So I said "No."

The rest of the day passed at a snail's pace. I kept
imagining Bronco being taken away when I should have
been drawing plants and my exercise books became covered with his head instead of facts and figures. When at
last it was time to rush outside to get into the bus, I
found Ben waving with his good arm. "Mum's come for
us," he yelled. "The film people have turned up."

"Already?" I said.

"I'm afraid so."

"Couldn't they have waited?" I cried, breaking into a
run. "They're like vultures, aren't they? They want their
pound of flesh."

"Not a pound, two thousand pounds," replied Ben.

"Two thousand, then. I wish the Trippets had never
come," I said.

Mummy was wearing her best coat and high-heeled
shoes.

"I suppose it's the girls with the horse box again," I
said, getting into the car.

"No. It's two charming men," replied Mummy.

"They are waiting for you. They won't budge from the yard until you come. They won't even have a mug of tea in the kitchen."

"Are they taking Bronco on the roof-rack, then?" I asked.

"They want to talk to you. So try and be pleasant, please," Mummy answered.

"They're only prolonging the agony," I replied. "Are they waiting until they've built a cage for Bronco? I suppose that's it; they haven't got his prison ready yet."

"You're not going to blubber, are you?" asked Ben.

"Shut up," I said.

The yard was full of winter sunshine. An elegant Mercedes was parked in front of our old-fashioned tack room, which still has the fireplace before which a groom

once sat, boiling kettles for fomentations and bran mashes – or so I like to think.

The men were not as I had expected. One was dressed in riding-clothes, the other wore jeans and a denim jacket over a polo-necked sweater. He had brown eyes and dark curly hair, which kept flopping forward. Lisa was admiring them from a distance.

"Harriet," said the one in denims, holding out his hand. "I'm Mike Mitchells." I heard Ben give a small gasp and I thought: He must be famous.

Mummy said, "Will you come inside and have some tea? It really is teatime now."

"Thanks a million," they replied. "Your other daughter has been showing us around. I hope you don't mind."

"Not at all," replied Mummy, leading the way to the front door, which we never normally use.

"Harry here is the horse expert. I'm just the producer," said Michael Mitchells as we crossed the hall. "I'm sorry you've had so much trouble with the horse. Gordon Trippet is one of our scouts and he thought he had spotted a winner, but he forgot temperament."

"When are you taking him away?" I asked in a voice which was meant to be cool, calm and collected but which came out with a croak in it.

"That is what we want to discuss," replied Harry.

"He isn't fit to travel," I said.

"Well, actually we don't want him to travel," replied Mike Mitchells with a smile.

"You're going to kill him, aren't you?" asked Lisa, suddenly white and tense.

"No, darling," replied Mike Mitchells, "we're not vicious. We want him to stay *here*. We want your big sister to train him, for which we will pay her and, subject to one or two things, we want to make the film here; we've been looking for a location and this is it. It's perfect, absolutely right, down to the last detail."

"Here?" cried Ben. "You mean, in this house?"

"Yes, and in the stables. We'll have to build the odd arch, of course, for the coaches coming in and out."

"Coaches? You mean drawn by horses?" cried Lisa.

"That's right."

"Oh lord!" cried James. "You don't mean it?"

Mummy had been listening from the kitchen; now her hand was shaking so much she spilt milk on the sitting-room carpet.

"You'll have to move the guests out, of course," continued Mike Mitchells.

"When will it be?" asked Ben.

"End of May, beginning of June. We usually pay very high rates per day for a property like this, and it could take a month."

I thought Mummy was going to faint.

"In the meantime, I want you, Harriet, to train Prince – he's going to be called that in the story, so stick to it, please," he continued. "He must be able to pass anything, particularly trains. And he must be able to swim across a river. Can you do it, Harriet?"

"Yes," I said firmly.

"He must learn to carry a sidesaddle and you may have to stand in for Miss Edwards once or twice . . ."

"You don't mean Julie Edwards?" asked Ben.

"That's right."

"Oh good lord," cried James again.

"We'll draw up a proper contract, of course, and more people will have to come down to sort out the house. The staircase is perfect but we may have to alter the front gates. Do you think your husband will mind, Mrs Pemberton? We need a wide sweep to the front door, and pillars."

"Definitely not," replied Mummy, sipping tea. "We never did like the gates, anyway."

"And we'll be bringing in things like period beds. If you have to move out we'll pay any hotel bills. We will need the old stables, so some of your horses will have to be moved."

"No problem there," said Ben.

"We'll draw up proper contracts and let you have them in a few days," said Mr Mitchells. "This place should look perfect by May, but we will be planting extra flowers; it will be in the contract . . ."

I wanted to throw my arms round their necks, to shriek with joy.

"Prince has done us a good turn. I would never have seen this place otherwise; it's so unspoilt," said Mike Mitchells, stepping outside and smelling the air. "It hasn't been tarted up. And the atmosphere is just right. I knew it the moment I got out of the car. It's the right period too. It really is a lovely old place."

"He's famous," cried Ben as they drove away.

"So is Julie Edwards," added James.

"I thought I was going to pass out," exclaimed Mummy.

"How shall I teach Bronco to swim – I mean Prince?" I asked.

"And you are going to be paid," cried James. "You're so lucky."

"I feel sick," said Lisa.

"And here comes Dad," shouted Ben, and we started to dance and shout like lunatics. "Everything is all right," I screamed.

"We're going to be rich," yelled Ben.

"Just wait until you hear," said James.

I shall never have time for two horses I thought. "You can have Lorraine now, Lisa," I said. "You're big

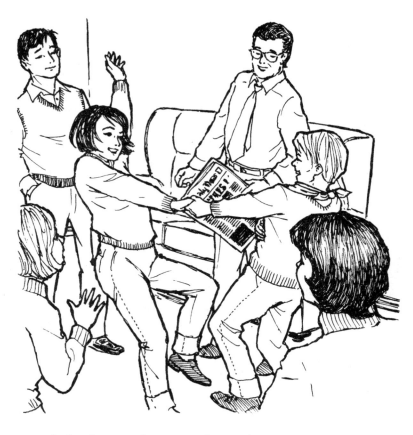

enough for her, and I'm too big. Okay?"

"Okay," she said. "And I'll lend Jigsaw to Rosie. She'll pay us to keep him and she does need a pony desperately. And she's my best friend at school."

So suddenly all the cold and the agony we had been through seemed worthwhile.

"We're made," said Dad when at last everyone had stopped talking. "We can advertise Black Pony Inn as the house used in such-and-such a film. People will come in droves, we'll never be half empty again."

"We must celebrate," said Mummy. "Steve and Janet have just left and Colonel Hunter loves a celebration."

"We must do the horses first," I said. "After all, it began with them, didn't it? Because if it hadn't been for Bronco, I mean Prince . . ."

"But what about the Trippets? We hated them but look what's happened!" said James.

"I don't know where it began or where it will end but it's wonderful just the same," cried Mummy, putting her arm through Dad's. "Let's all go out. Let's blow Steve's money. He paid in cash. I'm sick to death of cooking. Let's have a super-duper dinner at The Old White Lion."

"But who owns Bronco – I mean Prince – now?" cried Lisa.

"Them, I suppose," I said. "But he's going to stay here and who knows what may happen between now and the end of the filming?"

"We may all be film stars," shouted Lisa.

"Colonel Hunter will have to move out," said Dad. "Now get on and wash. I don't want you all smelling of horse at The Old White Lion."

We chose what we wanted for dinner, and the dining-room was lit by candles and was full of people in evening dress. The waiters were Spanish. We were all a bit tatty in appearance except for Colonel Hunter who came too and wore a dinner jacket.

Three days later a fat envelope containing two contracts came from the film company, one concerning the house and one concerning Prince, as we now called him. Prince's had my name at the top. It was very long and full of terms like "vested interests" which I didn't understand. But the gist of it was something like this: Hillingdon Prince remained the property of the film company until he was of no further use to them when he became mine. He had to reside with me but I had to agree to let them use him at any given time for filming, them being responsible for my travelling expenses and his, and a daily fee for any time I spent on location, the exact sum yet to be decided. I would also receive an outright fee for schooling him, and a weekly fee for his keep as long as he was with us. This would, of course, cease when he became my property. I would also be required to swim a river on Prince and perform some of the parts Julie Edwards couldn't, for which I would be paid.

It was the most exciting letter I had ever received. Dad was equally pleased with the contract concerning the house.

And best of all, Prince would now be with us for ever, a Prince at Black Pony Inn, insured against injury, mine as he grew older, a horse in a thousand to grace our stables. So suddenly the future looked brighter than the brightest day. And May glowed in the distance, a magic month when Julie Edwards would come to act out a script in our ancient house, and Prince would make his debut as a film star.

We walked about in a dream. All our troubles suddenly over. Our happiness seeming to stretch to eternity and now, at last, money didn't matter any more.

Catastrophe at
Black Pony Inn

CONTENTS

One

They're very rich

The summer was almost over. The winter's hay for the horses had been delivered; the garden chairs put away. School was about to start again. And we had only three elderly guests at Black Pony Inn. That was until Mummy dropped the bombshell, or rather Mum, because recently, for various reasons, we had stopped calling her Mummy. Smiling at us now, she said, "We've got a whole family coming to Black Pony Inn next week. Isn't that fantastic? They're not old either, so they'll sharpen us up a bit."

I didn't want to be sharpened up. I wanted life to go on the same for ever. Colonel Hunter had been with us for years. The other two guests were sisters, and always had what you needed suddenly, like sticking plaster, and needles and thread for plaiting manes. They were more like relations than paying guests.

Now Lisa, who is younger than me and more down to earth, asked, "Will there be children and if so, how many?"

"A boy and a girl," replied Mum, still smiling.

Ben, my younger brother, looked at me and said, "There go our rooms again, Harriet."

At the same moment James, who was seventeen, said, "I don't think it matters what they're like, if they bring in some money."

"I agree," said Dad. "It's money we need and they're bringing horses and dogs too. If they stay long enough we'll be able to build a swimming-pool."

"And think how nice that will be," Mum said, patting me on the shoulder. "You can swim every morning then, Harriet. You and Ben can train for the Pony Club tetrathlon too, can't you?"

"And their horses? What are they like?" I asked, unable to keep the excitement out of my voice.

"Show horses is how they described them," replied Mum. "The family are called Abbott, by the way – Grace and Pat Abbott, and their children are Justin and Tracey. They are waiting to move into a house they've bought. They're very rich. This was the only place they could find which would take their horses and dogs as well. I'm sure you'll like them."

Dad must have met them too, for now he added, "They are very positive. They showed us snapshots and everything they have looks wonderful – dogs, horses, cars . . . well, everything."

"And their children?" asked Lisa.

"Very neat," Dad said.

I looked at our parents. Dad has a round face with dark hair which curls when it's wet. Mum has nut brown hair and brown eyes. Dad is bulky, a bit like a dark-haired teddy bear, while Mum is quite small. Now they looked happy, which made me think of the bills in red dropping through the letterbox every morning. Three paying guests were hardly enough to keep Black Pony Inn going, so they had reason to smile.

As Ben suspected, he and I had to move out of our rooms, so we spent that afternoon, which was Saturday, moving our belongings into the attic bedrooms where Lisa usually reigned in solitary splendour. James didn't have to move. He has the smallest room in the house and it's always in chaos.

"It's going to be an invasion, isn't it?" asked Ben, pushing a lock of fair hair out of his eyes. "And I bet we never get the swimming-pool."

"They'll hate James. They won't like him spilling coffee and forgetting things. You know how cross Colonel Hunter gets, and he isn't particularly neat," I said.

We dragged our bedclothes up the attic stairs and made our beds. "Perhaps they'll give us tips if we carry their suitcases," suggested Ben, straightening his duvet.

"Tipping's out of date," I said.

"Not among the rich," argued Ben.

Later we went outside to check our horses. They were still living out. Liver chestnut Prince and grey Lorraine were gnawing at each other's manes. Ben's dark brown Welsh cob Solitaire was grazing alongside piebald Jigsaw, whom we sometimes drove in a governess cart. Our first pony, black Limpet, cantered across the front paddock to greet us. They were not just our ponies, they were our friends.

"It's been such a fantastic summer," I said.

"They may be nice, Tracey may be quite old. We don't know their ages yet," said Lisa, joining us.

"James may fall in love with her," suggested Ben.

"Or you," I added, laughing.

"No way," retorted Ben, throwing grass at me.

We had tea in the kitchen, while Mum waited on the guests in the sitting-room with a new spring in her stride. We ate lots of lardy-cake and home-made flapjacks.

"You look so gloomy. They're a lovely family, you'll like them. And think of the dogs, you know you've always wanted dogs. Well, now you'll have them," Mum said, washing up cups and saucers.

"How long will they be here?" Ben asked, eating his fifth flapjack.

"Between six and twelve weeks, they're not sure yet," Mum said.

"But that means they might be here at Christmas," I cried. "Won't I have my room back by Christmas Eve?"

"Yes, of course, long before that I expect," Mum replied, but she didn't sound certain.

"Think of the dogs," Ben said later, mimicking Mum and laughing, while we sat staring at a television programme without really seeing it.

"I hope the dogs are small and sweet," said Lisa, counting her pencils. "Dad says that Justin and Tracey won't be going to our school. They're going to St Peter's. They are too posh for the local school," she continued scornfully.

"We mustn't hate them before they're even here," James said.

It was dark outside by now. We were sitting in the room which years and years ago was the servants' hall. It looks out towards the stables and is next to the kitchen, which still has an old pump in it, a bread oven and a huge dresser running the entire length of one wall. Often while we are in the old servants' hall, which is now called the playroom, we imagine servants sitting there – cook, butler, kitchen maid and all the upstairs servants as well. They sit round the large table where we do our homework, eating; the butler at the top is lording it over the others, while a tiny kitchen maid waits on them.

In years gone by Black Pony Inn was quite an important house. It was called The Manor then. Newly prosperous Mr Black had built it for his wife and five children. When Mum and Dad turned it into a guest house we called it Black Pony Inn because we already had Limpet. But it's not the sort of inn which sells intoxicating liquor or dinner at pounds and pounds a head. It's just a guest house, really, where people can stay as long as they like, for a reasonable amount of money.

"I need a rubber and has anyone pinched my calculator?" said Lisa. She was the only one of us preparing for school, which started on Monday. James would simply throw all his things into his briefcase after breakfast on Monday morning. Ben had put his things ready days ago. He had even cleaned his school shoes. I had washed my school blouses and a skirt which was shiny with wear.

I didn't want to go back to school. The summer had been long and heavenly. Prince had won the Novice Jumping at our local show and come second in the Pairs Jumping with Lisa on Lorraine. Ben had won a Working Hunter class on Solitaire, who isn't a working hunter, but was the only horse to jump a clear round. Lisa had won numerous gymkhana events. And I had won the Open Musical Poles at the Pony Club gymkhana. We had been to the sea. And James had gone to France with a friend called Charles. Dad had done reasonably well selling double glazing, so in spite of the bills dropping through the letterbox, we had all had new school blazers except for James who didn't need one. Going upstairs to find things for school, I thought: It's the lull before the storm. Now we're to lose everything – our rooms, our stables, our privacy.

Presently Mum appeared and sat on my bed. "Don't be gloomy, Harriet darling," she said. "The time will soon pass. And you may actually like the Abbotts. They are horsy after all. You mustn't always look on the black side; it's a bad habit."

"It's all right, I don't mind giving up my room," I lied, looking into Mum's tired face. "Of course I don't. I just hope they're nice. I suppose their horses will have to be stabled. How many are they bringing?"

"Four."

That meant that all the old loose boxes would be oc- cupied, leaving only the two new ones empty. So now I saw our own ponies standing outside, waiting to come in, as the days grew shorter and the nights colder. Soon they would start neighing and rattling the gates, expect- ing feeds in their mangers and deep beds of golden straw or pale shavings.

"I feel like a poor relation. I always feel like that when we have children staying," I said, going to the window and looking out into the darkness.

"That's a terrible thing to say," replied Mum.

"And where will the dogs sleep?" I cried, turning round.

"Heaven knows. We'll have to play it by ear. Oh, don't look so glum, Harriet. We'll find somewhere for them," Mum said.

But I already knew where that would be. They would sleep in the two remaining loose boxes, the new ones, because they would be that sort of dog, neither small nor sweet as Lisa hoped, but big and expensive, the sort of dogs rich men keep.

"The Abbotts are really very nice, darling, I promise you," Mum told me before padding away in knitted slipper-sox to console Ben.

At last I had everything ready for school. When I returned on Monday the Abbotts would have arrived. I could hear Mum cleaning my real bedroom below. I had emptied the contents of my chest of drawers into suitcases, which were now under the bed in the tiny attic bedroom. I had put my collection of china horses on the window ledge by my bed. Each of them had a name. My favourite books were piled on the bedside table. It was nearly suppertime. Next door I found Ben lying on his metal, hospital-type bed, staring at the ceiling.

"Once servant girls came here at twelve years old to live in these rooms and to work for Mr and Mrs Black, think of that, Harriet," he said.

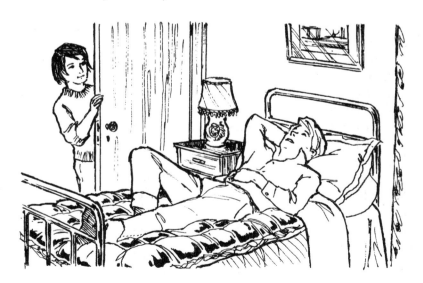

"Once Ben and Harriet Pemberton were turned out of their rooms and had to sleep up here," I replied. "So what?"

"The Abbotts are rich. Their children will give us their old clothes. Justin will play cricket in white flannels. They'll have rich voices and call us the hoi polloi," Ben said, smiling happily. "But will they change us or us them? That is the question."

"We'll change them," I replied firmly, before going in search of Lisa. I found her downstairs cleaning her shoes.

"I need a new pair. I need lots of new things. My satchel is held together by safety pins," she complained.

"That's why we are having the Abbotts. As usual we need the money," I said bitterly.

Lisa pushed her fair hair out of her eyes and looked at me. "But you know we couldn't have the ponies if we didn't have the guests. We would have to live in a tiny house with hardly any garden. Can't you see how lucky we are, Harriet?" she cried. And looking at her, so much younger than me and so stoic, made me feel suddenly ashamed.

"But it's all right for you, you don't have to move out of your room," I said.

"But I always live in the attic, that's why. If you did the same it would make life much easier for everyone, and you wouldn't have to move then," replied Lisa.

But I didn't want to live in the attic, because my room looks out on to the paddocks and the stables. It has a big beech tree outside where squirrels swing from branch to branch. It's my room and it always has been, and I love it. It's my lair too and full of memories and dreams and it's been like that almost as long as I can remember.

"I'm looking forward to going back to school. I want

142

to see Gillian and Rosie again. I shall be in the top form, and Rosie's moving to London after Christmas," Lisa said.

Lisa seemed to be growing older, whereas I felt just the same. I didn't want to grow up. I didn't want to be fourteen or fifteen and never sixteen. I wanted to go on being thirteen for ever.

Monday would be the start of a new year at school with different teachers and different classrooms. And every minute away from Black Pony Inn seemed a minute wasted. I didn't need friends, because I had Ben and Lisa and the ponies. And I would far rather be riding Prince than playing hockey or doing gymnastics. I'm being what Dad calls negative, I thought, laying the kitchen table for supper. But I'm going to make myself change. And I vowed that I would stop whinging about my room and like the Abbotts. But I had no idea then how hard it was going to be.

Two

The Abbotts arrive

On Monday, when Ben and I returned from school, Lisa met us in the stable-yard. "They've arrived. They came in two posh cars and they're drinking tea in the kitchen," she cried.

"You make them sound like an army of occupation," said Ben.

"What about their horses?" I asked.

"They're coming later in a horse box. And guess what, they've got a girl groom. And they absolutely insisted on drinking tea in the kitchen; they said they wanted to be treated as family," Lisa finished.

"It gets worse and worse," exclaimed Ben.

"At least they're trying to be friendly," I said.

Then Mum saw us and called, "How was school? Come in and meet the Abbotts, instead of lurking out there in the shadows like strangers."

There was a BMW and a Japanese car parked by the front door. James was examining the cars. A tall man opened the back door and welcomed us with open arms. "Ah, you must be Harriet," he cried. "I'm so very glad to meet you." He flung his arms round me in a crushing embrace. When he let go, I saw that he had greying hair, a dark moustache and blue eyes. Shaking Ben by the hand he exclaimed, "And you must be Benjamin. I'm glad to meet you too."

A woman who could only be Mrs Abbott, who wore slacks and an expensive jumper with a pattern of dogs on it, said, "Don't be shy, Tracey, come and meet Harriet." Tracey was younger than Lisa. There were gaps between her teeth. When she said hello she sounded as though she had a cold.

Justin was dark haired, with a closed expression which gave nothing away. He had a small mouth with tight lips. Looking at Ben he said, "Your trousers are a bit short, aren't they? They really do look most peculiar."

"Oh, Justin, what a thing to say! Don't be so rude," cried Mrs Abbott.

"Don't listen to the young pup, Ben. Your trousers are fine," said Mr Abbott, smiling indulgently.

Ben looked at his trousers. He had been wanting a new pair for ages, but hadn't liked to ask for some. Now he said, "Ankle length trousers are in fashion, didn't you know, Justin? St Peter's *must* be out of date, everyone's wearing them this year," and laughed. Then we heard a horse box arriving outside and we all rushed out to the stable-yard. A girl was driving the horse box and the horse box was towing a caravan.

"Whoa! Stop!" shouted Mr Abbott. "That's fine."

Suddenly I wished that Dad was with us, because Mr Abbott seemed to be taking over Black Pony Inn and Mum wasn't stopping him.

"There's a telephone in the BMW. It's very posh," said James, joining us.

"So what?" Ben muttered crossly.

Rugged and bandaged, with the initials G.A. on their rugs, the horses came down the ramps on the horse box one by one, each more beautiful than the last.

"Meet Seamus, Sultan, Scorpio and Stardust," said Mrs Abbott proudly.

We had prepared their boxes for them and they were soon installed, while our ponies looked over the field gate, their eyes agog with curiosity. Seamus and Sultan were large bays with beautiful heads and thoroughbred legs. Scorpio was black with one white sock and about fourteen hands. Stardust was about thirteen one, liver chestnut with a small star on his forehead. They were all geldings and beautifully turned out, their coats gleaming, their manes and tails perfectly pulled, their eyes shining. Looking over the field gate, our ponies suddenly appeared ordinary by comparison, their coats covered with fresh mud from rolling, their manes too long, their fetlocks untrimmed. They looked humble, like poor relations, I thought sadly, wiping tears from my eyes.

"What's the matter? Why are you crying?" hissed Lisa.

"I'm not crying, stupid. My eyes are watering, that's all," I retorted angrily. "I just hate looking at our horses out in the cold, that's all," I added.

"But it isn't cold," replied Lisa, missing the point entirely.

The girl groom was large and fair haired. She addressed the Abbotts by their Christian names.

"Wow, what a place!" she cried, smiling at Lisa, as soon as the horses were settled. "Let's see your ponies. Come on, I want a proper tour. Are you Lisa?" And I thought that Susan and Lisa seemed to be on the same wavelength.

We toured our mud-covered ponies. Susan called them all "poppets". Mrs Abbott said that Limpet looked like a tinker's pony. They all laughed at Jigsaw's large head and short legs. "His forebears must have been bred for the coal mines," said Mrs Abbott. She called Solitaire "a good sort", Lorraine a bit light in the neck,

146

Prince, she said, had character, "Bags of it." Then they showed us their horses in detail, if that is the right word, relating to us the prizes they had won, a whole catalogue of them. After that Tracey asked whether we would like to see her silver cups.

"We can't, we've got our homework to do," said Ben, making a face at me.

Justin said, "Have you started school already? St Peter's doesn't start until Wednesday. It's a first-class school with people from all over the world."

"I'm sure there are," said James seriously.

I knew St Peter's. It had wrought-iron entrance gates with a shield on them. It had a long drive lined with trees, huge playing fields and a lake. It sent crews to regattas and sides to cricket matches. James had once told me that it was full of wimps and that the girls talked as though they had plums in their mouths. So I didn't envy Justin. St Peter's had a preparatory school as well. I had seen tiny children being driven there in school uniforms, and once walking in a crocodile along a pavement. Poor Tracey, I thought. I bet it isn't any fun.

"Why don't you come and see our dogs now?" suggested Mrs Abbott, whose blonde hair was swept back, high off her forehead.

The dogs were called Rascal, Ruffian and Ruby. Ruffian was a Doberman, the other two boxers. Ruffian and Ruby were in one of our new loose boxes, Rascal in the other. So now there wasn't a single loose box left for our ponies.

"They win prizes too. Ruffian is a champion," Tracey told us.

"Ruffian isn't his name," said Mr Abbott, joining us. "They all have much more complicated names. But it's impossible to call them Rednight Ruffian or Roseware Renegade – far too long-winded."

Our ponies continued to lean over the field gate, their eyes shining with hope, or was it envy? Or jealousy? Or just plain curiosity? I wished I knew.

At last I went inside to look at Tracey's cups. She had unpacked them and put them on the window ledge in what I still thought of as my room. There were five, each with her name and the date engraved on it and she gave them to me in turn to look at.

"They're fantastic," I said, handing them back one after another.

Her dark blue riding-jacket was hanging on a hanger at the end of my bed. A photo of her on a pony bedecked with rosettes was on my chest of drawers.

"I won most of my cups on him," she said, pointing at the photograph. "He even went to Wembley. He's called Charcoal Burner. You may have seen his picture in *Horse and Hound*. We called him Burney for short," Tracey explained, and handed me another photograph.

He was bay and plaited and beautiful. "He's great. But where is he now?" I asked handing it back.

"Sold on. I grew out of him," Tracey said. "Can I see your cups now?"

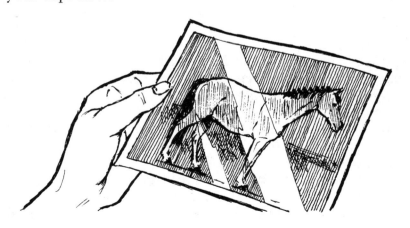

"I haven't any, only rosettes. But Lisa's got one," I said. And now I felt humiliated, because Tracey seemed to have everything – my room, fame, a girl groom, rich parents. And she was only eight years old! It was almost too much to bear.

"I had better do my homework," I said, standing up. "See you later." Envy is a sin, I told myself as I ran downstairs. And I've got Prince and he's ten times nicer than all the Abbott horses put together, but I wasn't sure, and I couldn't help imagining myself wearing a dark blue show jacket with a red lining, standing in the middle of the arena at Wembley holding a silver cup.

I helped Mum dish up supper in the kitchen. Dad wasn't home yet. James usually waited on the guests. The sisters, who are called Mrs Tomson and Miss Steele, were always pressing bars of chocolate into his hands. They called him "our boy". Miss Steele wore her grey hair short and straight, while Mrs Tomson's was long and in a bun on the back of her head. Miss Steele wore steel spectacles, Mrs Tomson plastic framed ones. They talked alike and were always together. Dad called them the twins.

Tracey had supper in her room, sitting up in my bed like a princess. The others ate in the dining-room, which is large and panelled. Justin appeared to be lecturing his parents on computers. The elderly ladies and Colonel Hunter sat at a different table, each with their own table napkin in its own special ring.

While we were putting the dishes in our recently acquired dishwasher, Mum said, "They've parked their caravan behind the stables and Susan is living in it and we haven't got permission."

"Do we have to have it?" I asked.

"Yes, of course, we're not a camping site," Mum said.

Ben was cleaning his shoes. "I should let Dad deal

with it," he advised, while Lisa interrupted, saying:

"You're looking for problems, Mum. It'll be all right. I think they're nice and Justin is great. I'm glad they're here. This place was becoming like an old people's home." We could hear Colonel Hunter talking, telling the Abbotts about his wartime experiences which had been the highlight of his life.

It was like any other evening, but different because the Abbotts were with us, which made Mum on edge, as she always is with new guests, for she's afraid they'll find the beds hard or the food not to their liking. She hates guests complaining. One complaint and her day is ruined.

I went upstairs to fetch Tracey's tray. She was reading *Pony* with a teddy bear beside her. "I love this room, it's so comfy," she said, smiling at me, wanting to be liked, while I only saw a spoilt little girl in my bed, with half the food uneaten on her plate.

"Yes, it's the nicest room in the house," I answered bitterly, taking her tray.

"And the bed's lovely and soft," she added as I shut the door after me.

I cannot remember how that particular day ended. I remember I did my homework in the playroom using oceans of Tipp-Ex, and I remember lying in bed looking at the eaves in my attic without seeing them, seeing instead myself at a huge horse show with television cameras looking down on me and the queen in the Royal Box.

"We've had so many guests, I can't think why you're whinging about the Abbotts, Harriet," said Ben next morning as we waited for the school bus. "They aren't any trouble and having a basin and shower instead of a bathroom isn't the end of the world. I know you don't

151

like giving up your bedroom – but there are people who don't have a bedroom, who sleep on pavements, or on the ground in mud huts."

"Thanks for the social lecture. But I know you're only trying to convince yourself, because you care as much as I do," I replied, with unusual perception. And I saw that I was right, because as I spoke Ben wiped a tear from one of his large hazel-coloured eyes.

That day at school seemed no more than an interlude between being with and being away from the Abbotts. Mr Abbott had left for London at 5 a.m. in his BMW. Dad had risen early to give him breakfast, then left himself in our ancient Volvo. Miss Steele and Mrs Tomson had had breakfast on the stroke of eight in the dining-room. I know because James overslept, so I had waited on them and remember them saying, "Where's our boy then?" The rest of the day seemed endless. But at last we were climbing into the school bus again, which goes miles around the countryside dropping pupils off at remote villages before leaving us on the edge of the common.

When we reached home at last it was to find Tracey riding round and round our small paddock on Stardust. She was cantering circles, then popping Stardust over our one and only cavaletti. Mrs Abbott was watching. Seeing us, she called "Halt" in a loud voice. Then beckoning to us she added, "You'll have to get some more poles and uprights, Harriet. What's here is totally inadequate."

"We have a few more poles and some oil-drums somewhere," answered Ben vaguely. "And some cross-country fences if you look."

"Your mother doesn't seem to know anything about the horses. She says it's your business," grumbled Mrs Abbott, who was beautifully dressed in an expensive jumper with a silk scarf at the neck, elegant slacks, and smart boots. But whatever she wore, she would always look wonderful, I thought enviously, admiring her slim figure.

"I'll find you a pole," offered Ben, handing me his school case.

"I need more than one, six at least," she shouted back in a voice used to being obeyed.

It seemed to be Susan's day off, for as we searched for poles we could hear music coming from her caravan. I can't remember what it was now, except that it was loud and modern, the sort of thing James listens to with his girlfriend Virginia. At last we found some poles lying in a bed of nettles.

"I'll just take off my school clothes, then I'll be right back," Ben shouted.

"Mrs Abbott didn't ask us whether Tracey could ride in our paddock. And now she's cutting it up," I grumbled, following Ben indoors.

Lisa was sitting in the kitchen stuffing herself with crumpets. "She wants poles," she said.

"Who's she? The cat's mother?" I asked.

"Tracey rides every day after school. She hasn't a single friend. She says she doesn't need them. She's too busy," continued Lisa, talking through a half-eaten crumpet.

"Lucky her. Where's Justin then?" I asked, taking off my blazer.

"Tacking up. He says that either you do things professionally and with dedication, or not at all. His school motto is: *Dedication Breeds Excellence* – in Latin of course. It's on his blazer," said Lisa.

"And on the school gates. When do they start school anyway?" I asked.

"Tomorrow. They've been buying things for school

today," said Lisa, starting to eat yet another crumpet.

We returned to the stable-yard. Justin was schooling by himself in the bottom paddock, riding round and round on black Scorpio. Ben and I dragged the poles to the schooling paddock. The nettles stung my hands, and one of the dogs chased our cat Twinkle to the top of a tall tree. Our ponies stood watching the schooling session like spectators at a cricket match.

"I think I prefer old ladies. They don't want poles, or to cut up our paddock, or use all our loose boxes," I said.

"You sound like an old person yourself – grumble, grumble," retorted Ben.

We watched Tracey schooling Stardust. Mrs Abbott was still standing in the centre of the paddock like an instructor. "Shorten your reins, keep contact. That's it, well done, steady, steady, don't let him lose cadence. I want you to lengthen his stride, Tracey. That's it. Well done." Then she turned to us and called, "Why don't you ride with Tracey, Harriet?"

"Go on, show what you can do," urged Ben. So I caught Prince and, after brushing him quickly with a dandy brush, tacked him up. Ben held my stirrup while I mounted.

"Go on, you show them," he said again, smiling in a silly way as he opened the paddock gate to let me through.

"Do up the harness on your hat, Harriet," called Mrs Abbott. "That's better. Now let's see how you're sitting," she continued, pushing me in the back. "Of course your saddle doesn't help. You need a deep-seated one," she added after a moment.

"And isn't she riding too short, Mummy?" asked Tracey in her bossy little voice, which I was beginning to hate.

"Yes, you're absolutely right, poppet, she is," said Mrs Abbott warmly. "Now come on, Harriet, hang your legs down, stretch, that's better. You young people never realise that you grow. You go on and on riding with the same length of stirrup. It's crazy. Two notches down I think. How does that look, Tracey?" she asked.

"Okay, Mummy, much better."

"Thank you, poppet."

Ben was leaning on the gate, splitting his sides with laughter.

"Okay, Harriet, off you go now on the right rein. Keep contact. Legs further back. Oh dear, oh dear, your leg position is still out of tune, Harriet," she called, standing in the middle now. "Halt. I want to show you something."

That's how it went on. Stop, start. Tracey's advice and comments treated like pearls of wisdom by Mrs Abbott. Ben grew tired and went indoors. Dusk darkened the sky. Susan emerged from the caravan. Justin put the dogs to bed. But I had to admit that Mrs Abbott was a marvellous instructor and soon Prince was dropping his nose and relaxing his back and feeling wonderful. It was Tracey who spoilt the lesson because she couldn't help adding her comments all the time. Things like: "She isn't looking ahead, Mummy," and "Shouldn't she change her diagonal now, Mummy?"

Justin and Scorpio joined us briefly towards the end. "Now, darling, show Harriet how a circle should be done," Mrs Abbott said. "Now watch, Harriet. See how Scorpio bends his body. Prince can't do that yet, he's too stiff. Asking him to make a circle is like asking a pencil, neither of them can bend. Harriet, are you listening?"

I nodded. I knew she was right, they were all right. But I was finding it hard to take, especially from eight-year-old Tracey.

As we untacked in the yard Tracey said, "Don't worry, Harriet. Prince will improve in time. I know he will."

"Lunging will help," Justin advised. "But you must keep up your schooling. Riding once or twice a week isn't good enough, not if you want to win, anyway." He sounded at least twenty years old.

"And you know you haven't won a single cup yet, Harriet. Wouldn't you like a row of them like me?" asked Tracey, smiling into my face.

Three

Where's Tracey?

I tried to like the Abbotts. We all did. They paid Lisa to exercise their dogs after school. Tracey followed me everywhere, often she sat on my bed simply staring at me. Mum said that she had a pash on me, poor thing. Tracey even wanted me to watch television with her every evening on the set she now had in what I still considered my bedroom. And the more she liked me, the more of a hypocrite I felt.

Susan pulled our horses' manes and tails without asking and free of charge, which upset Ben who thinks long manes are romantic, and me because I was afraid they would be cold living outside without them. But we said "How lovely" and "Thank you" all the same.

Susan chatted up James and invited him into her caravan, which wasn't any tidier than his room, being full of clothes thrown down everywhere and dirty mugs in the small sink. But James had his girlfriend Virginia already and wasn't interested in Susan. He only went into the caravan out of politeness. Mr Abbott worked incredibly long hours and we hardly saw him. James called him a worker-bee. Mrs Abbott rode their horses every morning with Susan. It turned out that she was a qualified instructor. She advised me to change Prince's bit and took away the martingale he had been wearing. She expected me to be absolutely dedicated to riding,

157

all the time. "That's the only way you'll succeed," she told me. So what with Tracey's demands and so much riding, I never had a moment to myself.

When Justin wasn't riding or at school he played chess on his computer, which was now in Ben's old room. Otherwise he watched television programmes, but only the ones which taught him something. He knew so many facts that Ben dubbed him a walking encyclopedia. "Don't any of them ever daydream?" he asked, when for a moment we were alone, leaning on a field gate, sucking blades of autumn grass. "Or stop to look at a sunset? And all this riding to win, I know it's important, but what about life being fun as well," he continued. "I don't believe they've ever played Charades, or any game which isn't in some way educational. I don't believe that Justin has ever been young."

"But he'll be famous, while we're nonentities," I countered.

"If he doesn't crack up first," replied Ben.

Mum had taken on an extra cleaning lady to cope with the Abbotts. She was called Peggy and always seemed to have lost her dusters or the polish. And I could see that she annoyed the Abbotts. "Why doesn't she get her act together?" demanded Mrs Abbott one day.

"Perhaps she hasn't got an act," I said.

"No wonder she's only a cleaning woman then," Mrs Abbott continued. "I've no patience with that sort of person. She needs to pull her socks up. Shall I speak to her?"

"No, thank you, she'll leave if you do," I said quickly. "Mum says that praise is the best spur. Anyway, no one wants to clean other people's houses these days; they think it's demeaning."

"Well, if they can't do anything else, they have no

choice," snapped Mrs Abbott.

The leaves were changing colour on the trees. Soon it would be too dark to ride after school. I wondered what the Abbotts would do then. If Tracey had a pash on me, Lisa had one on Susan, for now she spent every spare moment in the caravan playing cards with Susan or trying out her make-up. At weekends she helped Susan instead of looking after our horses. It was "Susan says this" or "Susan says that" all day long, until I felt like screaming. And when she wasn't with Susan, she was exercising Rascal, Ruffian and Ruby, keeping them on their leads, dragging them round the common in the dusk. Soon she was hardly ever in the house, and Mum

told her that she was treating it like a hotel. James spent
all his spare time with Virginia, who was red haired and
rather snooty. Our horses, meanwhile, continued to look
over the gate at the stables every evening, while I started
to pray that the Abbotts would be gone before the cold
weather arrived, for I desperately wanted life to be normal by Christmas.

Comparing this time with what was to come after, it
was a quiet time. And at least Lisa was happy, for she
was being paid ten pounds a week for exercising the
dogs and had already bought herself stripy socks with
the money, and a red woolly hat.

Our troubles really began on the day Tracey asked
whether she might ride with me. "Please, please. I won't
be a nuisance, I promise," she pleaded, watching me
tack up Prince.

I didn't want her. I wanted to ride alone. I love riding
alone. There was a little whispering breeze which picked
up the bits of the hay lying in the yard and whisked
them away. The first leaves were falling off the trees,
just a few, nothing like the avalanche which would follow in a few weeks' time.

"Must you? Well, you had better ask your mother
then," I replied without enthusiasm, hoping her mother
would say no.

"Thank you, oh thank you, Harriet," cried Tracey,
running towards the house to find her mother.

I pulled up Prince's girth and let down my stirrups.
I was sure Mrs Abbott would refuse, because she
wouldn't trust me, wouldn't believe I was capable of
looking after Tracey. But a minute later Tracey was
back, her glowing face relaying the news before she even
opened her mouth to cry, "I can go. She said yes."

Susan tacked up Stardust, saying glumly, "Rather you
than me, Harriet. And you'll have to see to him when

160

you get back. I'm off this afternoon. It is Saturday, you know. I have to have a half day off sometimes."

"That's all right. I'll see to him, don't worry," I said. Prince was on edge. He didn't like Stardust. And it seemed ages since I had ridden him out.

"We'll go through the woods. Are you sure you'll be all right?" I asked Tracey as Susan put her up, tightening her girth and adjusting her stirrups. Tracey nodded; she was still glowing with happiness which made me think she was really rather sweet and at least she didn't argue all the time like Lisa.

Stardust had to jog to keep up with Prince, who has a wonderful walk. Tracey's face was creased with happiness. I was surprised her mum hadn't appeared to see us off. Stardust wore a kimblewick bit and was afraid of his mouth. He looked at everything – pieces of paper, manholes in the road, dustbins left outside houses. But soon we were in the woods, which hold so many memories for me. In spring there is a carpet of bluebells under the tall beech trees there. Today there was a coating of orange leaves which rustled beneath our horses' hoofs. We trotted on and Tracey was still smiling. "I've never hacked like this before, Harriet. It's lovely," she told me.

Suddenly I was afraid. I slowed down. "We'd better walk then," I said. "We don't want you to do too much the first time, do we?"

But Tracey wanted to trot. "It's quite different from riding in the school with Mummy in the middle," she chirped happily. "I feel really grown up riding with you, Harriet. It's super duper."

We came out of the wood and rode down a lane. Then we reached the last of the year's stubble, which in a week's time would become dark, ploughed earth. "Are you all right for a canter?" I asked. "Just a slow one, nothing fast."

Tracey nodded, her hat pushed low on her forehead. We smiled at one another, and she gave a happy giggle as we set off gently side by side. "It's lovely, Harriet," she said again.

Prince was going well, he had dropped his nose and his hocks were under him. He felt as though he could go for ever. The wind blew gently in our faces. The sky was full of dancing clouds. It was a spring day in autumn – that's how it felt anyway.

I saw dogs in the distance and then, without warning, a gun went off and then another and another, and Stardust was galloping with Tracey screaming on top.

I shouted, "Sit up, sit back, pull on the reins, Tracey." But with an awful feeling in the pit of my stomach I knew that nothing would stop Stardust now. His head was down and he was heading for home. And if I chased him he would simply go faster and faster, so with my heart hammering, I cantered behind calling out instructions, while fear invaded my stomach and my brain felt clear and icy cold with an awful fatalism.

I could see the men with their guns. There were three of them and they were carrying dead pigeons. Stardust had reached the end of the stubble by now and was back in the woods, and I could hear Tracey calling, "I can't stop him, Harriet." It was a moment I would never forget, which would be engraved for ever in my memory, so that I would never gallop on stubble again without recalling it with horror. I pushed Prince into a gallop. I reached the wood, but the faster I went, the faster Stardust galloped. It was the old quandary: Chase a horse and you'll send him faster, stay behind and with luck he'll stop and wait for you. Only Stardust wasn't stopping and he had no intention of waiting for me. Stardust was heading for home and I knew that in a minute he was going to be galloping down a road full of

Saturday shoppers driving into town. Then he was going to sprint across the common and swing into the stable-yard at a flat-out gallop. And there was nothing I could do to stop him.

It was then that I started to pray, "God, please help Tracey, please make Stardust stop." But since I never go to church I could hardly expect God to do anything, and He didn't.

When I reached the road, several cars had already stopped. Stardust was disappearing into the distance and a young couple were kneeling over Tracey. I drew rein then, my heart hammering with fear, while Prince threw his head up and down with impatience. I dismounted before I approached the couple. "Is she all right?" I asked nervously.

"Yes, poor kid, but her mouth is full of blood," the woman said.

I imagined Tracey toothless, her parents wrath. And at that moment I wished that the earth would swallow me up.

Then Tracey stood up; her face was covered with a mixture of mud, tears and blood. "He wouldn't stop. I pulled and pulled. I really did, Harriet," she said.

"Stardust's a beastly pony who should be shot," I answered.

"We'll take you home, dear. Where is it?" the woman asked. I could see that they were a nice couple, he with dark hair, hers chestnut. They were nicely dressed too. James would have called them yuppies. Tracey pointed to Black Pony Inn standing beyond the common. The woman helped Tracey into their car, while I set off for home at a gallop.

There was a crowd waiting by the yard gate.

"Where's Tracey?" screamed Mrs Abbott.

"What's happened?" asked Mum, looking at me. She was frantic.

Ben was holding Stardust. He had scraped one knee, otherwise he appeared unhurt.

"She's all right. She can walk and everything," I said lamely.

"How dare you take her out without permission?" shouted Mrs Abbott.

"But Tracey asked you. I know she did." I dismounted and my legs felt weak and my head was still fuzzy with fright.

"She didn't ask. She just said could she ride with you. That's all, Harriet. She isn't good enough to ride Stardust out," said Mrs Abbott.

"Any fool can see that," Justin added spitefully.

Lisa was crying. Was she sorry for me or for Tracey, I wondered. The car was turning into the yard now. The young woman, who seemed to be called Margaret,

jumped out. "Your little girl threw herself off when she saw the cars. She could have been killed," she said.

I saw now that Tracey had grazed her chin. She looked pale and grimy and shocked all at the same time.

"I couldn't stop him, Mummy," she said. "There were guns. Men shooting. It was horrible."

I felt so ashamed now that I couldn't look at anyone. Feeling like an outcast I untacked Prince, while Ben saw to Stardust. "It was my fault, wasn't it? But Tracey's always telling me how to ride so I thought she was an expert. I must have been brainwashed," I muttered.

"You wait until Mr Abbott gets home,' replied Ben darkly.

When I had turned out Prince, I went upstairs and into my own bedroom without thinking. But of course it was full of Tracey's things, so I went to the attic and sat on my bed and cried.

Presently Mum joined me. "Don't sulk, Harriet, these things will happen. Time passes and they are forgotten," she said.

I looked at her face. "Why can't they just go," I replied. "They aren't our sort of people. They're so competitive and they think they know everything – and I mean everything. I was just beginning to like Tracey," I added and started to cry harder than ever.

"Oh, Harriet, you are too big for tears," Mum said.

"There's nothing nice about them," I continued, wiping my eyes. "Mrs Abbott's a bully. She bullies everyone. And the children have to win all the time. I know I haven't a single silver cup but I don't care."

"It takes all kinds to make a world. It's lunch in half an hour, Harriet," said Mum, getting off my bed. "Wash your face and brush your hair – please."

I didn't go down to lunch. Lisa brought me some stew on a plate. "Tracey's got a black eye and she's probably cracked a front tooth. You're in the dog-house now, Harriet," she said. "You must have been mad to gallop towards home on Mr Brind's stubble. Even I wouldn't have been so stupid."

Now I hated Lisa too.

Later there was a knock on my bedroom door. "Come in," I called, hastily straightening my duvet, then wiping my eyes.

It was Mr Abbott. He said, "We *are* disappointed in you, Harriet. We never thought you would be so foolish, or so devious." He was wearing a suit and a gold watch on a hairy wrist and highly polished shoes. I wasn't sure what devious meant. "We trusted you. We didn't think you would hurt our little girl," he continued.

"I didn't. She fell off. We all fall off sometimes," I answered. "It's inevitable. Anyway, Stardust is too much for her. She's too small for him."

166

"Exactly," agreed Mr Abbott, looking at me. "That's why you shouldn't have taken her out."

I didn't know what to say. I felt all sorts of things – humiliation, defeat, frustration, but most of all guilt. "She did ask. It was a misunderstanding. I wouldn't have taken her out if she hadn't asked her mother. I'm not that silly," I answered. "I never take children out riding without their parents' permission, not even Lisa's friends. It's a rule here." I felt quite calm for I knew what I was saying was true. Quite suddenly I didn't feel guilty any more.

"She'll have to have her front teeth crowned or capped when she's older and her nerves are all to pieces," continued Mr Abbott.

But I could look at him now. Suddenly I knew he had been sent by Mrs Abbott to tell me off, and he wasn't enjoying it.

"Ben has a crowned tooth. He broke it when he was ten. But no one knows or notices. Mum says you can't get through life without a few dents," I said. "Unless of course you never do anything exciting ever. And what sort of life is that, Mr Abbott?" I finished.

"A boring one," he said, beginning to laugh in spite of himself. "Well, don't do it again, Harriet," he added with a hint of a smile.

"No way. I'm not a complete idiot," I answered quickly.

He shut my door after him. I hoped that would be the end of it, but of course it wasn't. Mrs Abbott avoided me, and now Tracey only rode Stardust on a lunge rein. And whatever anyone had said, I knew that I was still blamed for what had happened, though I also knew it wasn't all my fault.

Four

It's fate

Things were to grow worse for the next evening Lisa came flying into the kitchen shouting, "I've lost Rascal. He slipped his collar and he's gone. I called and called. He'll get run over, I know he will, and the Abbotts will never forgive me."

I was trying to do my maths homework. Ben was reading again. Outside it was growing dark.

"He's the big one, isn't he?" Ben asked. "The one with white down his front?"

"He's one of the boxers." Tears were streaming down Lisa's face. "The most valuable one. The Abbotts will kill me, I know they will," she screamed.

Luckily the Abbotts had gone shopping, except for Mr Abbott who was away working as usual. They had taken Susan with them.

"I'll look on Prince," I offered. "I'll get some string and lead him back. I'll find him."

"And I'll look on my bike," Ben said.

"But it hasn't got any lights," I shouted.

"Who cares? You haven't, anyway, unless you call Prince's eyes lights," replied Ben, laughing.

We rushed outside. I caught Prince, tacked him up, and remembered my hat. Then I was gone, galloping in the dusk across a rain-sodden common. I went straight to the woods. I drew rein there and called, "Rascal,

Rascal. Come here, Rascal." Then I tried whistling. But the only answer was from the dripping trees: Drip, drip, drip. I rode on, remembering that I had left no message, told no one where I was going, not even James. And as I rode, I cursed the Abbotts again. They've brought us nothing but misery, I thought. Surely they realise that dogs need taking out more than once a day by poor Lisa, who has hours of homework to do every evening, who shouldn't be walking them at all. Then I thought that all the money in the world wasn't worth what we were going through. After that I talked to Prince. "They'll soon be gone," I told him, "then you'll have your own lovely loose box back again. You won't have to live out any more in the wet and the cold." He put back an ear and listened to me. And the trees went on dripping and there was no sign of Rascal anywhere. I halted Prince and called again and again, "Rascal,

Rascal, come here, good dog." And the tall, wet trees seemed to swallow up my voice and stifle it. "I'm sorry, Lisa, but there it is," I said to myself. "It's your turn to be in the dog-house now!"

I turned and galloped back through the woods and across the common. The houses there had their lights on now, glimmering in the murky dusk. I didn't want to go home. Already I was imagining the row – Lisa screaming, Mrs Abbott instructing everyone as though we were all kids at her special school for delinquents, Justin smug and self-righteous, Tracey standing behind her mother, not knowing what to say because, in spite of everything, she still liked me and Lisa. It isn't anybody's fault, I thought, riding across the common. It's fate. But Mrs Abbott will have to blame someone, she always does.

When I returned to the yard everything was unusually quiet. I turned Prince out and wiped my boots on some long grass before I went indoors. There was no sign of Lisa or Ben; just James reading *Hamlet* at the kitchen table.

"Where's everybody?" I asked nervously.

"Gone to see a vet. The Abbotts are still shopping. Rascal's been run over," explained James, without looking up from *Hamlet*.

"I don't believe it!" I cried.

"Ben found him. He caused an accident. Two cars bumped into one another. Mum had to sort it out. Lisa just screamed and screamed as usual," James continued, drinking tea out of a mug.

"Is Rascal going to die?" I asked.

"I shouldn't think so. His eyes were open, anyway," James answered.

"I think I shall hide somewhere because I don't want to see Mrs Abbott and have to explain," I said after a moment.

"Good thinking," said James. "She thinks I'm dotty, so she won't ask me anything."

"Sometimes I just wish they would all die," I said.

James looked at me in disbelief. "You don't mean that do you? You can't," he said.

"Not really, but half of me does. I want everything to be as it was before they came. It was so peaceful then," I said.

"Only by comparison," James answered.

Then we both saw car lights approaching. I ducked under the kitchen table and held my breath.

"I had better got their tea. I'll make them buttered toast and there's some chocolate cake," said James, putting down his book.

"Don't speak to me. I'm not here," I hissed, pulling the tablecloth towards the floor so that they shouldn't see me.

But it wasn't the Abbotts. It was Mum, Ben, Lisa and Rascal. Feeling stupid, I crawled out from under the table.

"What are you doing there?" Mum asked.

"Hiding from the Abbotts," I said, laughing.

To my surprise Lisa wasn't crying. "Rascal's all right. He's only suffering from shock," she said. "But I don't suppose I'll be allowed to walk the dogs any more, and I did like the tenner every week. Now I'll be poor again."

Mum made a bed with pillows and a blanket by the Aga for Rascal. "He's had a sedative," she told me. "I hope Mrs Abbott understands. I'm going to ring the insurance company about the cars. Don't do anything silly, meantime. Let me deal with Mrs Abbott, do you hear, Lisa?"

Lisa nodded. "I wish they would go away and never come back," she said.

"Same here," I added.

"Same here," said Miss Steele, holding out a hot-water bottle to be filled.

Ben filled the hot-water bottle while I laid the table for tea. James returned to *Hamlet*. Rascal was snoring by the Aga. But though we behaved normally, we were all on edge waiting for the row to begin!

Justin was the first to appear. He rushed into the kitchen; then stopped dead in his tracks. "What's he doing there?" he asked pointing to Rascal. "He should be outside."

I looked at Rascal and I must say he did look sweet wrapped in a pink blanket with his head resting on a blue pillow. He looked like a dog which is loved, instead of a show dog locked in a kennel half his life.

"He's had a little accident," said James, smiling at Justin. "But as you can see, he's all right now. He was a little shocked, hence the pink blanket. But he's going to be all right."

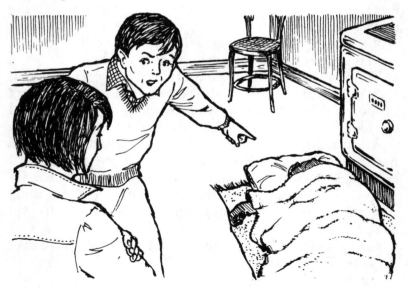

Mrs Abbott came in and put down her shopping on the kitchen table, just as though it was her house. Then she looked at James with dislike. "What about tea? We're famished," she said.

Justin pointed to Rascal. "Haven't you noticed, Mummy? Rascal's had an accident," he said, and he might have added, "And who's to blame? There must be a culprit," – for I swear that was what he was thinking. I thought then that he would make a good prosecutor and I could see him condemning people to life imprisonment. He would enjoy it.

"Oh no, what's happened now?" asked Mrs Abbott. "And who's responsible? Why isn't Rascal outside with the others? He's worth a lot of money, you know. When we're settled we mean to use him as a guard dog." Everything the Abbotts owned was worth a lot of money. They only bought the best, you see.

"He escaped. He slipped his collar, but he's all right," James said calmly, as though dogs slipped their collars and caused accidents every day.

"It was my fault. He wriggled out of his collar. He's been to the vet. He's been X-rayed. And we will pay for everything," said Lisa recklessly.

Mrs Abbott took off her beautiful mackintosh and, kneeling on the floor, looked at Rascal. "You were lucky this time, Lisa. But I don't think you had better walk the dogs any more," she said, getting up. "You're really not up to it."

Thinking of the ten pounds a week, Lisa wiped tears from her eyes. "I can manage the others," she said. "They're never any trouble."

But Mrs Abbott merely shook her head. "We'll have to pay Susan extra to walk them, Lisa. I'm sorry, but there it is. We let you try and you failed us, so that's that," she said.

So, no second chances I thought. Poor Lisa. No more stripy socks or treats for Lorraine. Lisa was looking out of the windows, where the curtains hadn't been drawn, and I knew she was crying. And I thought: I'm crying too, inside, and no one can see my tears.

Rascal loved being in the kitchen. Next day he had to be dragged outside by his collar and pushed forcefully into his loose box. Susan glared at Lisa. "So I've got to look after them now," she said. "Why didn't you hang on to him, you idiot?"

"But you're being paid for it," said Justin. "So you should be grateful. You'll have a nice little nest-egg by and by. You'll be able to buy a fantastic wedding dress with it."

"Speak for yourself," retorted Susan. "I spend all I get. I need to. I'll never have a nest-egg. And I don't want a fantastic wedding dress, thank you."

Our horses were already growing thick winter coats for the cold months which lay ahead. Normally, by this time, they would have been in at night, contentedly munching hay out of haynets. When I complained about it Mum said, "Oh, Harriet, just keep thinking of the swimming-pool." But I'm not a keen swimmer. I would rather be riding, so it wasn't much consolation.

There was nothing to tell us then of what lay ahead that Friday morning. Just the usual friction between us and the Abbotts, which seemed to spoil each day. Before I went for the school bus next day, I fed our horses. Lisa and James had already left. Ben had gone ahead to meet a friend. The horses blew hot breath into my hair. The hay smelled wonderful.

Susan was mucking out, her fair hair hidden by a headscarf. "You'll be late for school," she called, and then, "There's hay in your hair, Harriet."

Ignoring her I ran for the school bus. I was only just

in time. The back seat was full of pushing boys.

"There's hay in your hair, Harriet," someone said.

"And stuck to your socks," laughed a first year.

"Your shoes are muddy," said Rosemary, whom no one really likes, poor thing.

"I don't care," I said and meant it.

School dragged. But there wasn't the whisper of a breeze as I boarded the bus for home that evening, absolutely nothing to warn us of what lay ahead.

Ben was sitting at the back with a boy called Dave. It was still light, light enough to feed the horses when I got home if Lisa hadn't done it already.

The bus stopped to let pupils out and I thought: I'll go for a long ride on Saturday, for hours and hours. Perhaps Lisa will be nice and come with me, or Ben. But even if they don't, I'll take sandwiches and go for the day. I'll take a map and find new bridleways. And I saw myself riding on and on, down long lanes. I saw myself galloping, perhaps popping over an odd fence if no one was looking. I was beginning to feel really cheerful by the time we reached home. Our horses were waiting to be fed again. There was no sign of Lisa. I fetched feeds, then hay. A wind picked up wisps of hay and carried them away. Clouds were racing each other in a darkening sky. The leaves left on the trees quivered but already some were bare as skeletons against the evening sky. I fetched my tack and took it inside to clean. I told Mum of my plan for the weekend.

"Try to get someone to go with you. I hate you going so far on your own. Anything could happen," she said.

"But I always try to tell you where I'm going," I replied.

That evening is engraved on my memory for ever. Dad came in late looking disheartened. Justin had an argument with Ben. I helped Lisa with her homework. She wasn't doing very well at school and her end of the year report had been bad. James rang up Virginia and talked for half an hour. The elderly ladies were both knitting in the sitting-room. Colonel Hunter was watching television with a glass of whisky and soda beside him.

At nine-thirty it started to rain. I know the time because I was setting my alarm clock for seven-thirty the next morning. My curtains were drawn back and, looking at the falling rain, I thought: Prince's back will be wet, too wet to ride tomorrow, so I shan't be able to go, and I felt like screaming with disappointment.

Then I heard Mr Abbott coming back from work. He was laughing and talking about a deal. He called for champagne, but Dad couldn't provide him with any.

Later I lay in bed listening to the rain lashing against the windowpanes, and again I kept thinking of our horses outside in it, and I started to hate the Abbotts all over again.

And then at last I slept.

Five
The hurricane

It was a terrible dream. Tracey was disappearing into the distance on Stardust all over again, but now his hoofs were clattering on tarmac.

Then there was the sound of a train rushing faster and faster towards Stardust, while Tracey let out an ear-splitting scream and Mrs Abbott called, "It's all right, poppet. It's only a storm." Next there was a sound like paper tearing and now I knew that it wasn't just a dream – most of it was real. I leaped out of bed. My window was rattling as though the devil himself was trying to get inside. Mrs Abbott was talking to Tracey below in my real bedroom. I drew back my curtains which jumped and jerked, spurred by the wind coming in round the window, as though they had a life of their own. Outside, clouds were riding the sky like galleons on a tempestuous sea. Branches were flying across the drive as though possessed by demons. A pine tree lay split down the centre on the gravel. The bay trees which normally stand outside the back door in pots had disappeared. And there was a wild moon which vanished, leaving me in total darkness. I switched on the light and called out to Ben, "Are you awake? Wake up. Come and look."

Then there was a tremendous crash and all the lights went out.

"The horses! What about the horses?" shouted Ben from next door as I fumbled my way to the door.

Ben was emerging from his bedroom. Lisa was screaming, "What's going on? Is there a war started or something?"

"It's a hurricane," cried Ben, who always has an answer. "And it's throwing trees about like ninepins. Listen! There goes a chimney pot."

"How do you know it's a chimney pot?" I asked crossly, because Ben seemed to be enjoying himself while my teeth were chattering, half from fright, half from cold.

"Can't you hear the clatter of bricks falling?" he asked. We were all on the landing by now and we could hear the guests talking in excited voices downstairs. Colonel Hunter was walking about guided by a lighted match. Tracey was shrieking. Dad was shouting, "No one is to go outside. Do you hear? No one!"

"I'll make some tea," offered James. "I take it the Aga is still working?"

Someone had found a torch.

"What about the horses?" I asked, entering the kitchen. "We can't just leave them to their fate. We must do something."

"There's nothing we can do, not until the wind stops. Listen, there goes another tree," Dad said.

"But . . ." I began, as my imagination started to run riot, seeing horses crushed to death, the stables in a heap, blood and confusion everywhere.

"No buts, Harriet. Your father's right, you'll only get killed by a falling tree, and that won't help anyone, least of all the horses," said Mr Abbott.

Miss Steele appeared now. "I had to feel my way downstairs. There's all sorts of stuff coming down my chimney. I can't stop there, it isn't safe," she said talking in a funny way because she wasn't wearing her false

178

teeth. Then Mum drew back the kitchen curtains and we saw that dawn was breaking, a wild, mad dawn.

We could see each other now: Colonel Hunter in an ancient red dressing-gown and leather slippers; Miss Steele and Mrs Tomson in thick nighties which reached to their feet, talking to one another about the war, when London burned and they picked up the bits. Mrs Abbott was there, too, wearing a wonderful dressing-gown with peacocks on it. Mr Abbott was in silk pyjamas and a turquoise towelling dressing-gown. Justin was in nothing but pyjamas, and shivering. Tracey was in pyjamas with an anorak over them. Mum and Dad had dressed, but Mum's pullover was on back-to-front and Dad was wearing different-coloured socks. James was in a striped pyjama top and trousers and Ben wore much the same; while I was still in pyjamas and, as we sipped tea out of mugs, slowly day broke outside, revealing a terrible picture of destruction and devastation.

Mr Abbott pulled open the back door. Above the noise of the wind we could hear him shouting, "We can't get out, there's a tree down. Have we got a chainsaw?"

"No, it's broken," Dad shouted back, before, with one accord, we rushed towards the front door. Ben pulled it open. Mrs Abbott's car was upside down. The front gate had gone. There were fallen trees everywhere, trees I had loved. Suddenly it seemed like the end of the world. And then the wind unexpectedly stopped roaring. I rushed for boots and a coat with Lisa close behind me. "Our poor horses," I shouted.

"Yes. They may be dead, squashed to bits," shouted Lisa, rushing outside, struggling into her boots as she ran.

The roof and one wall had gone from the modern loose boxes and the Abbotts' dogs had gone too.

"They can't blame me this time. Oh God, what are we going to do? What's happened?" shouted Lisa.

We stopped and stared. The caravan was upside down, and there was no sound coming from it. Then Lisa yelled, "Susan! Susan! Are you all right?"

Mr and Mrs Abbott were close behind us. "Leave this to us," said Mr Abbott and kneeled down by the caravan, his grey hair blowing in all directions. "She's there. She's unconscious but she's there," he said after a second. "Someone telephone for a doctor. Hurry up."

I rushed indoors, my boots leaving a trail of mud and debris behind me. "We need a doctor," I screamed.

James picked up the telephone. Then he shouted, "It's dead. Everything's dead."

"What are we going to do then?" I screamed. "Susan could be dying. And now we won't be able to get a vet either."

"We're on our own," replied James. "We'll just have to cope."

When I returned to the caravan it had been turned over and Mr and Mrs Abbott were lifting Susan out.

"I can't get a doctor, the telephone doesn't work," I said helplessly.

Susan looked pale and there was blood on her fair hair.

"We'll take her into the house. Keep away from the trees," advised Mrs Abbott.

"Is she going to die?" asked Lisa, who is always expecting the worst to happen.

"No, she's not," snapped Mrs Abbott. "And don't stand there staring. Get a blanket and a hot-water bottle."

For a moment we forgot all about our horses. I rushed back to the house again, climbing over fallen branches on the way. James filled a hot-water bottle.

Mum found a blanket. We laid Susan on the sofa in the sitting-room. Lisa was crying. "I really liked her. She was my best friend," she sobbed.

"Don't be ridiculous. She's not going to die. Pull your socks up. Stop blubbering, Lisa," thundered Mrs Abbott.

"How do you know she isn't going to die? She may have internal injuries," Lisa replied, still crying.

"Because I'm a trained nurse, that's why."

We left Susan and returned outside. A big old syca-more tree had fallen across the field shelter. Our first pony, Limpet, was inside and he whinnied anxiously.

"He'll be all right for the moment," called Mrs Abbott. "Let's look at the others. Leave him there. Do as I say. I know what I'm talking about."

A huge branch had blown into Seamus's box and he was cowering at the back of it, one leg streaked with blood. "Steady there, steady there, old boy, whoa, steady." Mrs Abbott slipped quietly into the box.

"Is he going to bleed to death? What about a tourni-quet?" I asked, anxiously watching his bed of shavings slowly turning red.

"Get a stable bandage from the tack room and some wadding. Hurry!" said Mrs Abbott.

I ran. Justin was calling from inside another loose box. "Stardust is lying down, Mummy. I think he's hurt."

Lisa joined him. I could hear Prince neighing from the field. Then Mum appeared with a bucket of warm water and antiseptic. "Thank you. But we don't need it yet. I've got to stop the bleeding first," said Mrs Abbott. "Where's your first-aid box, Mrs Pemberton?"

"We haven't got one; only things like sticking plaster and Dettol. Nothing large," Mum said, and she sounded defensive.

I handed the stable bandage and a wad of lint over

the loose box door. Mrs Abbott sighed. "I'll do my best with this then," she said.

No one knew what was the matter with Stardust. He wouldn't get up. There were branches in his box too and in the end we decided that one of them had hit him on the head.

Mr Abbott had found Dad's old chainsaw and was mending it. The dogs were still missing. Scorpion, Prince, Lorraine, Solitaire and Jigsaw were unharmed and wanted breakfast. Sultan had a nasty cut above one eye, which was shut.

Then James appeared and said, "I'm going to see if I can get anywhere. I want to see whether Virginia is okay. I'll try to get a doctor and a vet. And I shall keep an eye out for the dogs. What are they called?"

How typical of James not to know their names, I thought. "Rascal, Ruby and Ruffian," I said.

Mrs Abbott had stopped the bleeding. She patted Seamus while he stood pathetically holding up his injured leg which was now encased in a stable bandage. "That's the end of his show-ring career, of course. Thank God he's insured," Mrs Abbott said, washing her hands in the bucket of antiseptic. "We'll have to sell him; he'll be scarred for life. Will one of you check on Susan, please?"

I ran indoors. Miss Steele was feeling Susan's pulse. "It's very slow. I nursed during the war, so I do know what I'm talking about," she said. "We need a doctor, dear, if you can get one, we really do."

"James is trying," I said, rushing back to the stables.

The day seemed to have lasted for ever already, though really it had only just begun. Everything seemed very quiet because the wind had stopped blowing. Stardust was still lying down and, once again, Lisa feared internal injuries. Tracey was crying. Mrs Abbott was examining Sultan's eye, while I was counting the nine trees down in our main paddock, including my favourite oak, and then Justin appeared saying, "I've just heard on the news on Daddy's car radio, the hurricane has hit all of southern England. There're no trains running and all the roads are blocked. The emergency services are working at full stretch. And three people have died."

"Thank you, Justin," snapped Mrs Abbott. "But Seamus needs a blood transfusion. Any news of a vet?"

"James is still out on his bike, looking, but I think the road's blocked. I think all the roads are blocked. I suppose we could call in a helicopter," I suggested.

"But there's no telephone," replied Mrs Abbott. "Why aren't you doing something, for heaven's sake, Harriet? Take Limpet some hay and water."

"But we can't get into the shelter."

"Use a ladder, then, or haven't you got one? Oh,

God, you Pembertons, you don't seem prepared for anything – no first-aid equipment, no chainsaw working, no generator to feed into the electricity system. How do you think we're going to manage tonight, Harriet? Have you any candles? An oil lamp? Have you anything on hand for an emergency?" Mrs Abbott said accusingly before going into Stardust's loose box, her shoulders twitching with anger and frustration.

I shouted for Ben. "We need a ladder to feed Limpet," I said. "We can't get into the shelter without one, because of the fallen tree."

Then James returned, saying, "The road's completely blocked by fallen trees. The electricity and telephone wires are down all over the place. Nothing is working, absolutely nothing, and half the chimneys have gone off the almshouses."

"No vet, or doctor, then?" I asked.

"No, not a hope."

"Did you see the dogs?"

"Not a sign."

Ben helped me put a ladder up against the shelter. He climbed up it and I gave him armfuls of hay, which he dropped through the holes in the roof. Then we filled up a bucket with water and lowered it into the shelter the same way on the end of headcollar ropes joined together. Lots of water slopped out, but there was a little left as it landed on the ground inside the shelter. Limpet watched us with startled eyes.

"The Abbotts are running the place," I said. "Listen, the chainsaw's working. Dad couldn't have mended it in a month of Sundays."

"Mr Abbott trained as an electrician. He's furious that we haven't a generator. He's torn a few strips off Dad. I don't know how it will be tonight. He doesn't suffer fools gladly," said Ben.

"You think we're fools, then?" I asked.

"No. But you must admit we do seem to be woefully unprepared."

Lisa was checking our ponies, running her hands down their legs, watched by Tracey. Justin was helping his father. Dad was clearing up branches, putting them in a heap which grew larger every minute. Then Mum called, "Coffee-time."

We went inside. Colonel Hunter was leaning against the Aga. "It's the only warm place in the house and I'm so cold," he explained. He looked very old. Suddenly he had become a tired old man. Miss Steele and Mrs Tomson were knitting with hot-water bottles on their knees, bulging under blankets. Susan was sitting in a chair and shouting over and over, "Where's Jim? I want Jim."

"She's concussed, no one knows who Jim is. She may go on like that for hours. I think I'll go crazy soon," Mum said.

"Mrs Abbott is dealing with everything outside. Our ponies seem okay," I told her. "But hers are banged about. Stardust won't get up."

"Perhaps he's concussed too," replied Mum with a wan smile.

"And we need a vet."

"Perhaps you could go to get help on a horse," she suggested.

"But if I got there, how would the vet or doctor get back?" I asked.

"I've tried biking. It isn't possible," said James, coming into the kitchen. "There are trees down on the road. Nine in a row and all enormous, I counted them, and even a horse couldn't get over them."

"Thank heaven for the Aga. At least I can prepare a meal," said Mum.

"Until the food runs out," I suggested.

"Yes, we'll be on tinned milk by tomorrow morning," Mum said. "And there's no more bacon."

"Porridge. We'll live on porridge," said Colonel Hunter. "The Scots live on porridge, damned good stuff, porridge."

Miss Steele was stroking Susan's forehead. "It's all right, dear, Jim is quite safe. He will be here presently, not to worry, dear," she said.

I drank my coffee. "I'll go and help with the mucking out now," I said.

Mrs Abbott inspected every loose box as I mucked it out, saying things like, "You've left some muck in the corner over there, Harriet," and, "I think you need a little more straw, Harriet. It should be banked up round the sides of the box; that's better."

Ben was enjoying himself with a bonfire. Lisa and Tracey were on the common calling the dogs.

"If horses stay lying down for more than a few hours

they die," said Ben presently, looking over the loose box door where I was cleaning around Stardust.

"I think Stardust has given up," I said.

"I think we should make him get up, that's what I think," argued Ben.

"Not without asking Mrs Abbott," I answered.

"The Abbotts are running the place," Ben said.

"There was a vacuum, no one filled it, so they did," I said. "And anyway, Stardust belongs to them."

I squatted on the straw and stroked Stardust's ears. They were hot, and there was sweat behind them, and on his neck.

"I think he's in pain. I think it's serious," I said slowly. Ben joined me inside. Together we felt him all over. There was nothing wrong with him as far as we could see, and yet he still lay there as though he was afraid to stand up, and the sweat behind his ears could only mean one thing – fever or pain.

"We ought to get him up," Ben said again.

"Not without Mrs Abbott," I insisted once more.

Then a small voice said, "He's mine. Get him up, please."

I looked up at Tracey and Lisa who were leaning on the loose-box door. Tracey was crying. Lisa had an arm round her shoulder. "We can't find the dogs anywhere," Lisa said.

Ben handed me a headcollar. I slipped it over Stardust's neat, well-bred ears. I was frightened of what might happen and of what we might see. I think we all were.

"He's such a lovely pony," Tracey said slowly. "He was going to Wembley next year. I was going to ride him there. He would have won, I know he would, and then I would have had another cup."

"Who cares about damned cups?" Ben snapped back.

"Mummy likes me to win cups," Tracey replied, wiping her eyes.

"You can't go on doing things for Mummy all your life," said Ben.

"Shut up, she's only eight," I said.

I pulled gently on the headcollar rope. Then Mrs Abbott's shadow appeared across the doorway. "Who said you could get him up?" she said.

"I did, Mummy."

"You don't heed an eight-year-old child, do you, Harriet?"

"But if he stays down much longer, he'll die," Ben told her.

"You're right, of course. Pull gently on the rope, Harriet, gently. Give him time to think about it."

I was sweating now. Supposing he can't get up, supposing his legs are broken, supposing he needs putting down and we can't get a vet? I thought.

Stardust grunted. He stretched out his forelegs. They looked normal, clean tendoned with neat fetlocks and lovely round hoofs. Yes, he would win at Wembley I

thought, if he could walk, if he wasn't maimed in some hideous way for life. If he didn't have to be put down, as soon as a vet could be found.

"Pull gently, Harriet."

"I am, Mrs Abbott," I said.

"I don't think his hind legs are working properly," suggested Ben, kneeling down to talk to Stardust, to say, "Poor old Stardust. What is it then? What's the matter?" to find a few crumbs of oats in the pocket of his old husky, to hold them out to Stardust, who wouldn't touch them, who hadn't touched any food all morning.

"Shall I pull a little harder, Mrs Abbott?" I asked.

She was in the box too, now. "Yes." She wasn't crying. Perhaps if you've been a nurse you can stand more than other people, I don't know. But she was quite calm, she had been calm all morning. She had lost valuable dogs; Sultan was scarred for life and could at any moment start bleeding to death. Seamus's eye might never recover, and now Stardust didn't want to move his hind legs.

Mum would have been at breaking point. I felt like crying myself and he wasn't my pony. But Mrs Abbott remained dry-eyed.

"Get him up, Harriet. Pull him up. I want to see what's the matter with him," Tracey cried suddenly.

"He'll die if he stays down much longer," Ben reminded me.

"Come on, Stardust. Stand up, hup," I shouted while Ben pushed at his quarters and the others stood watching, as though we were the servants and they the bosses.

Stardust threw his head up. His front hoofs clawed at the brick floor beneath the straw. His eyes rolled, his hind legs strained and then he was up, a trembling liver chestnut pony, one hind leg out of line, dragging behind the other.

190

"He's broken his leg. Look, Mummy, look," shouted
Tracey. "It's his off hind. What are we going to do? Will
he have to be put down, Mummy? Will he?" Then
Tracey stared at Ben. "Can you put a horse down?" she
asked in a shaky voice. "Because he's in agony, isn't
he?"

Ben shook his head. "It's out of the question. I'm not
a vet," he said.

Then Mrs Abbott walked up to Stardust. "Whoa,
pet," she said. "Steady." She felt his injured hind leg
with gentle hands, talking to him all the time. "He's
slipped his stifle," she said finally. "We can't put it back,
unfortunately. Get him a feed, Lisa, just damp bran and
pony nuts. I'll go indoors and get a sedative for him. I've

got a syringe. I'm always prepared for anything." And I knew that it was true, which was doubtless why the Abbotts were rich and we were poor; they had proved to be superior by their actions because none of us could have mended the chainsaw or stopped a wound bleeding or injected a sedative into a horse's neck – more skilfully than a vet as it turned out.

"He'll be all right now for a bit. Give him his feed, Lisa," she said a few minutes later.

Colonel Hunter was outside now, dragging bits of fallen tree about. He was wearing bedroom slippers and with his white hair standing up round his ancient face he looked very old and fragile. I could hear Dad saying, "Take it easy, Colonel. You don't have to help. I'd stay in the warm if I were you."

"Must do my bit. I've always done my bit," Colonel Hunter muttered, his blue-veined hands dragging a branch towards a gigantic heap of them.

Seamus's wound had started bleeding again. The dogs were still lost; it was eleven o'clock now and there was still nothing moving outside the gates of Black Pony Inn, not a car nor a lorry, not the milk-float nor the post van, and already I was longing for normality.

Six

No *way round*

Once again Mrs Abbott tried to stem the blood streaming down Seamus's leg, using a clean sock this time to
plug the hole which was there.

"He's worthless now. He'll never be sound again,
Harriet," she said, sounding tearful. "Please try calling
the dogs once more," she added.

Outside one could hear the distant whine of chain-
saws. Across the common people stood aimlessly at their
gates. Outside Lilac Cottage a car had been crushed by a
fallen tree. There was no sign of anyone inside it.

I stood and called the dogs until I was hoarse. I asked
people whether they had seen them. But they only shook
their heads, and a woman wearing a headscarf told me
that Mr Brind's cows were down on the railway line, but
the line was blocked so it didn't matter. An old man,
walking with the aid of a frame, said that he had never
known anything like it. The new telephone box had
blown over. An old, dilapidated barn lay in pieces on the
ground. Heaps of tiles lay beneath a bungalow's hanging
gutters. People were cutting up fallen trees. Bonfires sent
grey smoke into the grey sky. The storm had changed
everything. No one had gone to work. We were cut off
and some of the new houses near the church relied on
electricity for everything! Somehow it made all my previous fuss over the Abbotts seem trivial. This was life,

real life. All the rest was unimportant, I thought, going back to Black Pony Inn across the familiar common, where trees lay like fallen giants, trees I had known nearly all my life, trees which had stood there for centuries. Somehow it put everything in perspective, made Tracey's love of silver cups seem even more ridiculous, and my sadness over the loss of my bedroom futile and selfish. It made me understand why Colonel Hunter harped on about the war; for ordinary life must appear rather trivial after you have faced death for so long and watched your friends die.

Lisa was calling my name. I started to run. "I'm on my way," I shouted. "What do you want? I can't find the dogs, I've looked and looked."

"Mum wants you and Ben to try and get a doctor. Colonel Hunter's had a stroke," she called. "Hurry. She won't let me go, but Ben is tacking up Solitaire and Prince. And Mrs Abbott wants a vet. Hurry up. Run. It's a major catastrophe."

I was breathless when I reached the yard. "We'll never make it," I gasped.

"We've got to try," Ben said.

"Is he very bad?"

"I don't know. He's not talking and his face is twisted. Mrs Abbott is dealing with him. He should be in hospital, of course," Ben said matter of factly, though I sensed he was upset.

Lisa fetched my riding-hat. Suddenly I didn't feel like talking.

"Dad and James are trying on foot. They're heading for the railway line," Ben said, mounting Solitaire.

"It's blocked by fallen trees, everything's blocked," I answered glumly, mounting automatically, turning Prince round, riding out of the yard across the changed common, which was suddenly like a mouth with all its

194

teeth gone. "The roads are blocked, we'll have to try the fields," I said.

"Miss Steele is crying. I think she's in love with Colonel Hunter," Ben said.

"And Susan?" I asked.

"She's still shouting for Jim."

"And Mum?"

"She's near breaking point."

"And the Abbotts?" I asked, dismounting to open a gate.

"He's trying to clear the road; she's exhausted. Tracey is screaming because she can't watch television, and Justin is waiting for the next news bulletin on the BMW's car radio," Ben said.

Our horses kept stopping, suspecting an enemy behind every fallen tree. Prince was on edge; he wouldn't walk and stared round him as though seeing everything for the first time. The air still smelled of burning wood. In the distance the railway line was empty of trains, and the roads were empty of cars. It felt eerie and frightening as we cantered across a ploughed field on our nervous horses, who were only waiting for a chance to carry us back to their friends at Black Pony Inn.

A tree lay across the gate out of the field. Ben looked over it. "We can jump the hedge further down, there's quite a good roadside verge," he said.

"And then?" I asked.

"Heaven knows. But we must remember that while we hesitate, Colonel Hunter may be dying and Seamus bleeding to death," replied Ben.

I imagined us attending Colonel Hunter's funeral. Or would some distant relative whom we had never seen and who had never bothered about him, appear to claim everything and have his remains removed to some distant crematorium? I wondered gloomily.

We collected our horses together and rode them at the hedge. There was a drop on the far side and we only just missed landing on the road.

"Hurray, now we can go on," cried Ben, pushing Solitaire into a trot.

"Funny, there are no cars on the road," I said.

"They're probably holed up in their garages," replied Ben optimistically. "It can't be more than two-and-a-half miles to the Health Centre now."

"Let's hope there are doctors there waiting for their patients. But it doesn't seem very likely, does it?" I replied. "And what about the vet? He won't be in his surgery either."

"The town may be different and it's only two miles on along the main road now. And I'm sure that will be open. It must be," said Ben.

"I don't want Colonel Hunter to die," I shouted above the clatter of our horses' hoofs. "I should miss him too much."

"Miss Steele would miss him even more," replied Ben.

Now we saw that two enormous sycamore trees lay stretched across the road. Two men were looking at them. "Can't we get through?" shouted Ben.

"What does it look like?" shouted one of the men.

"Haven't you got a chainsaw?" asked Ben, halting Solitaire.

"Ours isn't big enough. Besides, they're too heavy to move. It's a job for the council, if they ever get round to it," the other shouted.

"We need a doctor. It's urgent," I said.

"I'm sorry to hear it, but we all need something we can't get."

"Are the telephones working round here?" asked Ben.

"No way. I should have been on the six-thirty train to London for a conference," said one of the men. "And here I am. And I can't even inform them that I won't be there. It's a joke."

After a moment the other man said, "It's a rum old job, isn't it?" He looked as though he had lived in the country all his life and had never been to London or the sea.

"Isn't there a way round?" asked Ben.

"No, there's no way round, not until the council have cleared the trees."

"A man's had a stroke and we need a doctor," insisted Ben. But they were tired of us and turned away and trudged towards cottages further down the road.

"We'll have to go back," I said to Ben.

"And admit defeat," Ben replied, making defeat sound like a dirty word.

"At least we tried," I answered.

"There must be a way," insisted Ben, but he didn't sound convinced any more.

"If only the telephones worked," I said.

"What difference would that make; they still couldn't get to us," retorted Ben.

"Yes, they could – by helicopter," I cried, and imagined Colonel Hunter being taken inside a helicopter on a stretcher.

"It'll be dark soon," said Ben, pushing Solitaire into a trot.

It took us ages to get home. We were both filled with a sense of failure and our horses stopped at every fallen tree again. Then Solitaire refused three times before he would jump the hedge.

"There's no decent run, that's why," explained Ben, when at last he was over and we were crossing the plough again.

"Mrs Abbott will call us feeble," I said as we rode across the common.

"She can try herself, then," replied Ben.

When we reached home, we turned our horses out and watched them roll. Everything was quiet in the stable-yard. Without electricity, we'll have to feed early and go to bed early. What a bore, I thought.

"There are fallen trees all along the railway line. And no one's clearing them," said James, appearing as we removed our boots. "So it's going to be a long while before we can go anywhere."

"You're preaching to the converted. In other words, we know," Ben snapped back.

Mum appeared next calling hopefully, "Any luck? Did you find a doctor?"

I shook my head while Ben said, "We did try, Mum."

Someone had brought a bed downstairs for Colonel Hunter. He was sitting up on it, looking incredibly old. His face was still twisted but he could talk out of the corner of his mouth, though not very clearly.

"He mustn't get excited," Lisa told us. "He'll be all right if he doesn't have another stroke. He's very lucky." I had the feeling that Lisa was quoting Mrs Abbott.

Mum had kept us some lunch. "You really couldn't get through, then?" she asked.

"Not a hope in hell," replied Ben.

"After you've eaten your lunch, I want you to light fires in the old ladies' bedrooms; otherwise they'll die of cold. There's plenty of wood now. If they have fires, they'll have a bit of light too. They won't be so nervous then," Mum said.

"But the fires haven't been lit for years. What about the chimneys? Shouldn't they be swept?" asked Ben, whom Mum often says has an old head on young shoulders.

"Never mind the chimneys. Just try," she answered. "Please . . ."

So after lunch we gathered sticks and wood and prepared to light the fires. First of all we had to sweep up the mess which had fallen down the chimneys during the hurricane. Then Ben laid the fires, carefully criss-crossing the sticks in the small Victorian grates. Mum had told us not to use many matches. "I've only got three boxes left," she had said. "So don't waste them, please."

While Ben worked, I fetched more logs and put them in old coal scuttles which had not been used for years. Then Miss Steele appeared and started to advise us in her plaintive voice, which James had once, unkindly, likened to a cat mewing. "You must have air underneath the kindling," she said. "Here, let me show you."

"But look, it's going!" cried Ben triumphantly. "And the one next door is going too, so now it's up to you and Mrs Tomson to keep them alight. Mum says I'm to put some of the Aga fuel on later, then they'll stay in all night. But we must see to the horses now, because it's getting dark outside," finished Ben.

"What about the Colonel?" Miss Steele asked anxiously.

"He's going to have a bed in the kitchen. And Mum has found a nightlight she bought for Lisa when she was ill years ago, and never used, so he'll be all right. And anyway, I think Mum and Dad are going to sit up with him all night, poor things," Ben said.

"I don't mind doing a shift," said Miss Steele.

"Lovely," said Ben. "You're an angel, Miss Steele," and with that we escaped out to the stables and more problems.

The chainsaw had broken again, so no one had released Limpet from the shelter where he now stood, anxious, hungry and neglected. Mrs Abbott had revived after two hours in bed and was doing what Mum calls laying down the law again. Partly recovered, Susan was going through her things in the caravan, assisted by Lisa. They were both crying. Tracey was feebly brushing Stardust. Justin was sitting in his father's car, listening to the radio. He had done little else since the hurricane. Mr Abbott had disappeared. Mum said that he was looking for a pub where he could buy some whisky. James was trying to reach Virginia. And above us all, the grey sky was darkening into another night.

Mrs Abbott stared at me angrily. "Your mother says she only has a few candles left, Harriet. How are we

going to manage? I cannot understand it, I really can't.
A house full of old people and no emergency form of
heating; it's incredible," she said. She looked changed.
Her hair had lost its bounce, her eyes were no longer en-
hanced by eye shadow, so that now she looked wan and
rather ordinary, and not at all rich. Suddenly I wasn't
scared of her any more.

"We only have three old people with us, as you know,
we have a further four beds for guests, and we're all
quite young," I answered. "So the house is hardly full of
old people."

"Well, have it your own way, Harriet, but I still think
it's incredible," she said.

"But we've never had a hurricane before," I
answered.

She made no reply, and now the wind had started
blowing again and it frightened me, for the roofs of the

loose boxes were a constant reminder of what it could do. Then Justin appeared. "They've brought in men from all over Britain, even from Northern Ireland, to re-connect the electricity," he said. "But there's more gales on the way."

"What about the telephones and the roads?" I asked.

"The authorities are doing their best." Justin was beginning to talk like the radio news.

"Aren't you going to help with the mucking out?" I asked.

He shook his head. "I never help. It's Susan's job," he replied.

"But Susan's hurt," I answered.

"She can do them tomorrow, then," I looked at his small set face and I thought: He's ruthless. He's a hard-headed company director already. Perhaps people are born suitable for certain jobs. Perhaps we're already programmed before we ever enter the world.

Meanwhile Lisa and Ben fed and watered Limpet and the horses in the fields. It was nearly dark now and Stardust still didn't want to move so I took his food to him – just damp bran and nuts and an armful of hay. I took his water to him too, holding the bucket under his nose while he drank.

"The vet will put his stifle back, but it may not stay back," said Mrs Abbott watching me. "I think we're going to have to start all over again."

"What do you mean by that?" I asked anxiously.

"Put them all down, and buy another lot."

"But they're not washing-machines, they're alive, friends," I cried.

"Oh, Harriet, one has to be realistic, however much it hurts," she said.

"But can't his stifle be strapped up?" I asked.

"Have you ever tried bandaging a stifle, Harriet?"

I shook my head.

"You can't," she said.

"Plaster then . . ." I suggested, but she only smiled grimly.

By now it was dark. Justin drove his father's BMW into the yard and switched on its lights.

"No more than five minutes, Justin dear," Mrs Abbott told him. "Because we don't want a flat battery, that would be the last straw."

In the lights from the headlamps I swept up the yard and topped up the water buckets in the loose boxes. None of the Abbott horses had been out and their legs were beginning to swell. They were all on bran mashes and Mrs Abbott had started to demand carrots. But now, as we walked indoors together, there seemed to be a strange sort of friendship growing up between us; we were opposite in nearly everything, but somehow we were meeting halfway. I suppose one could call it an unexpected affinity growing between us. Mrs Abbott had opened a new window on life for me and I was beginning to see it from a different angle. I was beginning to see us from the outside, from someone else's point of view, for the first time. And it wasn't comforting.

"I've seen Virginia and she's all right," James was beaming as we returned indoors. "I even got as far as the village shop, but it has no candles left, or milk, or matches."

Tracey had found one of my old pony books and was reading it. Dad and Mr Abbott were lighting a fire in the open fireplace in the hall, which we had never used before. Ben stood nearby with a pair of ancient bellows in his hands. We are going back in time, I thought, back to the 1800s. Colonel Hunter was talking incoherently to Miss Steele. Mrs Tomson was talking to Justin about the early days of radio. Lisa was outside, calling the dogs again. She seemed to be forever calling them and her voice was growing hoarse.

I helped Mum serve tea. Then we drew all the curtains and lit our few candles and I think we both were praying that the lights would come on soon, before the candles were burned out.

The fire cast shadows across the hall. It lit up the paintings there. It was an evening I would never forget. If we had been on our own, I might have been happy. But with our demanding guests this was impossible. "I can't see to read," shouted Tracey. I fetched a torch and gave it to her.

Mr Abbott paced up and down the hall. "Are you sure we can't get to a pub?" he asked presently.

"We can try again," Dad replied.

"I feel so dirty. Is the bathwater hot? And is there any light up there?" Mrs Abbott asked.

"No, sorry, the immersion heater isn't working and the Aga doesn't run to baths," Mum said.

And Mrs Abbott sighed and her sigh said many things.

Then Mrs Tomson and Miss Steele started to play cards by the light of a candle while Ben sat twiddling his thumbs. Then Lisa came indoors saying, "I can't find the dogs. I've looked and looked, and now there's a wind blowing and it's pitch dark. What are we going to do?"

"Nothing," said Mrs Abbott, which surprised us all, because she had never said anything like that before.

James sat silent, thinking, I suspect, about Virginia.

"We'll eat early tonight. It'll only be soup, I'm afraid," Mum said apologetically, stirring the contents of a saucepan by the light of a candle.

"But I never eat soup," cried Tracey.

"You can eat bread and cheese then," Mum snapped back.

Mrs Abbott was sitting with her head in her hands now. I felt sorry for her.

"At least we are still alive and so are the horses," I said.

"But not the dogs. We've lost the dogs," she replied.

"They may turn up. We mustn't lose hope," I answered.

"I expect someone's shut them in a barn," suggested Ben.

"And while there's life there's hope," added Lisa.

And it seemed strange that we were all comforting Mrs Abbott.

We ate our soup out of bowls in semi-darkness. We

left the washing up until morning. Ben and I had a torch between us. There was no moon. It was one of the blackest nights I have ever known and the wind was starting to howl again like some poor, demented animal trying to get inside the house.

"They won't be able to mend the electricity tonight," Ben said, climbing into bed before handing me the torch.

"I always thought the old days must have been lovely with horses everywhere, now I'm not so sure," I said. "I can't see how they managed without electricity."

"What you've never had you don't miss," Ben said.

The torch was flickering now. In another minute it would need a new battery and we had no batteries in reserve and no means of getting any. I could hear Dad and Mr Abbott arguing downstairs. Dad was shouting, "You'll get a reduction in charges, of course you will, so what are you griping about? I'm sorry about the drink. We just don't keep a lot. We don't have a licence."

I pulled my duvet over my head and prayed. God make them mend the electricity soon. God bring back the Abbotts' dogs and make Stardust sound again. But I knew God wouldn't listen to me, because I never went to church. So why should He?

Seven
We'll be ruined

I hardly slept that night. The wind shook the window-panes and howled. My room had grown cold during the day and was even colder in the night. I was dreading the next day. I imagined the last candle burned, stocks of food growing low. And now we had Susan to feed as well. What if we ran out of everything? I had seen inside the bread bin; we were down to two large loaves, and we had no yeast to make fresh bread, no strong flour, no more candles, no more meat, and only powdered milk. We wouldn't have minded. But the Abbotts would. They would go on and on about it. And Colonel Hunter might grow worse, he might need invalid food, steamed fish, semolina pudding, that sort of thing.

Next door Ben was moving about in his bed, too. And twice Lisa called the Abbotts' dogs' names in her sleep. I couldn't help worrying about them, for Ruffian was barely recovered from his accident. How was he managing? Would we ever see any of them again? It seemed unlikely, for they could be so easily captured and sold.

At last morning came with rain driving across the fields in sheets, driving water under the back door, soaking everything outside. I sat up in bed and thought of our horses out in it. I imagined Limpet trapped in the shelter with the rain pouring in. I dressed and went downstairs, and in a sudden burst of hope tried the telephone, hoping against all reason that it had been repaired, so that we could call assistance – vet, doctor, food van. But of course it was still dead. Everything seemed dead at the moment. The milk had not been delivered. The postman was nowhere to be seen. I went outside. Our horses were standing together in a corner of the bottom field, their backs to the rain, their tails tucked between their hind legs, their heads low, their ears back. There was nothing to recommend the day, absolutely nothing. I looked over the loose box doors. Stardust was lying down again, the others were resting various legs. Only Scorpio's head was restlessly hanging over his door.

I went outside, through the archway on to the common. Nothing had changed there, the trees still lay where they had fallen, the road was still empty of traffic. The rain stung my face. My eyes ran, my hands turned to ice. At that moment there seemed no reason why the weather should ever change. I dragged hay into the bottom field, while Limpet whinnied pathetically from the shelter. My boots squelched in mud, the rain ran off my husky on to my trousers and into my boots. My hair dripped rain down my neck, and there was no crack in the grey sky, no hopeful sunlight, just the pouring rain, as endless as an ocean. I swore then that, when life was normal, I would never grumble again. I would never be nostalgic about the past, or long for the days when all the houses were old, and the motor-car had not been invented. I will thank God for the telephone and electric power every day, if only it will return, I thought, before I heard Mum calling, "Harriet, where are you? Come in out of the rain. Come in at once."

"In a moment. When I've fed Limpet," I shouted back.

I fetched hay and climbed the ladder which still leaned against the shelter, and my feet kept slipping on the wooden rungs. Limpet raised his head and whinnied. He was soaking wet and shivering. I pushed the hay through the cracks in the broken roof and my coat sleeve caught on a piece of wood. Suddenly the ladder was gone and I was falling down and down to the wet earth . . .

I lay under the ladder. Dimly I heard Mum calling again, "Harriet, where are you? Come in at once." She

sounded miles away. I felt dizzy. I felt sick. I couldn't move without wanting to vomit. And still the rain poured down.

Quite soon after that I realised Ben was bending over me. "Oh, Harriet. Why didn't you wait? Why are you such a fool?" he asked.

"Actually, I'm quite all right," I replied carefully, trying to sound normal though there was a buzzing in my head.

"I'll get help," Ben said and disappeared.

Presently Dad carried me indoors. "Another casualty," he said, putting me down on a chair in the sitting-room.

"Poor Limpet, he's shivering," I told them.

"Shivering's a good thing, it's nature's way of keeping something alive," replied Mrs Abbott briskly. "It's when a horse is cold and doesn't shiver that you're in trouble."

I lay looking at the dust which was gathering everywhere. And when Dad helped me out of my wet coat, bits of hay fell on to the chair and carpet, and now there was no cleaner to pick them up because it, too, needed electricity.

"How are you feeling?" asked Mum, handing me a mug of tea.

"All right. I can't think why I'm being so feeble. I think it must be shock. One minute I was feeding Limpet, the next I was on the ground," I answered. "It all happened so quickly."

"Don't ever go up that ladder again, unless there's someone on the bottom rung," Mum said.

"We must get Limpet out. Surely we can cut the tree up bit by bit," I suggested.

"My chainsaw can't handle a trunk that size," Dad replied.

"We'll have to take the shelter to bits then, plank by

plank, because he can't stay there another night," I said.

"Let's wait until the rain stops," suggested Mum.

Colonel Hunter was shuffling about in slippers now. Susan was recovered and wondering about her boyfriend who lived in Kent.

I ate cereal for breakfast, with powdered milk. Ben was relighting the fires in the fireplaces upstairs. James was bringing in logs, dripping rain on to the hall carpet.

"They'll never burn. They're too wet," he said.

Tracey was still in bed, reading. Justin was still sleeping, cosy under Ben's duvet. Mr Abbott was pacing the hall fuming. "This is absolutely typical of this country. One small hurricane and everything packs up. Listen, there isn't even a train running. It's pathetic."

"Perhaps one should unwind occasionally," Mum suggested.

"Unwind! We're all too laid back already," Mr Abbott stormed. "That's what's wrong with this country."

The rain beat against the windowpanes. Our horses were still out in it. Limpet was still trapped in the shelter. Some days seem endless and this was one of them. We seemed suspended in time. The sense of frustration was enormous and everywhere. I saw Mr Abbott kicking at the wellington boots lying in the back porch in rage and frustration.

James tried the telephone again and then hurled a mug across the kitchen, which smashed against a wall. Ben was biting his nails to pieces. Mum's face was drawn with worry.

Later, as the rain slowed down, I went out to clean the stables with Susan and Mrs Abbott. Lisa had gone upstairs to play Monopoly with Justin and Tracey. Ben found a hammer and started dismantling the shelter.

The horses were a little better. Stardust stood up with difficulty. Seamus's wound had stopped bleeding.

Sultan's injured eye was half open. "You see, we've managed. Nothing's died. Perhaps doctors and vets are not so important after all," said Mrs Abbott.

"We couldn't have managed so far without you," I said, and meant it.

"But I haven't done much, not anything really," she replied.

"But you were here when we needed you. You knew that Colonel Hunter and Susan weren't going to die. You knew what was wrong with Stardust. The rest of us thought his leg was broken. Without you we would be crazy with worry," I said.

"Thank you, Harriet. That's the nicest thing anyone has said about me for years," Mrs Abbott replied, and kissed me. I was so surprised that I nearly dropped the fork I was using. "And you're all right, Harriet. You'll go a long way one day. I know that. Just a little more dedication. And you're going to be beautiful, a really beautiful girl."

"Me beautiful? That's a joke," I answered, but was pleased all the same.

"I mean it. I always mean what I say."

"Thank you."

The sky had cleared. A watery sun looked down on us. Everything began to seem a little better. Ben led Limpet out of the shelter. "I'm going to give him a warm feed. I think he deserves it," he shouted.

"He's a good boy. I hope Justin grows up as good," said Mrs Abbott, her eyes following Ben across the yard

"But Justin is so dedicated and so clever," I answered. "He can even programme a computer already! It's amazing."

"Yes, that's true," Mrs Abbott said with a sigh.

Then James appeared shouting, "There's a helicopter landed, there are men mending the wires. Come and

look. We're going to have electricity again."

The helicopter was parked on the common. There were half a dozen men. Two of them were already re-connecting cables.

"When will the electricity come on again?" called James.

"Not yet. Not for some time. There's over fifty poles down," one of them called back.

"It's a beginning anyway," said Mrs Abbott.

There were baked potatoes topped with cheese for lunch. Mr Abbott left half his. Colonel Hunter still couldn't talk properly. The chainsaw had broken down again. It was very cold in the dining-room where the guests ate. Susan joined us in the kitchen saying, "I'm not one of them. Never have been. Never will be."

Tracey demanded ketchup. Justin demanded pickle. Mr Abbott seemed to be sitting surrounded by a magnetic field of anger. When we left them alone to eat their pudding of stewed apple I could hear him shouting at Mrs Abbott, "You chose this place. You wanted to move. It's all your fault."

Tracey was crying. Justin said, "Leave Mummy alone, Daddy. You wanted to move too. You wanted somewhere smart to entertain your business associates. Remember?"

The Abbotts had seemed so perfect. Now I realised that they were just as flawed as the rest of us, and I didn't envy them any more, not their horses, nor their equipment, nor their clothes, nor their individual television sets; not even Justin his computer. I was happy to remain careless, clumsy, untidy Harriet Pemberton without a penny to her name. I didn't even want their swimming-pool, and with this feeling came a great sensation of happiness for I realised that the saying "Money doesn't buy happiness" is probably true.

"They're cracking up," I said.

"They can't be," replied Ben without asking who "they" were.

"Mr Abbott is used to things running his way. He wants to push on and he can't," said Mum.

Later, when it was dark, we played games by the light of the open fire in the hall. Then we told stories. Justin's was about a world ruled by computers. Lisa's was about a pony which no one could ride but a girl who turned out later to be a ghost. Ben wouldn't tell a story but James's was called "Murder at Black Pony Inn", and went on and on, growing more and more spooky, so that when it finally ended no one wanted to go to bed.

"Why don't you tell nice stories?" Mum asked.

Finally I went to bed without a light, feeling my way upstairs, undressing in the dark. I didn't wash or clean my teeth, just crawled under my duvet and waited for daylight to reappear, my mind thinking back over the last two days, thinking of all the things we might have done but hadn't.

Next morning nothing seemed changed except that life seemed to be moving at a slower pace; only Mr Abbott was functioning at the same speed as before. Susan and Mrs Abbott rode out on Sultan and Scorpio who, after too much time cooped up, were full of bucks. Ben and I carted logs into the house where we stacked them by the Aga, while Mum removed the last piece of meat from the freezer.

Stardust wasn't any better. Seamus's injured leg was enormous. Suddenly there seemed no end to our worries. Miss Steele would no longer go up or down stairs in the dark. "I can't risk a fall," she said. "I'll have to have a chamberpot in my room, what my mother called 'an article'." And we hadn't a chamberpot for we had never imagined such a catastrophe.

At eleven o'clock I found Mum sitting alone in the kitchen, her head in her hands. "There's going to be an accident," she said looking at me with a tear-stained face. "I know there is. And then we'll be sued. And the insurance will wriggle out of it, they always do, and we'll be ruined. I can see it happening, Harriet. Miss Steele will fall downstairs or Colonel Hunter will fall out of bed, or Tracey will trip over something and hit your bed with her face and break all her front teeth. I can see it clearly, Harriet. And there's no more food in the deep-freeze, and no way of getting any. And it's all my fault. I should have forseen this situation. I should have had a generator installed. The Abbotts are right. We've failed everybody."

It was a terrible moment. I didn't know what to say. I'm not used to grown-ups crying.

"It could go on for another week, do you realise that, Harriet? Then the old people here will die of hypothermia. One by one in their freezing bedrooms," Mum continued in the same hopeless voice.

"But they have got fires," I said, putting my arm round her shoulders. "So they'll be all right. Don't worry."

"Yes, thank God for grates and fireplaces, and the Aga. Without them we would be finished. At least we can cook, and there are still a few potatoes left in the sack in the pantry. What about the horses?"

"We've got plenty of hay, but everything else is running a bit low. Luckily, since most of them are standing idle, they don't need a lot of oats," I replied.

I suppose in every catastrophe there's a low point, when hope is abandoned and all seems dark and hopeless. And this was it. The Abbotts refused to drink powdered milk in their coffee or tea. Colonel Hunter was very cold. Mum plied him with hot-water bottles and hot drinks, but nothing seemed to help. Looking at him made me afraid he might die at any time, and what would we do then? Once again it would be Mrs Abbott who would decide.

Mrs Abbott seemed changed too; there were new lines etched on her face. She talked about the dogs in the past tense. "We had hoped Rascal would win at Crufts in February." I imagined other cups, even bigger ones this time. She talked of having Stardust put down. "He's finished," she said. And none of us could bear to look at Seamus's leg any more because it was enormous now and he held it up all the time, looking at us pathetically, as though saying, Do something – please. "He needs a shot of penicillin and I haven't got any," Mrs Abbott said. Justin wearily told her that everything was going to be all right and she snapped back, "Don't be a fool, Justin, and don't treat me like one either."

Mr Abbott was at a loose end. He constantly disappeared in search of something – a mended telephone? – a cleared road? No one was certain. "I'm losing thousands every minute, do you realise that?" he shouted at lunch-time, banging the table with his fist. "And what's this?" he continued, staring at the almost meatless hot-pot which Mum had prepared. "Is this all the grub we've got left?" No one answered him.

Miss Steele refused any lunch and sat feeding Colonel Hunter mashed potatoes with a spoon. Mrs Tomson kept on about rationing in a war which only herself, Miss Steele and Colonel Hunter remembered. Dad went without lunch, too, saying, "Leave the food for the guests. I need to lose some weight."

Susan sat, getting in everyone's way and grumbling. She had managed to salvage two bags of crisps and a tin of baked beans from the caravan. Now she ate them like a hungry dog.

"Why didn't they tell us it was going to happen?" Ben asked presently. "I mean, why do we have weather bulletins if they can't get it right? What's the point of them, Mum?"

"They do their best. The wind must have changed at the last minute," replied Mum, who seemed prepared to forgive anyone everything at the moment, if only they would forgive her for her lack of foresight.

Then, after lunch, I started to feel sick. It wasn't a usual sort of sickness. It was to do with fear. I was sick because I was afraid that we were going to be cut off for weeks, that our old guests would die, and the Abbotts go crazy with frustration. Odd though it may seem, I was not afraid for us. We seemed to have an enduring strength, which the Abbotts with their drive and boundless energy didn't possess for they were tiring themselves, and burning up everything they ate, with anger and frustration. Even Justin seemed to be losing his nerve, for without electricity he had no computer to play with and no television to watch. Lisa was cracking up too. Now that Limpet was all right, she worried endlessly about the dogs. Every hour she seemed to be on the common calling their names, on and on, and there still wasn't a sign of them anywhere.

We went to bed early that night for without lights there was no point in staying up. Dad still had a torch working, which he used every hour to look at Colonel Hunter, asleep in the hall now beside the big, still smouldering fire. Dad too was afraid that he might die, just slip away in the night, leaving us to deal with his remains as best we could.

Later that night I heard Mr Abbott shouting, "It's a disaster, an absolute disaster. If this goes on another week we'll have lost everything." Mrs Abbott was crying.

218

I was glad now that we hadn't any money to worry about and that Dad wasn't raving like a lunatic over his assets. I was glad I didn't go to St Peter's too, where I suspected houses and money were a major part of conversation. After a time I found myself praying again. "God, please bring back the dogs and save Seamus, Stardust and Colonel Hunter." And I was ashamed because without thinking I had put Colonel Hunter last.

Then Lisa appeared like a ghost and, drawing back the curtains, said, "Look, there's a moon outside. What's going to happen, Harriet? I'm so frightened. Will Seamus and Stardust really be shot?"

I didn't know what to say because I didn't know either. "Things happen; it's fate," I said at last.

"Tracey's been crying all evening. Mr Abbott is being horrible. Justin won't speak to anyone, not even to me, and I haven't done anything to him," Lisa said wearily. "When do you think the lights will come on again?"

"Soon, very soon," I said without conviction.

Lisa curled up at the bottom of my bed. "I suppose wars are like this," she said.

"Worse, much worse," I answered.

"I wish I could find the dogs. I really liked them," she said presently.

"One day we'll be able to laugh about this," I answered. "I'll say, do you remember the hurricane –?"

"When Colonel Hunter died, and the dogs died, and Stardust and Seamus were shot. Oh yes, what lovely memories!" cried Lisa, sitting up again. "Oh, Harriet, you're just as mad as everybody else."

"Well, why talk to me then?" I asked.

"I won't," she said, and went back to her own room in a huff.

And when sleep came at last to me, it was like a friend, shutting out the fears and anxieties which were everywhere.

Eight

My heart sings

I had stewed apple for breakfast next morning. The Abbotts hadn't appeared by eight o'clock, only Mum was in the kitchen making tea. I went outside and found Susan mucking out.

"God, I'm sick of this. I feel as though I'm in a cage," she said.

"But why?"

"I can't ring up my mother. I can't ring up my boyfriend. And there's no post, that's why," she shouted, pushing the wheelbarrow with such force that it keeled over.

"We can still ride," I said.

"Ride, ride, that's all I ever do."

"Lucky you."

Seamus's leg was so big now, it made me sick to look at it.

"He's getting blood poisoning, that's what he's getting. Look at the lump under his elbow, go on look," thundered Susan.

"I don't want to," I replied.

"And Stardust's finished too. And no one's doing anything. It's so damned pathetic. Surely someone could walk to the vet and bring him here," Susan continued furiously.

"Why don't you go?" I answered.

"I am. This morning. You can come with me, we'll take bikes," Susan said.

"Okay. Great. As soon as I've finished feeding," I said.

So half an hour later, we pumped up the tyres on James's and my old bike and set off. And, as we pedalled, miraculously the roads seemed to be clearing in front of our eyes. Men were everywhere with huge machines and gigantic trucks. They waved cheerfully as we passed. And the bikes didn't shy or buck or stop at every fallen tree, and so suddenly we were on the main road, pedalling like mad. "It's open and we never knew," I shouted.

"Oh, I feel so free," shouted Susan laughing. "I feel as though I've been let out of prison. I feel terrific."

"And so happy," I yelled back.

I liked Susan, but at that moment I was in the mood

to like anybody, such was my feeling of relief. Suddenly the main road and the cars passing along it were beautiful. Everything was beautiful. We reached the suburbs. Lights were on; everything was working.

"We've wasted so much time," I shouted, pedalling faster and faster. "And won't the Abbotts be furious? There they are, lying in bed, not knowing that the road's open."

"Oh, the Abbotts!" shouted Susan. "It's money, money, money, with the Abbotts. And win, win, win."

I could see the vet's surgery now. Another minute and we were throwing down our bikes and rushing inside. "It's urgent. We need Roy," I cried to the receptionist.

We always have Roy to tend our sick and injured animals. He's a friend as well as a vet.

A minute later he was standing in front of us saying, "Hello, Harriet, what's up?"

I was so excited that I could only gabble, "We need you straight away, we've been cut off. We've got blood poisoning and a slipped stifle, the lot."

"Can you come at once?" Susan added, smiling.

"Will do. Give me twenty minutes. I must finish surgery first," he said, the same bluff, down-to-earth Roy we love.

We leaped on our bikes again and pedalled another hundred metres to the human Health Centre. The receptionist wanted us to sit down but we refused and soon we were seeing a new, young doctor with lovely dark wavy hair and blue eyes. I explained the situation to him. ". . . so one stroke and a lot of pending nervous breakdowns," I finished.

"Including me. We've been cut off for days and it seems like years," said Susan, smiling into his eyes. "We're all going mad."

But he didn't smile. I suppose that doctors don't find

madness funny, and I don't blame them, because the real thing must be awful.

"I'll be there as soon as I can," he promised, while the receptionist, who wore a white coat and plastic-framed glasses, wrote down our address saying, "Are you sure the road's open? Doctor's very busy this morning and we mustn't waste his time."

"Of course it's open. How do you think we got here?" replied Susan. "We haven't got wings, we can't fly, unfortunately." I wished she wouldn't be so rude, because we will have to talk to the receptionist long after she's gone.

We went outside together. "Stupid old cow," said Susan, mounting her bike.

We pedalled full speed for home, standing on our pedals, hoping to race Roy there, laughing and screaming at one another, like two horses turned out after being shut in for weeks on end.

"I'm so happy," shrieked Susan.

"Same here," I cried.

"And wow, what a doctor, you are lucky," shouted Susan, her fair hair streaming behind her.

"I'll hit you with something, then we'll call him out," I shouted back.

"Oh yeah. I bet he wouldn't come. I bet they would send some old boy who's been a doctor for years," laughed Susan.

All the fallen trees had gone from the road. All the telegraph poles were up again. The sky was blue. Birds were singing. People were starting up cars, clearing up their gardens, laughing. A milkman was delivering milk. The red post van was rushing from house to house. I felt as though I had been away for a long time and come back. Tears of joy ran down my face as I pedalled. My heart sang.

"I'm moving back into my caravan tonight," said Susan. "I'm tired of sleeping on your sofa. And I'm going to ring up Jim. Your mum won't mind, will she?"

"Not if you put some money in the box and time it," I said.

We could see Black Pony Inn now. Wood smoke was rising from the high Tudor chimneys.

James was waiting by the back gate. "How dare you take my bike without asking!" he shouted.

"You were in bed. You weren't up," I shouted back. Susan was laughing. I started to laugh too. "We're saved. The road's open. Is the telephone working yet?" I asked.

"No. And Mum needs the doctor. Colonel Hunter's had a relapse," James said.

"Well, he's on his way. So's Roy. The emergency is over. Everything's going to be all right from now on. Isn't it fantastic?" I shouted.

"You had better tell crosspatch Abbott that; he doesn't know yet. He's fuming over breakfast, because there isn't any milk, or bacon and egg, or sausages. He's being absolutely foul," James said.

"But listen, there's the milkfloat. Can you hear it?" I yelled in triumph before I rushed indoors shouting, "Everything's all right, the road's open. The doctor's on his way, and the vet. We're saved."

Mum stood in front of me with tears of relief streaming from her face. Mr Abbott leaped to his feet shouting, "For goodness sake, why didn't you tell me before, Harriet? Look at the time I've wasted."

"Because I've been visiting the doctor and the vet. That's why. How's Colonel Hunter?" I asked.

"Very poorly," Mum said.

"I'll go into town right away and find a telephone," said Mr Abbott, leaving the house at the double.

"I'll go and get some food for us all," Dad said, hugging me.

"I can't believe it. But it's too late isn't it? The dogs have gone. And Seamus is going to die of blood poisoning. Oh God, I can't bear it," cried Mrs Abbott, with her head in her hands. "I can't bear another minute of it."

"But it's over," I said.

"Not just that – the move, the work, the bills," she cried.

Luckily there was a knock at the door then and we found Roy outside. I introduced him to Mrs Abbott and we hurried to the stables together, Mrs Abbott wiping her eyes and saying, "I'm sorry I'm such a wreck." (As though Roy was looking at her or cared!)

Then Mum opened the back door to call, "The electricity's on again. I can't believe it, everything's working."

Roy talked quietly to Seamus, while the big horse smelled him. "Poor old fellow, what a shame," Roy said slowly, squatting in the straw and feeling his leg. Then he went outside to his car.

"Antibiotics?" asked Mrs Abbott.

"Yes, and a pain-killer, for starters," Roy said.

And Lisa appeared from nowhere to ask as usual, "Is he going to die?"

"Not if I can help it," replied Roy, filling a syringe. "But he isn't well, not by a long chalk."

No one else can give an injection like Roy; he just slips the needle under a horse's skin so gently that the horse hardly feels it. "Okay, we'll have the bandage off. He needs walking out. He shouldn't be standing still," Roy said. He looked at the wound. "I've got a new type of dressing I'll put on, it's part seaweed and very good," he said, returning to his car.

Tracey had joined us now. "Justin's gone into town with Daddy,"she said.

"Right," said Roy now. "Lead him out in an hour's time, just gently. He'll be a bit sleepy, but not to worry because if he's too energetic he'll start the bleeding again. Now let's see the other patients." Stardust looked a pitiful sight, almost a case for the RSPCA. His sides were run up like a greyhound's, his eyes were dull, his head hung low.

"More sedative," said Roy with a sigh, going to his car. "I don't know whether I can get his stifle back in place; if not he'll have to go to the Equine Centre at Newmarket for an operation."

While Roy waited for the sedative to work we showed him the other horses. "You've done quite well considering," he said. "At the stud they've lost one of their best mares. A tree fell through the roof of her box. And she was in foal too. The foal would have been worth thousands."

"Is Stardust going to be all right? That's what I want to know," cried Tracey, staring up at Roy, her eyes full of tears.

"I'm going to do my damnedest to save him. But no promises," Roy replied.

"To save him?" cried Tracey.

"Well, he can't live in pain, can he?" Roy said. "He can't be left as he is either, I must do something or he'll have to have an operation. There's no other way. And even the operation may not work; nothing is one hundred per cent in my trade. We just do the best we can."

Mrs Abbott watched Roy with glassy eyes. She was so tired that I don't think she was really with us. Something had happened in the night. Something between her and Mr Abbott – that was obvious. But no one knew what.

"Oh, Harriet," she said now. "The horses pull at your heartstrings, don't they? Mine too. Will you keep Stardust for us, for ever?"

"Not if he's in pain," I answered, wiping a tear from my eye.

"I don't think I can bear to have him put down. I shall go away for a day and leave it to you," she continued. I seemed to be seeing the real Mrs Abbott for the first time, the mask had gone. Perhaps we all wear masks at times.

"Ben's stronger emotionally than I am. I'm not being sexist, but he's the person to deal with such things," I answered, but even as I spoke I wasn't sure that this was true, because Ben *will* deal with anything; but afterwards his hands come up in a rash, or he has to reach for his asthma spray. Then I thought that the results of the hurricane would be with us for ever; and that any future wind would revive memories and fears.

Later Roy drank a cup of tea in the kitchen. The young doctor had arrived and was arranging for Colonel Hunter to be taken to hospital by ambulance, which made me think that if only he hadn't tried to help us, he would be all right now. Miss Steele stood in the drive watching him leave. Colonel Hunter waved weakly to us all, calling in a voice crackling with age, "It's only for assessment. Keep my room, will you?"

"Of course. It'll always be ready for you," Mum called back, wiping tears from her eyes.

Then Susan asked the young doctor to look at her head. "I'm sure it should have been stitched. The caravan fell on top of me. It was horrific," she told him with a smile.

I went back to the horses with Roy, and I kept thinking that if the Abbotts hadn't been with us it would have been our horses trapped in the loose boxes instead of theirs, so that in a way we were lucky. Ben joined us and led Seamus out of his box, gently talking to him all the time. He was very stiff, but gradually, as he walked slowly up and down the drive, he improved, until after some five minutes he was almost sound again.

"He's going to be all right," said Roy, smiling at Mrs Abbott.

"But not for showing," she answered.

"No, he'll have a scar, of course."

I couldn't bear to watch Roy working on Stardust's stifle. But Ben did. Outside the back door Susan was saying goodbye to the doctor. Tracey was playing some sort of ball game with Lisa. The sun was actually shining, and the clouds in the sky were small and cheerfully buzzing about like strange ships in a blue sea.

"I've won," shouted Lisa.

"No you haven't, I have," shrieked Tracey.

Then Mum appeared to say, "The dogs are found. They're all right. They're in a dogs' home. They were found nearly ten miles away searching for food on a garbage heap."

"Excellent, we'll fetch them after lunch, shall we?" Mrs Abbott said, smiling at me.

"If you want to, that's all right by me," I replied.

"There's a special lunch – roast lamb, roast potatoes and all the trimmings, to make up for the last few days," Mum said before going back to the house.

"I've put his stifle back, but I don't know whether it will stay. I've strapped it up the best I can. I'll be back tomorrow," said Roy, whose car telephone was calling him urgently to another job.

Susan appeared then asking for instructions. I went indoors to lay the table for lunch. It seemed to have been a very long morning.

"We're out of the wood," said Mum happily.

"I seem to be going to collect the dogs after lunch. Mrs Abbott suggested that I should go with her. I can't think why," I said.

"She likes you, that's why," Mum replied.

"Oh yeah," I said.

Everyone except poor Colonel Hunter was present for lunch. Dad opened two bottles of wine. "It's on the house," he explained. "A sort of celebration. After all, several people have died, but we are still here, in spite of everything."

"Just," said Mrs Abbott. "But I can't drink because I'm driving."

"I suppose we have to go back to school tomorrow?" asked Justin.

"It's been lovely and awful at the same time," said Tracey, smiling at me as I poured wine into glasses. "And I don't want to go back to school. I wish I could go with Lisa to her school. It sounds much more fun."

"Don't be silly, Tracey," snapped Mr Abbott, scowling at her.

"She may have a point," said Mrs Abbott.

"What point? You can't compare the two schools, they turn out different people," replied Mr Abbott.

"What rubbish, Dad," cried Justin.

I returned to the kitchen unable to believe my ears. Was it really the Abbotts talking – Justin? Tracey? Mrs Abbott? Had we changed them after all? Then I heard Mr Abbott say, "I've seen the solicitor. Completion is next Tuesday. So we'll be leaving then, lock, stock and barrel."

"On Tuesday? As soon as that?" asked Mrs Abbott. "But supposing we can't move the horses?"

"They'll have to follow later, then."

"I don't want to go," cried Tracey. "I want to stay here with Lisa and Harriet. I like it here. I want to stay here for ever. I don't like the new house, it's too big and empty and I don't want a swimming-pool, or a Jacuzzi. I want to stay here, Mummy. Are you listening? I like it here."

There was a short silence. We could hear everything from the kitchen. Ben looked at me and said, "What a turnabout!"

"She's a spoilt brat. I wouldn't say no to a swimming-pool," said James. "And think of the Jacuzzi! Wow!"

Then we heard Mrs Tomson say quietly, "Money isn't everything."

"But it makes a hell of a lot of difference," answered Mr Abbott.

"Perhaps we could leave Tracey behind," suggested Justin with a snigger.

Mum started rattling the dishes then. "Stop eaves-dropping," she said. "It's a disgusting habit."

"We're not eavesdropping. We just can't help hear-ing," I answered.

"And I feel like crowing," added Ben, smiling.

"I don't want Tracey and Susan to go, especially Susan," said Lisa. "I want them all to stay here for ever, and the dogs."

"Where will our ponies live in the winter, then?" I asked.

"We can build some more loose boxes," Lisa said.

"No thank you. I want a rest. I've had enough of the Abbotts," Mum told us, dishing up trifle. "Mr Abbott is a pain, and I don't suppose Peggy will return, she hates them too much. She says they treat her like dirt."

"I don't hate them any more. I'm sorry for them. I'm just glad Dad isn't like Mr Abbott. I would hate having to win all the time," I said.

"He beat Justin for not winning last year. Tracey told me," Lisa revealed. "And Justin didn't shed a tear."

"I don't believe you," I said.

"It's true. He beat him in the horse box. Ask Susan," Lisa answered.

Suddenly I was seeing Justin differently too. I couldn't imagine dear, good-natured Dad beating anyone or any-thing. He simply isn't made that way. But what if he had beaten us? We would be different then. Meaner for a

start, crueller too, withdrawn. Like Justin? I didn't
know for sure. We're not perfect, far from it, but supposing Dad had beaten us? It was too awful to contemplate. And supposing he hit Mrs Abbott too?

"It's only gossip," Mum was saying. "You mustn't
listen to gossip."

"I don't think Lisa gossips. I think it fits," Ben said
slowly. "Poor Justin. And I've been hating him. I've refused to talk to him, and I've refused to bowl for him or
put up stumps. I feel guilty now, because he probably
needs someone to talk to."

"And Tracey hates St Peter's. She wants to go to
school with me. She says she's going to run away," Lisa
continued, sounding important because we were all concerned and listening, and we rarely listen to Lisa because
we think of her as the youngest in the family, a sort of
perpetual toddler.

"They're leaving soon. We may never see them
again," said Ben.

"I know. And we've hated them, most of the time
anyway," I replied.

"And envied them their money," Ben added.

"You don't have to feel guilty. Lots of fathers beat
their children. Justin will surely repeat the pattern and
beat his," replied Mum sadly. "That's the way it goes."

"It doesn't have to," said James.

Our guests were filing out of the dining-room now. I
missed Colonel Hunter, who would always look into the
kitchen before going into the sitting-room for coffee. He
would smile at Mum and say, "That was very nice, Mrs
Pemberton. Thank you."

Miss Steele and Mrs Tomson were talking to each
other. The Abbotts were now silent. Soon they'll be
gone, I thought, and I didn't know whether to be
pleased or sorry.

Nine

Time to leave

We checked the horses again before we set off to bring home the dogs. Lisa and Tracey sat together in the back of Mrs Abbott's car. I got into the front. Everything was normal again, or almost, and it was like a miracle. The only black spots were the trees still lying everywhere, the houses with gaping holes in their roofs, the fallen fences and smashed sheds.

"It was the worst hurricane ever in this part of the world," Mrs Abbott said, driving at high speed. "We're lucky to be back to normal. In parts of Kent they're still without electricity."

"We'll be better prepared next time. Dad's talking about getting a generator. We were to have a swimming-pool, but he thinks the generator will be more use to the guests," I said.

"He's probably right. I can't see your present guests using an outdoor swimming-pool," said Mrs Abbott, while Lisa and Tracey giggled in the back. As thick as thieves, Mum would have called them.

There were dogs everywhere at the kennels. Lost dogs, dogs no one wanted, dogs which had never known a home. Bitches in whelp. Puppies and high-spirited dogs. Misunderstood dogs. They were in pens watching us, some begging to be taken away, others looking for beloved owners, only to be disappointed. They were all shapes and sizes, some pedigree, some not.

"Where do they all come from?" cried Lisa in despair.

"From all over the place. We have most soon after Christmas. They are given as pets then, and are soon found to be too much trouble," said the lady who was showing us round.

"And if no one ever claims or wants them?" asked Lisa, her voice shaking with emotion.

"We find them homes."

"And if you can't?"

"If they're old or vicious, or diseased, we put them down." The woman, who was called Mrs Chivers, seemed very matter-of-fact. I suppose she had to be, for to be involved emotionally would break one's heart.

The Abbotts' dogs were all together. They welcomed Mrs Abbott with wagging tails, while I stood staring at a black and white dog whose nose was pressed tight against the bars of his pen, who had eyes as soft as velvet, with so much sadness in them that to look at them was to weep.

"Hasn't he got a home?" I asked.

"Apparently no one wants him. He's been here a month and no one's taken him," said Mrs Chivers. "Why, do you like him, dear?"

"Yes, I do." The dog was wagging his tail now, slowly, uncertainly, his eyes on my face.

"We need a dog," I said. "We really do."

"But you haven't asked our parents," cried Lisa.

"He's half Labrador, half collie. He's a real sweetie and very clever," said Mrs Chivers.

Lisa was looking at him too now. She had always wanted a dog, more than me. At times it had seemed an obsession.

"We can ring up Mum," I said. "Have you got a telephone we could use?" My heart was racing inside me

236

with hope, and I was seeing the dog in the kitchen lying
by the Aga. And watching me leave on the school bus in
the morning, and still there when I returned in the
evening.

"It will be a very good home. I can vouch for that,"
said Mrs Abbott. "I can give you a written reference if
you like."

In the end we went indoors and rang up home. Mum

wasn't certain at first and kept saying, "You must ask Dad first."

"But we need a guard," I replied. "And he's quite big, but not too big, big enough to frighten people anyway; and he's got a lovely face. Please, Mum. Please."

Then Lisa grabbed the telephone and cried, "You promised we could have a dog, you know you did, and Dad did. Please, Mum."

I knew it wasn't true. No one had promised, but Lisa's not above inventing things which have never happened, when it suits her that is.

When at last it had been agreed and we had put down the telephone, Mrs Chivers said, "I shall have to ask you for a donation. We always do." I hadn't any money with me, nor had Lisa.

"That's all right. He's going to be my present to you both. I owe you a lot and I was going to buy you something," said Mrs Abbott briskly, taking a cheque-book out of her bag. "Shall we say fifty and something for my dogs' keep?" she asked, writing the date on a cheque.

"We'll pay you back," I said. "Truly."

"Yes, truly," agreed Lisa, jumping up and down with joy.

"I just hope we can fit them all in the car," replied Mrs Abbott, signing her name. "Four of us and four dogs, it's quite a lot."

We wrote down our names and addresses, and Mrs Abbott signed a form.

"He answers to 'Bob'," said Mrs Chivers. "He belonged to an old man who died. He's six years old." She put a lead on him. "You can keep it if you like," she said.

I helped Mrs Abbott with her dogs. They were very excitable, pulling and choking in their haste to get into the car. Fortunately it was a very large car.

Bob sat on the floor in the front with me, while the other dogs sat in the back part, panting.

"I don't know what to say. You've been fantastic, Mrs Abbott. Thank you so much . . ." I began, wishing to be polite.

"Don't say anything then," replied Mrs Abbott, driving on to the road. "The best things are left unsaid."

Bob pressed his nose against my knee; then he put his paws on my lap and tried to lick my face. I can't believe he's ours, I thought. We've wanted a dog for so long. And now, thanks to the Abbotts, we've got one. The Abbotts of all people!

"A penny for your thoughts, Harriet," said Mrs Abbott.

"Nothing fantastic. I was just thinking how much we had all changed. Somehow the hurricane changed everything, not just the landscape but us too," I said slowly, hoping she wouldn't laugh at me as James would have done.

"Yes, you're right. It blunted the sharp edges, put things in perspective. All that need to win seems pretty silly when things are crashing all about you, and the food's running out," replied Mrs Abbott, turning to smile at me. "We were all pretty uptight, weren't we? You didn't like giving up your room; and I don't blame you. We didn't think the arrangements were good enough," she continued.

"How did you know about my room?" I asked, turning red.

"It was on your face, all the time. And you didn't like giving up the stables either."

"I didn't know it was so obvious," I said.

"It doesn't matter. It's over now. Let's just be friends. God knows we all need friends. And remember this, Harriet, if any of you ever need help with schooling your horses, I'm around. We're only going to be twenty miles away and that's nothing in a motor-car. So just ring me up day or night," she finished.

Bob settled in very quickly. Everyone loved him. The Abbotts began packing. School started again. Seamus's bandage was taken off for good. Stardust was turned out in our smallest paddock for a few hours every day. His stifle was still in place and he was no longer in pain.

"I won't call again unless you call me. I think we've won," Roy told us as he left for the third time.

The first frost came and the last of the flowers in the garden wilted away. The new loose boxes were mended. But nothing could replace the trees. It would take a hundred years to do that. And without them we could see things from our windows which we couldn't see before – the church, the road, even sometimes the railway line. Bob seemed to like us all equally, and our elderly guests loved him. Mum visited Colonel Hunter in hospital with Miss Steele. They took him flowers and chocolates and orange squash.

"We should have taken him whisky," Mum said afterwards. "But we were not sure whether it was allowed."

Mrs Abbott gave me a last lesson on Prince. Ben put up a small course of jumps, and before I jumped them I trotted over poles on the ground, trying to get him to relax. I had learned more than I can possibly describe with Mrs Abbott. Prince had been hollowing his back and rushing his fences; now at last he was taking them steadily, his back rounded.

"You've got a winner there," Mrs Abbott told me when the lesson was over. "He's clever, he's fast and he's careful. You don't often get those three altogether in one horse."

240

As we walked indoors that day, I told her his history. How he had come to us as unrideable, and then refused to live anywhere else. How he had appeared in a film with me when we swam a river together.

"So he isn't really yours at all?" she asked when I had finished.

"Not completely. He really belongs to the film company," I said. "If they want him for a part we have to let him go."

We went out to dinner with the Abbotts that last evening. Mr Abbott paid for everything. I had nothing suitable to wear. In the end I wore one of Mum's dresses which was corduroy and blue. She lent me a necklace to go with it. Justin stared at me all through dinner. I didn't know what to say for no one had ever looked at me like that before. Tracey and Lisa giggled together and pretended to be drunk. Ben talked to Mr Abbott about his future. James wasn't there, preferring to spend the

evening with Virginia. We drank to all sorts of things, to eternal friendship, to the end of the catastrophe, to the Abbotts' new home, to our future. We felt sad and merry at the same time. It was a fantastic evening when no one said a cross word.

Afterwards Ben, Justin and I sat talking in the playroom. Cider had loosened Justin's tongue. Words poured out of him. He asked me to go to the Christmas disco at his school. I didn't know what to say. I thought of telling my form at school about it.

They wouldn't believe me at first. "You, go to a disco, Harriet? At St Peter's?" they would cry in disbelief. "You? How will you bear to leave your horses?"

Because of that I said yes, for I was tired of being considered old-fashioned, and I knew I would enjoy their envy. At the same time I was worrying about what I would wear.

"You don't have to bother too much about clothes," Justin said, reading my thoughts. "Jeans will do."

Then he told us about his parents, how his father had started as a labourer, then became an electrician, how hard it had been until he had invented a new sort of foam for cushions and upholstery which wasn't inflammable. He had invented a lamp, too, which was shaped like a lozenge. He had borrowed money and gone into business and made a fortune. "But he's always wished he was educated, that's why we're at St Peter's," Justin finished. "He wants us to have what he didn't have. He wants us to have an easier time than he did. People laughed at him, you see, or so he says. They laughed at his clothes, at the way he spoke."

"You wouldn't think it now," Ben answered.

"No, he even has his hair set. It's that important to him. If I told the chaps at school that, they would laugh their heads off," Justin said.

When we said goodnight to one another it was lovely to be able to switch the lights on in the attic, and wash, and go to bed and read. To know that tomorrow the lights would still be working, that the fear and the discomfort were over. Already Mum was looking years younger, while Dad was praying for a cold snap so that people would start wanting double glazing. It seemed years since the Abbotts had arrived, though it was really only a few weeks. Their visit had caused a watershed in our lives, Dad was to say later.

I couldn't sleep that night. It was a very still night, without a whisper of wind, silent now. Not the rustle of a bird or the squeak of a mouse, with the branches on the trees quite still at last.

When we returned from school the next day Mrs Abbott and Susan were loading their horses. Lisa was watching them with tears streaming down her face.

"Don't for goodness sake," I cried, seizing her by the shoulder.

"I don't want them to go," she sobbed. "Not any of them."

"You'll start me off in a minute," I said, wiping my eyes.

Their horses loaded one by one without a backward glance, while ours watched, their eyes glowing with interest.

Mum and Dad appeared to shake hands with the Abbotts one by one, saying things like, "All the best," and, "You know we're here if you need us."

Justin and Tracey stood saying nothing.

The cars were loaded with computers and suitcases. The dogs were leashed and ready to leave. Bob stood with us watching. Susan had cleaned out the loose boxes. Everything was tidy. It was like an end of an era.

"Right," said Mrs Abbott at last. "Time to leave. Come on, kids." Justin shook hands with Ben. Then he kissed me.

"See you," he said and walked away without looking back and I swear he was crying.

Mrs Abbott kissed us one by one. "You know the door is always open. Come whenever you like. Here is our change of address card," she said, her voice shaking with emotion.

There was nothing left to do now but wave and wave until they were out of sight.

"I hate farewells," Mum said then. "Come indoors. There's a surprise."

"What surprise? I don't want a surprise. I want them back again," Lisa cried tearfully.

We found presents for each of us on the hall table – a picture for Ben, a book on riding for me, a china horse for Lisa, and an address book for James. Then Mum

said, "Follow me." And there in the old pantry was a
generator. "So we're all right now whatever happens,"
Mum said happily.

"But they gave us Bob," I cried. "We didn't need
other presents. We didn't need anything."

"They've left one for Peggy too," Mum said. "And

for Colonel Hunter. They've been very generous."

"So in spite of the catastrophe they *did* like it here," said Lisa, sniffing.

When we returned outside, our horses were standing waiting by the field gate, and I knew they were asking, "Can we go into our loose boxes now?"

We fetched feeds and put them in their mangers. Then we opened the gate, and with one accord they hurried each to his own box and own manger.

"They're pleased anyway," said Ben, shutting the gate after them. "Now I'm going to move back into my own bedroom. I feel just like they do. As Colonel Hunter would say, enough is enough."

"Same here," I said.

My room had been left tidy and propped against the mirror was a note which read: *Thank you for letting me have your room, Harriet, it's the nicest in the whole world. Luv from Tracey* XXXXXXXXXXXX

Bob followed me upstairs. I sat on my bed and he put his head on my knee and licked my hand. I sat remembering the emotions and trials of the last few weeks. I remembered how I had hated the Abbotts and how the hurricane had made us friends, changing us all. And I thought: Perhaps we need disaster to make us see life as it really is. To get rid of jealousy and envy and offence and all the other awful things which beset us.

Then Mum called, "Tea. There's lardy-cake." And drying my eyes, I thundered downstairs with Bob at my heels.

"We have a new guest arriving next week. He's a young army officer on leave. He's called Captain Matthews. His favourite aunt lives nearby and he wants to ride," Mum told us cheerfully.

And helping myself to lardy-cake, I thought: Here we go again.

246

Ben said, "He can ride Solitaire if he likes, because I haven't much time this term."

"I want to visit the Abbotts soon, Mum," Lisa said. "Please."

"We'll all go," said Ben. "We can swim in their pool, because I know we'll never have one whatever Dad says."

And now the future stretched ahead full of hope. Christmas, a disco, the beginning of another year – they lay before me like a landscape waiting to be explored. "I don't know why, but I feel as though I've grown older," I said, taking another piece of lardy-cake.

"About time too," replied Ben, laughing.

Good Deeds at
Black Pony Inn

CONTENTS

One

A matter of life or death

"Gillian is going to die. Are you listening?" shouted Lisa with tears streaming down her face. "There's no hope. And she's only ten."

Lisa is the youngest in our family and much given to exaggeration. Because of this none of us believed her at first.

"Don't be silly," said my brother Ben, who has fair hair. "People of ten don't just die. They go to a big hospital and are cured."

"Not always," said James, who was hoping to go to university soon.

We were just home from school. We had thrown our school bags down on the kitchen table. The paying guests had had their tea and were in the garden, sitting in chairs catching the afternoon sun. In the fields the ground was parched and dry. Our horses were in their loose boxes, because of the flies buzzing everywhere. The holidays were just around the corner, waiting to be enjoyed.

"She's my best friend, she and Rosie," continued Lisa, still weeping.

"How do you know she's going to die?" asked Ben.

"Everybody knows."

"That's a stupid answer."

"I heard old Forby and Miss Fletcher talking about it.

They said there was almost no hope. They looked very upset. They said that her only chance was to go to the United States for an operation and you know the Rosses haven't any money, everybody does. Gillian doesn't even have a father and her mum goes out to work cleaning other people's houses for money," Lisa sobbed. "She needs a special operation which they don't do in England, that's what Miss Fletcher said anyway."

"How much does it cost?" asked Ben slowly.

"I don't know, thousands I expect, and then there's the fare," answered Lisa, wiping her eyes.

"We'll raise the money," I said.

"But how?" asked Ben.

"Exactly," agreed James.

"We could hold a raffle," suggested Lisa. Now she wasn't crying any more.

"It wouldn't make enough," replied James, making tea for us all.

"A horse show then," I suggested.

254

"They don't make much, and supposing it rains?" asked Ben.

"It's got to be something big, really big," said James, sipping tea.

"A fête, a really big one, with a jumble sale as well," cried Ben triumphantly.

"With a dog show," said Lisa.

"And clear round jumping at two pounds a time," I said slowly.

"And all the village involved," added James. "Because it's got to succeed."

I remember how I felt elated and afraid at the same time. "What if it rains?" I asked.

"We can insure against it," Ben said.

"Too expensive," said James.

"We can have things indoors too. Things like counting the sweets in a jar," suggested Lisa.

"We need a committee," said James.

"We haven't asked our parents yet; and what about the residents?" I asked.

"They can be the committee," said James.

"They'll talk and talk. Committees are hopeless," said Ben.

"We can give pony rides and rides in the governess cart," suggested Lisa.

"I think we need a pencil and paper," said Ben, rummaging in the case he takes to school, which is mended at the corners.

"There isn't much time. It's late already for the operation," said Lisa, sniffing again.

Ben wrote FÊTE on the top of a lined piece of paper.

"We need a date," said James.

I fetched a diary which lives in the hall by the telephone. "It'll have to be a Saturday," I said.

"And not a Bank Holiday weekend," said Ben.

"And soon, or she'll die," cried Lisa.

We chose a Saturday near the end of July. I wrote down BLACK PONY INN FÊTE in large letters on the appropriate day in the diary.

"Can I tell the Rosses?" Lisa asked.

"Not yet, not until it's all decided," replied Ben.

"I'll draw the posters. I'm good at posters," said James. "I'll make them funny. I'll put dogs and horses on them and Virginia will help; she's very efficient."

Virginia is James's girlfriend. She has red hair, is rather aloof and not at all like us. She's very tidy for a start and she hates horses. I think she feels we're a bad influence on James, whom she would like to be perfectly turned out, whereas he often has his elbows out of his sweaters, and different coloured socks. But I may be wrong.

"Does she have to be on the committee?" Ben asked now.

"No. It's up to her," replied James.

We left it at that. Our parents were out. We put our mugs in the dishwasher and went outside. Our horses were looking over their loose-box doors, each one so different from the others: rangy, grey Lorraine who once was mine, but now Lisa rides her; solid, tireless Solitaire who stops at nothing and is Ben's; Prince, liver chestnut with an Araby head and a brain as quick as a high-powered car, whom I've ridden for more than a year now. Our first ponies, black Limpet and piebald Jigsaw, whom we lend to other people from time to time because we've outgrown them, greeted us over the gate with welcoming nickers. Other horses have come and gone at Black Pony Inn, but we had decided never to sell the ones we have now because they became part of the family.

When I leave school I intend to train horses. I want to

buy the unwanted ones and turn ugly ducklings into swans. James says that I'm mad to even consider such an occupation. Ben says it will mean I'm poor for ever. Mum believes I'll grow out of my fixation, as she calls it. But in a strange way Dad understands, for he has never wanted to be rich, only to have enough put by to live on and a little for a rainy day. He had a business once which went bust, which is why Black Pony Inn is now a guest house. When this story begins we had just four guests, two sisters called Miss Steele and Mrs Tomson and Colonel Hunter who is incredibly old and just recovered from a stroke. They are the permanent guests. There was also Captain Matthews, who liked to be called Peter.

But now we tacked up our horses before riding across the common and into the beech-woods, which are shady in summer, and windproof in winter. Soon our horses were walking like old friends under the leafy branches on the tall trees, which cast shadows like lace across our path.

We talked about the fête as we rode, imagining a fine day and a thousand people paying to come in. Lisa saw herself presenting a cheque to Mrs Ross, the joy on her face, and Gillian returning from the USA miraculously cured. She started to laugh as the summer sun grew cooler and our horses hurried homewards. "We'll put posters everywhere. We'll invite the whole of my school," she cried.

"And the whole of mine," cried Ben.

"It's going to mean mountains of work," I said, pushing Prince into a trot.

"But it'll be an advertisement for Black Pony Inn," said Ben. "It'll put it on the map."

"We'll need ring ropes and tents," I continued as though he had never spoken.

"And loos," shouted Lisa, riding ahead.

And so the idea was born: a fête at Black Pony Inn in aid of Gillian Ross, and it took off like wildfire; it didn't smoulder, it flared and raged and took over our lives until the whole house was involved and nearly all the village as well. Dad has a saying: Big oaks from little acorns grow. And that is how it was, for from that moment the fête consumed us.

As I untacked Prince I recalled Gillian Ross; small and pale. Mum said she resembled a small bird. Her fair hair framed a thin face, her dark eyes were set back in her head, so that Ben had once called them sunken eyes, and Lisa had been furious. Her mother was a larger copy of Gillian, with the same fair hair and thin, exhausted face. Had they been born that way, I wondered now, or had life made them so?

Reading my thoughts, Lisa said, "Gillian will look different when she comes back cured. She's been ill for a long time, Harriet. She's been in and out of hospital, she's even been ill enough for lessons at home. The trip to the USA is really her last hope; or it could be the end for her and then her mother will die of a broken heart, because she hasn't anyone else, only Gillian."

Lisa said it with such finality that I had to believe her. Putting my tack away I remembered Gillian running round the yard with Lisa; then riding Limpet. It seemed like yesterday; but in reality it must have been months ago, if not years.

Prince was rolling and the sun was going down behind a row of trees, and the sky was slashed with red, promising another fine day. Peter's car was parked in front of the house, and I could see Mum dishing up dinner in the kitchen. I rushed indoors to help. Washing my hands I said, "Have you heard about the fête, Mum? You don't mind, do you?"

259

"Not now, later, darling," she said.

So after we had eaten dinner, sitting in the old-fashioned kitchen, while the guests rolled up their napkins and left the dining-room, I said, "Now we can discuss the fête, can't we? You don't mind, do you? We can hold it here, can't we?"

And Lisa added, "It's for Gillian. She's very ill."

And Ben said, "It won't make a lot of mess. We'll clear everything up afterwards."

And James, who was making coffee for everybody, said, "Virginia wants to help," as though her help mattered more than anything else.

Dad, who had just helped Mum clear the table and was washing his hands at the sink, said, "What fête?" in the maddening way he has at times.

"Not what fête! The fête," cried James, exasperated.

"In aid of Gillian Ross," added Lisa once again.

"Where?" Dad asked next.

"Right here," said Ben.

"But you haven't asked me."

"That's what we're doing now, Dad," I said.

"It's a matter of life or death," added Lisa.

"Do I know Gillian?" asked Dad, hunting for the hand-towel.

"Of course you do, darling; she's been here enough times. She's the one who looks like a little bird. We can't say no, darling. We must help, for goodness sake, and it's my place too, I'll have you remember," Mum finished, glaring at Dad.

Dad held up his hands in surrender. "Yes, of course. I'll help. We must save Gillian. When are you holding it? How many people do you expect? What do you want me to do? I'm game for anything," Dad said.

I fetched the diary again. Ben fetched his piece of paper. We explained the general idea. Then Mum said,

"I'm not running a cake stall. I'll run a dog gymkhana."

"A dog gymkhana? Bags I enter Bob," cried Lisa, while Ben wrote MUM: DOG GYMKHANA on his piece of paper.

"Virginia says she'll run a nearly-new clothes stall," James said.

"And we must have pony rides and pony cart rides," said Lisa.

"But we haven't got enough helpers," I cried, "because I want to run the clear round jumping and lots of other things."

"We must get the village involved, everyone, even the rector," Mum said seriously. "How much money do we need to make?"

"Thousands," replied Lisa grandly.

"But how many thousands?" asked Mum.

"I don't know, just thousands and thousands," Lisa replied.

"We'll need judges too," I said.

"And someone on the gate," said Dad.

"And stewards to put up jumps when they fall down," added Lisa.

And now our little acorn really did seem to be growing into a most enormous oak. As we looked at each other Dad said, "We are taking on one hell of a lot."

"We can't do anything else. We must try to help Gillian, can't you see, darling?" replied Mum.

"Exactly," agreed Lisa.

"And we've only got three weeks," I reminded them.

"You can move mountains in three weeks," replied Dad. "You can die or be born. You can make a fortune and lose it again. We'll work better with a deadline."

"We'll have to tell the police because of the traffic coming in and out. And arrange for the St John Ambulance Brigade to be present," Mum said.

Two
Making plans

The next day was Saturday. After breakfast Dad called the guests together. Ben, who is older than me, explained the situation. He was very diplomatic, he always is, not like James who rushes into things without thinking.

"First of all we hope you won't mind; we are not going into this idea lightly but, as Lisa will tell you, it is important and we personally feel that we should help little Gillian to recover, even if it means going to the USA." (At this moment Lisa hissed, "She's not little, she's my age.") "So we're planning a fête, which means there will be hundreds of people here; so if you don't agree, please speak now," Ben finished.

There was a short silence before Mrs Tomson said to her sister, Miss Steele, "We'll run an arts and crafts stall, won't we, dear? We'll start knitting right away, we must help the poor mite, we really must."

Then Colonel Hunter said, "I'll run a croquet game, highest score wins a tenner, I'll give the tenner, fifty pence a go. I think I know a feller with a croquet set, great game croquet."

And I knew we had won our first battle.

"You'll judge the dog gymkhana, won't you, Peter?" Mum asked, smiling at Captain Matthews.

"It'll be a pleasure, I've got a stop-watch, if you need one, and I'll donate a cup," he replied.

Then we all started talking at once. Mum explained about the dog gymkhana: "There'll be jumping, and a best trained dog class and funny classes too," she said, and I knew she was working it out as she went along.

"Virginia says we've got to have a jumble sale," James said.

"Ben and I are going to give a display in the main ring at three o'clock," I announced.

"It must be after the dog gymkhana," replied Mum.

"At four o'clock then," I suggested.

"If we have too many things, we'll get in a muddle. And that could be disastrous," said Ben.

"We'll have our arts and crafts under the cedar tree on a big table," Miss Steele said firmly.

"With a white cloth on it," Mrs Tomson added equally firmly.

"I'm afraid that will be in the way of the croquet," said Colonel Hunter. "Think again, ladies."

"I'll roll the lawn for you, Colonel," Peter offered, looking very much at home in a cotton jumper, jeans and old trainers.

During the afternoon Ben, Lisa and I rode to the Rectory, which is small and modern and not at all as rectories once were. The rector is the Reverend Leonard Smythe. According to the postmistress, because he is a Christian he likes to be called by his Christian name; so we knew if we were to make any progress we had to call him Leonard and his wife Gloria.

"Or should we call him Len?" asked Ben, giggling, as we rode across the common.

"No, don't be silly, that's far too familiar. But what on earth are we going to say?" I asked.

"Leave it to me," replied Ben, trotting ahead.

Sensing our mood our horses pricked their ears and hurried. The Rectory drive was green with weeds.

Leonard was washing his car. He was wearing a dog-collar on a grey shirt, and grey trousers and wellies. But for the collar he might have been anyone; so that Lisa complained straight away, saying, "He doesn't look at all godly, does he?"

"Shut up, he can hear you," I said, halting Prince.

"What can I do for you?" asked Leonard, putting down the hose he was using, then turning off a tap.

"We are on a sort of crusade," replied Ben, dismounting. "A crusade to help Gillian Ross, whom you may or may not know. And we want your blessing."

Leonard has fair hair, fair eyebrows and a small thin-lipped mouth. He looked at us now with amazement in his blue eyes. "Do I ever see you in church? Because I cannot recall your faces," he inquired without smiling.

"I knew it would be like this. I just knew it," whispered Lisa. "It's so embarrassing." Lisa is easily embarrassed, unlike my brothers.

"Yes, well," began Ben, before Lisa interrupted him.

"We've come about Gillian Ross. You've got to help. We need you. She's ill and we need money. Thousands of pounds. Please, please help." She was crying again.

"We just want your help, that's all," I added.

"She hasn't got a father," interrupted Lisa.

"And she has got to go to the USA," I continued, "because she's got to have an operation."

"Of course I'll help," replied Leonard, smiling at last. "What do you want me to do?"

"Lots of things," cried Lisa.

"Manage the money," said Ben.

"Just be there," I replied.

"Will do. And I'll have prayers said for her in church, this very Sunday," promised Leonard, still smiling. "Just let me know what you want nearer the time."

"We will," said Ben turning Solitaire.

"Thanks a million," Lisa cried as we rode away. "He was lovely, wasn't he?" she continued as we trotted across the common. "I thought he would be stern, you know what I mean. But he wasn't a bit. We'll have to go to church now, because we can't not go if he's saying prayers for Gillian, can we?"

When we reached home we found Mum standing in the stable-yard, her hands full of apple peelings for the horses. "Colonel Hunter's finally decided to leave," she told us. "He's only staying until after the fête. He wants nursing care available, and I'm not a nurse. I shall miss him terribly."

I think I had better explain that Colonel Hunter had been with us for several years, so that now he was almost part of the family.

"So we'll have to advertise for more guests, otherwise we'll be bankrupt," Mum continued, "because Miss Steele and Mrs Tomson are already talking about moving to Oxford, so that they will be near shops, and you can't blame them, can you?" she asked.

It's always like this, I thought. Always the same panic

when guests leave. "What about Peter?" I inquired.
"He's only here as long as his leave lasts."
"But then we won't have anyone," cried Ben.
Mum nodded. "It'll be all right for a week or two, but after that . . ."
"We'll think of a really good advert, Mum, don't despair," Ben said.
"It's the overdraft. We owe the bank quite a bit already," answered Mum, feeding each of our horses the apple peelings in turn. "But don't think about it for the time being, just get on with the fête."
I was already thinking about it, seeing a FOR SALE notice outside on the common, people coming to look at the house, touring the rooms, making comments. The paddocks full of bungalows, the stables converted into houses. And where would we go then? But I had heard it all before so I wasn't giving up hope, not yet anyway.
In the afternoon we went on foot to see Mrs Eastman who was chairman of the Parish Council. We took our black-and-white half collie, half Labrador dog Bob with us. Mrs Eastman was sitting in a chair in her garden where flowers grew straight and tall and the lawn was perfect. She had a Yorkshire terrier on her knee. She was very large and the terrier was very small. We told her about Gillian and the fête. She told us that she was chairman of all the committees in the village.
Ben said that ours wasn't that sort of committee, "It doesn't really have a chairman," he explained nervously.
"We just muddle along," I added.
Mrs Eastman suggested that Gillian's parents should do more for her.
"But she only has a mother," Lisa cried.
"Silly woman," said Mrs Eastman.
The sun was hot on our backs. The terrier ran round and round Bob, yapping wildly, while he stood looking

the other way, pretending that she didn't exist.

"We thought the Women's Institute might help. We need a cake stall, you see," I suggested vaguely.

"I'll put it to them. I'll do my best," Mrs Eastman promised. "Keep in touch. I'm sure we'll do something. We won't let you down, I can promise you that."

And that was better than nothing we decided, running home across the common. Everything was still, and very beautiful, without a breath of wind or a cloud in the sky.

We found Miss Steele and Mrs Tomson were in the sitting-room knitting socks non-stop for their stall. Suddenly we all seemed to be racing against time.

Later Mum said, "I've booked the St John Ambulance Brigade with two-way radios, a first-aid tent and an ambulance, so we'll be all right if anyone's hurt."

Dad was out. "He's seeing estate agents," Mum explained. "Just testing the water."

"What water?" I asked anxiously.

"The property market's water," Mum replied.

"You're always on the verge of selling Black Pony Inn, but if you do I'll run away and never come back," I said.

"And so will I," shouted Lisa.

"The whole place needs modernising. Guests want their own bathrooms. No one wants to share these days," Mum told us. "They ring up and ask for a room with bathroom attached and ring off when I say we haven't got one. They want a bar downstairs as well where they can drink with their buddies. Times are changing. We've been left behind, and we can't catch up because we haven't the money."

"Can't Dad do the place up himself? I'll help him," suggested Ben.

But Mum shook her head. "Nothing's settled anyway

so let's get on with the fête," she said. "Put it out of your mind. Nothing is definite and we may still stay here for ever."

But I couldn't put it out of my mind, for I love all of Black Pony Inn, not just the house, but the fields too – the trees, the hedges, the wild garden which we never managed to tame; the arch above the entrance to the yard; even the old rooms above the stables which are never used because the floors are no longer safe. I couldn't imagine life anywhere else. It was unthinkable.

The next day was Sunday and Lisa and I went to church. We hadn't been for ages. Everybody looked at us as we walked in and we kept losing our way in the prayer book. Then, as we reached the sermon, Bob barged his way in and sat down at the end of our pew,

and Lisa couldn't stop giggling. But later, official prayers for Gillian were said. I prayed for Black Pony Inn to be saved. Afterwards, when we stood outside in the sunshine, we apologised for Bob's appearance but Leonard only laughed, saying that it was all right because he was wearing a dog-collar. So walking home, we agreed that Leonard was indeed lovely.

"And the prayers were lovely too. I just wish Mrs Ross had been there to hear them," Lisa added.

"I expect Leonard will call on her now," I suggested. But Lisa said that she would slam the door in his face.

"But why?" I asked.

"Because she's that sort of woman. She hates vicars and doctors and schoolteachers. She hates nearly everyone," Lisa told me. "She only likes poor people, down and outs, unmarried mothers, squatters, those sort of people."

"Poor Gillian, where is she now?" I asked.

"In hospital. Having medicines which don't do any good," replied Lisa.

"How do you know?" I asked.

"Because I keep my ear to the ground," replied Lisa, looking at me defiantly as though I might not believe her. "If you want to know, when you were cleaning your tack the other day, I went and saw Mrs Ross. She told me that Gillian was in hospital and I told her that we would be raising the money needed for the operation. She didn't believe me, of course. She kept on about the government. Then she said that it was sweet of us to try anyway and, though she knew we could never make enough, she appreciated our goodwill. But we will make enough, won't we, Harriet? We've got to."

"We can only try," I said. "But thousands of pounds is an awful lot of money."

"Let's have a box for donations. Leonard can sit by it

in his dog-collar," suggested Lisa. "Then everyone will know it's legal."

"Yes, we can use a vacant table. We can stick a notice on it saying *Donations to the Gillian Ross Fund*," I said slowly.

"And rich people will put in pounds and pounds," cried Lisa.

"We need a photograph of Gillian. We can blow it up, a really nice one. You'll have to get it, Lisa," I said.

I was seeing hordes of rich people pushing ten-pound notes into a collecting box, while Leonard bowed his head in thanks. I was seeing the end of the day, the money growing in front of our eyes as we counted it. Then my mind switched to an airport, to a jumbo jet waiting on the tarmac, to us waving and waving as Gillian disappeared into a departure lounge on her way to the operation which would save her life. But I knew I was going too fast. I was seeing the end before the beginning, for the race had hardly begun, and there was nothing to say we would win it.

"Nothing is that easy," I said to Lisa. "We can't guarantee anything. We can only try and try and keep on trying."

"And hope and pray," replied Lisa as we reached home.

Three
Riding without reins

Next day we returned to school, bearing posters made by James which read: SUMMER FÊTE in aid of THE GILLIAN ROSS FUND – Stalls, Dog Gymkhana, Pony Rides, Displays, and lots more – Entrance 50p. Children and OAPs 25p. There was a drawing of a horse in one corner and a dog that looked like Bob in the other. Almost at once, someone pointed out that there was no place or date mentioned, both of which I then added in ink.

"It's not the proper one," I said defensively. "It's just for the last three days at school."

"I suppose your loony brother did it," said someone. I always wonder why people call James loony. Eccentric, inspired, out of the ordinary, untidy, looking like a poet – but not loony, surely?

I said, "I haven't got a loony brother. If you're alluding to James, he can't be loony, because he's off to university in the autumn, so just shut up will you."

"Well, only he would forget the day and place," said someone else.

Several teachers said that they would put the date in their diaries. One offered me some bric-à-brac, another offered plants. A third, called Mrs Cooke, suggested a car boot sale.

"We've got the room, but not enough people to

272

help," I said.

"But I will organise the whole thing," she said, gazing at me through pink-rimmed glasses. "I know Gillian and I want to do something. All right?"

"All right," I agreed, wondering what Ben and Lisa would say, because Ben has often compared Mrs Cooke to an insect which has just emerged from beneath a stone.

Several first years wanted to know more about the dog gymkhana, and I promised that there would be schedules in the village shops and the pet shop in the town. The fête seemed to be growing very fast.

We had put TEAS on the posters, but who would dispense them I wondered, waiting for the bus home. And where would the cups and saucers come from, and wouldn't we need soft drinks too and what about ice creams? Ben was with his friends and ignored me as he always does when he's with them. The sun beat down on the tarmac, melting the tar. My bag was so full it wouldn't shut. I seemed to be the only person standing alone in the hot sunshine. They must think I'm loony, too, I thought glumly, looking at my bitten nails and ink-stained fingers.

I told the others about Mrs Cooke later on, when we were eating doughnuts in the kitchen.

"Oh no, not Mrs Cooke, she's such a drip," exclaimed Ben.

"No she isn't, not if she's going to help, she can't be," cried Lisa.

"Exactly," I replied.

Then Mum appeared with the dog gymkhana schedule typed out. "Peter's been rolling the lawn and the croquet set has arrived and he's going to set it up for Colonel Hunter. He is a poppet. I'm going to have entries on the day for the dog gymkhana and use raffle tickets. Okay?" she asked. We nodded in unison.

"We'll do the same for the clear round jumping," Ben said.

"Mrs Eastman rang when you were out," Mum continued. "She says you can hire chairs, tables and crockery from the village hall. She sounded really nice. She's looking for more helpers. I think she's a sweetie."

"You're very complimentary today," said Ben.

"Dad says that he'll get a float," Mum continued, ignoring Ben.

"What's a float?" asked Lisa.

"Money, change, people must have change," Mum said. "Mrs Tomson says she will serve soft drinks and ice creams and what about a raffle? We'll need some prizes, won't we?"

"We hadn't thought about the raffle. Perhaps Leonard will give a prayer book," suggested Ben, smiling in a silly way.

"Don't be so objectionable, Ben," said Mum, glaring. "We must get cracking; there are only nineteen days left."

"I've got to work on my display with Ben. We haven't even decided what we're doing yet," I said.

I must have sounded desperate because Mum said, "Not to worry, darling. Peter will give a raffle prize, and Colonel Hunter, and Dad can get one from his employers and we can try Roy, your vet, and the Health Centre. No one can decently refuse, not for Gillian. It's such a worthy cause."

Ben and I spent the evening working on our display. We agreed to use only Solitaire and I suggested that afterwards I would do a jumping display on Prince, without any tack, not even a halter.

Then we decided where the ring would be and that spectators would enter through the arch to the stables. We decided to ask James to make signs pointing to the Croquet Competition, Bric-à-Brac, Teas and so on.

"Cardboard arrows," Ben said, tacking up Solitaire, who was not pleased to be working again since Peter had ridden him earlier. There were flies everywhere and the earth seemed to be crying out for rain and turned to dust under our feet, while the grass was parched and yellow. I marked out a ring with stones while Ben tried vaulting on and falling off. He vaulted on to Solitaire over his tail. Then he took off his saddle and rode bareback.

"I want to jump him over fire," Ben said. "We'll have to dig a trench."

"Isn't fire dangerous?" I asked.

"Not if we're careful."

"But it's so dry everywhere," I said. I watched Ben, praying that it would rain soon, as long as it wasn't on the day of the fête.

I soon realised that Ben simply wanted me there to watch and to shout things like, "That's lovely. Perfect, smashing." He also wanted me to pick up the things he dropped – the balls he was attempting to juggle with, the bucket of water which always seemed to be empty. I

was no part of the display. It was solely his. "I'm going to tack up Prince," I said after twenty minutes had passed. "I'm going to practise riding without reins."

Prince was marvellous, I knotted my reins and soon we were cantering with me steering him by my legs and weight alone. I only had to lean back and he would halt, to use my legs and he would turn. I stopped and stared at the sky, longing for rain because I wanted to jump, but the ground was like concrete and hard enough to ruin the toughest equine legs.

Presently we turned our horses out and fetched spades and dug a trench, our arms aching, sweat running off our faces. "Supposing the others don't want the main ring here?" I asked after some time, leaning on my spade.

"It's the obvious place. You come through the arch and here it is, right in front of you, and it's only a few minutes walk from the lawn and all the other attractions. There simply isn't anywhere else as good," replied Ben.

"And the dog gymkhana?"

"In the same ring. My display will be at four o'clock, followed by yours," Ben told me.

"If it rains this trench will be full of water," I said a moment later.

"We'll put something over it," Ben said.

We went indoors and found Lisa cleaning the harness in the kitchen.

"We'll have to take Jigsaw out for a drive. We must get him fit," she said virtuously.

"What, just for cart rides?" asked Ben.

Lisa nodded. "We don't want him to get harness sores," she said.

"We can use him to fetch things from the village hall then," suggested Ben.

"We haven't got enough people. I had a nightmare last night. I was doing everything. It was awful. I just couldn't do it all," Lisa told us, rubbing saddle soap into breeching straps. "And Bob won all the prizes. I've been jumping him. He's terrific. I'll show you later," she said.

There was a new batch of posters on the kitchen table, ready to be put up and this time the date and place had been included.

The dog gymkhana schedule was there too. It read something like this:

Class 1 – Jumping for dogs under sixteen inches.

Class 2 – Open jumping. Class 3 – High jump.

Class 4 – Best trained dog. Class 5 – Bun race.

Class 6 – Best veteran. Class 7 – Consolation Race.

Class 8 – Dog most like his owner.

"Mum's been to the pet shop. They're donating prizes," Lisa told us. "And Dad's been offered £50 if we agree to a double-glazing stand and demonstration, whatever that means."

"The fête's growing so big, it's frightening," I said.

"I know, but it's still not big enough to make thousands, is it?" Lisa asked sadly.

"I think that Cold Snap Double-Glazing should pay £100 for a stand," Ben said. "Dad never pushes hard enough."

So Black Pony Inn suddenly became a place of seething activity; even the air seemed full of plans, until the whole house vibrated with them. Mrs Tomson and Miss Steele were still working, making things like knitted hot-water bottle covers. The Women's Institute had telephoned to say that they would run a cake stall. James had written out an advertisement for the local paper. Mrs Eastman had telephoned again to say that her niece would help with the pony rides; various other people had called offering to help. Suddenly we seemed to be meeting the village properly for the first time. People we had never known before appeared saying that they had produce they would like to contribute. Mr Brind, a local farmer, offered us bales of straw for seats round the ring.

Soon we couldn't step outside the gate without someone calling "How's it going? Do you need anything? Can we help?" Overnight we seemed to have become part of a village we had hardly noticed before. Even Peter's aunt appeared with a pile of books in a carrier bag. "They're for the book stall," she said, though we hadn't planned one.

School ended. It rained. Ben put newspaper in the trench we had dug, then lit it and we jumped our horses over it without much difficulty. Gillian was sent home

again from hospital and we saw her sitting in her small council house garden looking pale and weak.

The lawn looked like green satin now. Mrs Eastman came to coffee and admired it.

The fête was to start at 1 p.m. and end at 6 p.m. Dad had booked an ice cream van. Mrs Eastman told us that the local Brownies would serve teas, since Gillian had once been a Brownie. Mrs Cooke arrived to discuss the car boot sale and went away to obtain permission to hold it on the common. The posters were everywhere. James started to make arrows. Two of them said LOO. Fortunately we have four loos, one just inside, another outside and two more upstairs. Peter brought Union Jacks to hang over the gate.

Ben practised his act over and over again. Mum screamed at him for riding without a hat. "It's not riding, it's an act," retorted Ben. "It's not the same. I don't have to wear a hat, Mum."

"I don't care what it is. I won't have you riding without a hard hat; you're setting a bad example," shouted Mum.

"I'm going to be a clown. And clowns don't wear riding-hats," yelled Ben furiously.

"You can wear a crash-helmet, then, and something over it. Do you want to hit your head and be ga-ga for the rest of your life?" stormed Mum.

"Ga-ga isn't a word. One is subnormal or mentally retarded," replied Ben, while Solitaire pawed the ground impatiently, smelling of sweaty horse.

I went to the tack room and fetched our one and only crash-helmet, which fits us all.

"There you are. You can put a clown hat over it," said Mum, turning away as I gave the helmet to Ben. "That's a good compromise."

"She spoils everything," said Ben rebelliously.

280

"Now you are being foul," I answered.

It's hard to describe the next few days. It rained and rained. The lawn grew soggy; the sky was permanently overcast. Our spirits were dampened. We saw a wet fête. We saw wet tablecloths and ruined cakes. We saw the fire in the trench going out, and the dogs jumping in a thunderstorm. And all the time Mrs Tomson and Miss Steele went on knitting and crocheting; even at meals they were working between the courses. Lisa visited Gillian and returned depressed.

"She keeps being sick," she said sitting down at the kitchen table. "And her wrists are like sticks."

"Don't despair," replied Mum, sewing rosettes for the dog gymkhana.

"I told her she would be going to the USA. I said that I wished I was going too, but I don't really, not with her like she is, anyway," Lisa continued.

"We ought to book the flight for her," Ben said.

"We ought, but we can't," replied Mum, biting cotton with her teeth.

By now the playroom was full of jumble and bric-à-brac. I had never seen so many used clothes before. Virginia, who had a job in the day, now came in the evenings to sort out things for her nearly new stall, which she had widely advertised without telling anyone, so that the village and surrounding area were now completely plastered with posters concerning the fête.

I schooled Prince until he would jump a course of jumps without wearing any tack at all. When he had done it, I had a bucket full of goodies waiting for him and, perhaps because of this, he seemed to enjoy his act more and more, until every time I mounted him he made for what was to be the ring.

We harnessed Jigsaw to the governess cart and drove him round the village. We lunged Limpet and cleaned

his tack ready for pony rides. Our repertoire of events grew as more and more people offered to help until we had everything from a croquet tournament to a guess the weight of the cake competition.

Colonel Hunter spent every afternoon playing croquet alone, because no one had time to play with him. Mum and Dad had made a course of jumps for the dog gymkhana, including a brush fence with laurel in it, and a gate. The event was to be judged under BSJA rules. Bob could now jump four feet and looked a certain winner of the high jump competition. Meanwhile Ben and I worked on the clear round course, which would be held in the bottom field. I hammered my right thumb with a hammer and it turned blue. We were permanently soaked to the skin.

Dad saw the police about putting up GO SLOW notices by the entrance on the day.

Then without warning, the skies cleared and the sun shone, raising our spirits once again until anything seemed possible, even raising thousands of pounds in one afternoon.

But life is like the weather, or so Mum always says, wet and fine. And as usual she was right, because suddenly everything started to go wrong.

Four
Worse things happen at sea

A day later I woke to hear the sound of hoofs below my window. I leaped out of bed and drawing back the curtains saw that it was still dark outside. We had left our horses in what we call the long paddock. Fenced by rails, it has a gate leading into the front field where the fête was to be held, and a gate leading into the bottom field, where the clear round jumping course was set up. Now I ran downstairs and unbolted the back door. Bob joined me, barking wildly, waking up the whole house in spite of my frantic cries of "Quiet! Shut up, Bob, be quiet." Soon I could see lights going on behind me and hear doors slamming. Another second and Lisa and Ben appeared, pulling on dressing-gowns as they ran.

"Is it burglars? What is it?" shouted Lisa.

"I think it's loose horses," I cried, pulling on my boots before switching on an outside light.

Ben, ever practical, shouted, "We need halters and a torch."

"And oats," added Lisa.

Colonel Hunter appeared on the stairs, looking like an old hound and carrying an old shotgun. "What is it? Burglars? I wasn't asleep. I never miss a thing," he said.

"No, it's horses, nothing to worry about. Take it easy," Ben said soothingly before grabbing a torch as we dashed outside. The gravel at the front of the house was

284

covered with hoofprints. A second later we found Prince
calmly grazing the lawn, while Solitaire tucked into cab-
bages on the vegetable plot and Lorraine stood in a
flower border eating roses.

"Don't run. Go slowly. Talk to them," advised Ben,
shining his torch on Solitaire.

"I'll get headcollars and some oats," said Lisa running towards the stables, then falling over something
and shouting, "Ow! Ow! Oh, my poor knees! Damn,
damn, damn."

In the distance a train raced towards London, its windows lit up. I examined the lawn by the light of Ben's
torch.

"They've ruined it. Oh, what are we going to do?" I
cried.

"Repair it," said Ben.

"Just like that?"

Ben nodded. But I knew we couldn't and already I was imagining the despair when daylight broke. I saw Colonel Hunter's old face crumpled with dismay and Dad furious.

"I fell over the damned wheelbarrow," said Lisa, returning with three headcollars.

When Solitaire saw us approaching, he whirled round and cantered across the lawn, giving absurd bucks and idiotic snorts while my spirits sank lower and lower. Lisa started to shout, "Catch him, Ben, he's ruining the lawn, for heaven's sake. Do something, Ben."

I slipped a headcollar over Prince's ears. But even at the best of times, Solitaire can be difficult to catch and now, under-exercised because we had spent all our time organising the fête, he bucked and zoomed across the lawn as though we were playing a game. Ben just stood there saying, "Whoa, steady, there's a good boy."

I led Prince round the edge of the lawn. Then Lisa caught Lorraine, who followed us with half a rose hanging out of her mouth. All the time I was thinking: This will break Colonel Hunter's heart. Bob followed us, and the way was lit up by lights which seemed to be shining from every window in the house. Then Solitaire flew past us with one final buck of defiance, which sent clods of lawn flying into the air.

"Everyone's going to be so angry. How on earth did they get out? Who left the gate open?" wailed Lisa.

Now our eyes had become accustomed to the dark, it was easier to see beyond the house, and besides, dawn was almost with us, the birds were already beginning to sing and there were pale streaks appearing in the sky, and that feeling of emptiness and a new beginning which belong to the early hours.

"There won't be any croquet, that's a fact," said Ben

286

as Solitaire clattered into the yard giving a succession of piercing snorts, and Limpet and Jigsaw neighed an anxious welcome from the schooling paddock.

"I wish day would never break because I don't want Colonel Hunter to see the lawn. I can't bear it. Supposing he cries?" I asked.

"Old soldiers never cry," said Ben.

"They'll all be furious," cried Lisa.

"And what about Peter, who's rolled it again and again?" asked Ben.

"The croquet match is on the posters," I continued.

"And in the newspaper," added Ben.

"So we can't cancel it," yelled Lisa.

We put Lorraine and Prince in their loose boxes. Then Solitaire rushed into his, looking for food in his manger, and Ben slammed the door shut after him.

Utterly crestfallen we returned indoors to Mum and Dad in the kitchen.

"The horses were out, weren't they?" asked Dad accusingly as we took off our boots.

Ben nodded while Mum handed us mugs of tea.

"I fell over the wheelbarrow and now my pyjamas are stuck to my knee by blood," Lisa said.

"Come here, let me look," said Mum.

"Yes, they've wrecked the lawn," said Ben at the same moment; while a guilty Bob watched us with his tail down and pleading eyes, fearing that he had caused the disaster.

"How did they get out?" asked Dad.

"We haven't looked yet," Ben replied.

No one was angry. I think the situation seemed too bad for anger. I'm sure we were all thinking the same thing – poor Colonel Hunter.

"It's enough to give the poor old boy a heart attack," said Dad at last.

"Don't," cried Mum, fetching sticking plaster for Lisa's knee.

"We'll start repairing the lawn at first light. I don't feel like going back to bed anyway," said Ben. "We can buy new turf, can't we, Dad?"

"Yes, but it won't be good enough for a croquet lawn. New turf takes months to settle," replied Dad.

While we talked the sky grew lighter. Soon we were fetching spades and rakes, and the heavy roller from behind the old potting shed. We banged down the churned and pitted turf with spades and flattened it. We added new earth where necessary and rolled it in. The sun rose; the chorus of bird song grew louder. Soon we could hear the hum of distant traffic which meant people were on their way to work. Later, when Colonel Hunter looked at the lawn, he seemed quite calm.

"I've seen worse things at sea. It'll do," he said.

"Are you sure?" asked Ben anxiously.

"Well, if people don't like the look of it, they needn't play," Colonel Hunter said. "It's not the end of the world, is it?"

We returned to the stables. The long field's gate was open. Either we had left it open, or one of the horses had learned to undo the catch. We decided that in future we would tie it shut with a headcollar rope. Then we found the horses had been in the ring. The dog gymkhana's brush fence had had all its laurel removed and scattered. The gate had been trampled on. I cut more laurel while Ben repaired the gate. Solitaire's huge hoofmarks were everywhere.

When we went in for breakfast Mum was serving the guests, helped by James. A bright sun shone through the windows, lighting up the dust which was everywhere.

"There's only a week left," Ben said, stretching his arms. "How will we manage when it's all over?"

288

"Well, there's three horse shows in August," I said.

"And pair jumping at two of them," added Lisa happily.

"And there's a hundred-mile ride in September which I'm thinking about," said Ben.

Then I remembered that Black Pony Inn might be on the market by then. We might even have moved. I imagined it empty, Colonel Hunter's room with its windows wide open and spiders' webs in the corners. I saw the stables turned into a house and the yard into a swimming-pool and I wondered why I worried so much about the fête when there was so much else at stake.

Later that day James said, "Virginia's changed her mind, she's not running the nearly new stall any more. She's competing with her poodle, Sophy, instead."

"But she promised, and she seemed so keen," I replied.

"I can't help it, she's made up her mind."

It seemed a blow of the first magnitude, for we had expected the stall to make at least one hundred pounds because there were some antique dresses to be sold as well as lots of newer garments.

"We'll have to find someone else. I'll talk to Leonard, perhaps his wife will do it," suggested Ben.

Then a boy rang asking for me. It turned out to be Richard, who wears glasses and is musical and not my type at all.

"I want to help. What can I do? Just tell me," he said.

Ben was listening. "Tell him to bring a mate and deal with the car parking in the long meadow at fifty pence a time," he said.

Richard said that would be a pleasure and that he would come before the day to sort things out.

"He fancies you, aren't you pleased?" asked Lisa, in the maddening way she has, as I replaced the receiver.

"No, not at all."

"I don't think you'll ever marry, Harriet," she said next.

"I'm not fourteen yet. Do you want me to be a child bride?" I asked. "Really, Lisa, you get crazier every day."

"She can run a dating agency when she's older and make lots and lots of money," said Ben before setting off in search of Leonard's wife.

One couldn't move in the playroom now for jumble; the pile seemed to grow every day. People kept bringing it in carrier bags. Some of it was filthy and smelled. Mum said that people should have sorted it out first.

"Supposing we're left with it all?" I asked.

"We'll take it to the tip," Mum said.

Later that day I decided to ride Prince. I rode across the common and down the old bridleway which has been there since the beginning of time. As I rode I prayed that Black Pony Inn would stay ours for ever. I prayed for new guests and new bathrooms. I forgot all about the fête and Gillian as I rode. Suddenly all that mattered was the survival of Black Pony Inn as it was, nothing more. Prince walked with a long swinging stride, his mane dark against his chestnut neck, his quarters rippling with health. I couldn't imagine life without him. I knew now how lucky we were and how privileged, but it hadn't seemed like that before, for we had all worked like fiends to keep Black Pony Inn going. Now we faced failure. I rode home. Mum was showing the horses to a woman with two children, followed by a man with spiked hair.

"Meet my eldest daughter, Harriet," she said. And then, "These are our new guests, darling. The children are going to have the attic, so you won't have to move."

The children were both boys. One had the face of a

weasel, the other heavier features with a large mouth. I
disliked them immediately. Maybe it was my mood;
maybe I would be proved wrong in the future. I fer-
vently hoped so as I dismounted and ran up my stirrups,
for hadn't I prayed for guests and here they were. So I
fixed my mouth in a smile of welcome and heard myself
say, "I hope you enjoy your stay here and like the
horses."

"He's Darren and he's Gary," Mum said, patting the
boys' heads.

"And we're Linda and Tony," added the man, with a
smile.

"And this is Prince," I said, smiling too.

"They're only here for three weeks," Mum explained
later.

"And we need the money."

"Colonel Hunter will hate them," Ben said.

"He's leaving, so it doesn't matter," replied Mum.

Our new guests were called Stamp. They insisted on
helping with the washing up and were awed by the
dining-room. They left their napkins on the floor and

their toys all over the house. If our older guests hadn't already decided to leave, they would have left anyway. We didn't grumble, but suffered in silence. And luckily the fête took up all our spare time. But however hard one tried, one couldn't really escape the Stamps for they were like flies, always in the way, buzzing. They hung around the stables making silly remarks like, "Why do you pick out their feet?" And, "Why don't you cut manes with scissors?" And, "Why do you call him Prince?" They were forever feeding the horses with biscuits, Polos and chocolates. Soon we stopped watching television because they were always in front of the only colour set in the house. The older guests began sitting in their bedrooms to avoid the Stamps. And Colonel Hunter seemed suddenly older and more decrepit. Miss Steele and Mrs Tomson went about muttering under their breath and Dad stayed out later and later. I don't think any of us trusted the Stamps, though I couldn't have said why.

Linda Stamp smoked, leaving her cigarette butts in flowerpots and saucers. The children threw sweet papers down without thought, anywhere. In a strange way I think we were all a little afraid of Tony and Linda. James said that they were simply townspeople. Lisa accused me of being a snob. Ben said that they smoked drugs in their rooms and we all would be sent to prison as a result. I tried to keep my feelings to myself; but whatever we felt, no one could deny that in two days the whole atmosphere of Black Pony Inn was changed. The peace was gone. Suddenly there wasn't a room in the house which was private any more for the Stamps followed us everywhere like bored dogs, and we were afraid to say, "Go away," or "Don't come into my room unless you're invited," because we needed their money. Life was as bad as that.

And all the time the fête grew nearer and our prep-
arations more frantic. Miss Steele made Ben a big
spotted hat to wear over his crash helmet. James wrote
out a programme which went like this:

BLACK PONY INN FÊTE, then the date and time
IN AID OF THE GILLIAN ROSS FUND
Admittance 50p – Children and OAPs 20p

MAIN RING
1 p.m. – Dog Gymkhana: Entries on the day
    Judge – Captain Peter D. Matthews
4 p.m. – Display by B. Pemberton riding Solitaire
4.15 p.m. – Display by H. Pemberton riding Prince
5 p.m. – Drawing of the raffle and presentation of
the prizes by Reverend Leonard Smythe.

OTHER EVENTS
Clear Round Jumping from 1 p.m. to 5 p.m.
Rides in Pony Cart
Pony Rides
Croquet Tournament – Front Lawn
Boot Sale – The Common 1 p.m. to 4 p.m.

OTHER STALLS AND COMPETITIONS
Guess the weight of the cake
Guess the number of sweets in jar
Arts and Crafts stall
Cake stall
Jumble
Bric-à-brac
Nearly new stall
Raffle

*   *   *

Now it was obvious that we still hadn't enough helpers.

"We could ask the Stamps," suggested Lisa.

"But can we trust them?" I asked.

"They wouldn't do it. They only do things for money. They say the State should look after Gillian. I've heard them telling Mum so," Ben replied. "They say that they don't believe in good works and that good works are for the idle rich."

I wanted to ride. I wanted to school Prince. It was like a dull ache inside me but the fête was taking up all our time. And though I longed to disappear on Prince and to ride and ride with my lunch in my pocket and return home in the dusk, there just wasn't time.

James had hired a loudspeaker system. He had also taken a job clearing up someone's garden at the other end of the village, so that now he left home at eight every morning, leaving Ben and me to serve the guests' breakfasts. I hated serving the Stamps. They wanted sauces on their table and put their knives in the marmalade instead of using the spoon provided. Ben acted the part of a waiter, bowing and scraping, calling everyone Sir and Madam in a loud, affected voice, while I felt like a second-class citizen. Bob followed us, eating spilt crumbs and bacon rind.

The telephone started to ring incessantly with queries about the fête; Limpet and Jigsaw remained unexercised and we were still woefully short of helpers.

"If Virginia hadn't let us down, Gloria could be running something else," said Ben crossly, for Gloria had offered to take on the nearly new stall.

"We can stick a notice in the village shop saying, Helpers needed for fête in aid of Gillian Ross," suggested Lisa.

"And then ring round," said Ben.

"We haven't got the sweets, and we haven't made a

cake, so we can drop them if we like," I said slowly.

"Exactly," agreed Ben.

"Mum's probably got them organised, so stop fussing," replied Lisa. "It'll work out on the day, you'll see."

Miss Steele and Mrs Tomson were marvellous. They had run fêtes before. They bought books of raffle tickets and helped Mum sort through the jumble once again. They laughed and said that it was just like the old days.

Richard appeared one evening with a friend called Joseph who was tall with a chain round his neck. They paced out the parking and asked questions. They stood

in the kitchen like the Stamps, talking while we were trying to get supper. James gave them coffee. Ben glowered. Later they followed me round the horses, asking more questions. I wished they would go away and never return.

"You're so unromantic," Lisa said when they had gone. "Can't you see that Richard fancies you?"

I didn't answer because I didn't want to be fancied by Richard. I didn't even like him particularly. And I didn't want to grow up, not yet anyway. And I was tired of being followed.

"You're getting awfully old, Harriet," Lisa said next. "Don't you think it's time you had a boyfriend?"

I threw a handful of hay at her and went indoors.

Now there were only two days left until the fête. I found James listening to a weather bulletin on his radio. "It's going to be stormy over the next few days," he said.

"We'll need tents then. How much does it cost to hire a tent?" I asked.

"Hundreds," replied James.

But it was too late to hire tents whatever the cost. So we would have to weather the weather. We looked at each other and imagined wet jumble and sodden arts and crafts.

We decided to ignore the weather. All sorts of people had delivered raffle prizes. The village shop had sent a box of groceries, the Women's Institute a bottle of home made wine and a chocolate cake. Mrs Brind had left a dozen free-range eggs and Dad's firm were donating two double-glazed windows. The local electrician had given us a television set. So suddenly everything seemed to be moving at a great speed again.

Because we were all involved, meal times became erratic, but no one complained. The Stamps even made jokes about it, or rather the same joke again and again, though I can't remember it now. Peter made bunting out of discarded jumble, found music to play over the loud-speaker system and rolled and mowed the lawn until it looked like green satin again without a hoofmark to be seen anywhere. Only the Stamps still wandered about doing nothing to help, insisting that the government should pay for Gillian's fare and treatment. "That's what they're there for," they said. They kept strange hours too, often being out for dinner and then on their return demanding snacks late at night when all the other guests were in bed. Linda usually cooked these, leaving the frying pan for someone else to wash up. Then next morning they would appear at breakfast, bleary-eyed and ravenous.

"I expect they go to a pub," Mum explained. "Some people can't exist without a regular pub life." Mum accepted the Stamps as she accepted everyone else and never complained.

Later on she made a ring out of binder twine and bean poles and a smaller collecting ring. Meanwhile Ben practised being a clown, rolling over and over in the yard, then turning somersaults. He put on a false nose

while I stood watching, wondering how it would be on the day, now a mere forty-eight hours away.

It seemed impossible that everything would be ready in time. Later that day I tacked up Prince and rode him round the clear round jumping course with my reins knotted. He went very fast but didn't put a foot wrong. I felt elated and sick at the same time. Lisa was teaching Bob more and more tricks. James was marking out pitches for different stalls. Oh God, let it be fine on Saturday, I prayed. Not for us but for Gillian, please.

Meanwhile Tony Stamp, ignoring the rest of us, tinkered with his ancient car which was so rusty we all wondered whether it had ever had a valid MOT; Gary and Darren watched television, while Linda sat smoking in the kitchen, making Mum's eyes water. You could almost feel the tension building up with nerves racing to breaking point. Without realising it, I think we were all waiting for someone to start screaming, like you wait for a storm when the sky is heavy with dark clouds and you seem to be gasping for breath. Looking at Tony Stamp, I think we all knew he was wrong somewhere. But Mum said that he had paid for three weeks in advance in cash, so we couldn't turn them out. She kept saying, "It's only for two weeks now." But if it hadn't been for the fête, I think they would have seemed the longest days of my life.

I had started to spend all my time now outside, dodging the two boys. The attic rooms were still strewn with clothes and toys, so that Peggy, our help, threatened to leave. And though the Stamps continued to ply our horses with titbits, they were still suspicious of Tony, as though they too knew that he wasn't quite genuine.

Ben and I were working non-stop on our two displays, which still weren't perfect. We were both keyed up and our horses knew it, which didn't help.

To comfort us Lisa kept saying, "Nothing matters except the money for Gillian. We simply need the people
to come in. Stop fussing." But I couldn't, for my nights
were scary with nightmares, where Solitaire rolled on
Ben and the Stamps set fire to the house and then stood
shouting, "It doesn't matter. The insurance will pay up."

Five

I wish it was over

The day before the fête it rained. I cleaned Prince's tack and our one and only set of harness yet again. Lisa cleaned Limpet's tack. Everyone was depressed. James disappeared to see Virginia. Dad went to work. Ben practised his act over and over again, growing wetter and wetter. Twice he fell off. Three times I had to catch Solitaire.

"You're hopeless. Give it up," I suggested.

"Bad rehearsal, good performance," replied Ben, vaulting on to Solitaire's wet back once again then sliding off over his tail, then vaulting on again and juggling with balls. He was wearing ordinary clothes and scowling and I've never seen anyone look less like a clown than he did. The yard was full of puddles now. When we went indoors Mum was putting the raffle prizes on the hall table.

"What if someone steals them?" asked Lisa.

"We'll put Leonard next to them," Mum said. "He'll stop them."

"You mean God will," replied Lisa.

Miss Steele and Mrs Tomson were still working, producing more and more lacy mats. Suddenly I wished we could call them by their Christian names, which were Irene and Helen. But, like Colonel Hunter, they belonged to another age when to use a Christian name was

300

to be familiar, so we went on calling them Miss, Mrs and Colonel.

Soon Lisa and I went outside again to measure the clear round jumping course. We had agreed that two foot six was high enough and that no one would be allowed to go round more than twice. Mum had ordered fifty rosettes which were red and had CLEAR ROUND printed on them. Now Lisa started to do sums in her head. "If there are a hundred entries we'll have two hundred pounds," she said, "and two hundred, four hundred pounds."

"Well done, but there won't be that many entries because no one will come far just for clear round jumping," I answered.

Suddenly I was depressed. I imagined a car park with no cars in it and Leonard sitting all day waiting for donations which weren't given. I imagined telling Mrs Ross that we had failed. I imagined again the wet cakes and soggy arts and crafts, and piles of wet jumble heaped in the playroom. Then, worst of all, I imagined Gillian getting worse.

"God didn't listen to us. We went to all that trouble and prayed in church and he just didn't listen. I can't believe it, I really can't," cried Lisa as though God was some sort of social worker sitting in an office sifting through appeals saying yes to this one and no to that one.

"Give him time," I answered.

"But look at the sky," cried Lisa dramatically. "Just look. I can't believe it, Harriet, I really can't. I mean, why did we bother?"

"There's still tonight and tomorrow morning," I answered, staring up at the dark sky which glowered above us, overbearing and immovable.

"I mean, you try and help and then this happens," cried Lisa. "It just isn't fair, and what about Leonard? He's a rector after all. He must have some influence, surely."

"You've got it all wrong, Lisa," I said. "Go away and read the Bible."

"Oh Harriet, you're just like everyone else – defeatist," cried Lisa.

"Me defeatist? What about you?" I shouted back, "I'm not moaning, it's you."

At this moment James returned from seeing Virginia. "The forecast isn't hopeful, but we can't cancel," he said, as though we didn't know. "Mum says we can move most of it indoors. Of course the croquet will be a wash-out, and the dog gymkhana will be wet, but never mind, we'll still make a few pounds."

"But not enough. A few pounds is no good, we've got to make thousands, James," insisted Lisa, "or didn't I tell you?"

The telephone rang all evening. There were people inquiring about the clear round jumping, about the dog gymkhana, about the croquet match.

A large couple appeared in a van with a load of jumble. They called everyone "Dear" and hoped we would save "the little darling". We were all on edge by this time and their jumble smelled of pig muck and Jeyes fluid evenly mixed. "We'll be there tomorrow," they promised on leaving. "We'll be bringing our lurcher dogs. Lovely dogs, they are. There won't be any better, I'm telling you that," they said.

"Virginia says lurchers fight. You had better watch it, Mum," James said later.

When they had gone Mum sat sorting through the prizes from the pet shop. There was a whole heap of squeaky toys, three balls and various chewy bones, doggy chocolate drops, three brushes and a dog lead.

Ben looked at them in dismay. "Bob hates squeaky toys and you know he thinks balls are silly," he said.

"But Bob isn't going to win them, is he?" asked Mum.

"I wouldn't be too certain about that," Ben insisted.

"He'll just have to put up with what he's given then," snapped Mum. It was still raining. Ben and I put our horses in their loose boxes.

"We can dry the ponies in the morning," Ben said. "But drying all four is just too much."

He looked tired. His act still wasn't going well. Solitaire was being difficult and Ben had split his clown's trousers and though Miss Steele was mending them on her sewing machine, he was afraid they might split again at some unsuitable moment.

"If they do it'll make people laugh. It won't matter. They'll think it's part of the act," I said.

"Very funny," replied Ben.

We had a fry-up for supper. Colonel Hunter was very quiet. Miss Steele and Mrs Tomson asked for a tent to be provided as though tents were waiting in lines to be hired. "You can be in the hall if it's wet. Don't worry," Mum said.

The Stamps were late for supper yet again. They said their car had broken down. Peter was having supper with his aunt. James had borrowed badges from somewhere which said JUDGE and STEWARD. Dad was still out selling double-glazing and the rain was still falling as endlessly as sea breaking against rocks.

"God, I wish it was over," said Ben suddenly. "I wish it was Sunday, and we didn't have to worry any more. Has anyone seen my inhaler? I think I'm getting asthma."

"It's by your bed. Just calm down. We're going to do our best. No one can do more than that," Mum said, dishing up sausages. "At least we're trying to save the poor child."

Then Richard telephoned to ask, "Is the fête still on if it's raining?"

304

"Of course. It's still on, whatever," I replied. "See you."

"God, what a wimp," cried Lisa.

Remembering her suggestion that Richard should be my long-awaited boyfriend, I made no reply.

Then Leonard rang asking, "What time do you want us tomorrow?"

"Noon, say noon," hissed Mum.

"Noon, you'll be in the house if it's raining," I replied.

"Oh thank goodness, I was going to bring a golfing umbrella," he said, laughing.

"He's so jolly. Are all rectors so jolly?" asked Ben.

"Tell him to pray," cried Lisa. "Go on, Harriet, just tell him to pray for a fine day, please. Is it too much to ask?"

But I had already put down the receiver. "I couldn't. He knows when he wants to pray. I can't tell him what to do," I said.

"God, you're mean," said Lisa. "Oh, just forget it."

Then Dad appeared, starving, only to find that we had eaten everything. And the rain beat against the windows and found its way under the back door and left a pool in the passage.

"I'll never speak to God again if it's not fine tomorrow," Lisa said.

"That will be very nice for him. I expect he's sick of your whiny voice," replied Ben disagreeably. "I know I would be if I was God."

So Lisa stormed off to bed, while I slipped outside to say goodnight to Prince who whinnied softly and didn't complain about anything. Everything smelled of the countryside, wet and leafy. I stood in the rain and shouted madly at the sky. "Stop, go away, clouds, please, please. Don't spoil everything tomorrow. Just dry

305

up." But standing in the dusk with everything so wet there didn't seem much hope and, as I walked in, I thought: Perhaps it's to do with Gillian, perhaps she's doomed and there's nothing anyone can do to save her, perhaps it's fate. I wished then that I believed in God or the stars or something because at that moment, as far as the fête was concerned, everything seemed hopeless, with nothing except failure ahead.

Next morning I lay in bed listening to the rain falling outside. It was seven o'clock, but as long as it was raining there seemed no point in getting up. Then Ben appeared.

"We had better get cracking. I had a nightmare last night and then a terrible attack of asthma, and my hands have come up in a rash. Look," he said.

I didn't want to look. Ben seems so calm outwardly, but often inwardly he's in turmoil.

"They look like raw meat. Are you well enough to do your display? Shouldn't you see Dr Jones?" I asked, looking reluctantly at his raw, red hands.

"Don't be ridiculous. Of course I'm well enough," said Ben, starting to cough.

"You don't sound like it."

"I dreamed that everything blew down, then Solitaire blew away. Even the raffle prizes blew away. The television ended up in a bed of nettles and Mum cried," Ben said, making Mum's crying sound the worst thing of all.

At that moment Lisa clattered down the attic stairs shouting, "It's past seven o'clock and it's the day of the fête. Get up. It's past seven o'clock."

"If only she wouldn't repeat herself," complained Ben wearily.

"And as if we didn't know what day it is," I said. "We'll never make enough, you know that, don't you? A couple of hundred if we're lucky," I continued. "And that won't even buy a ticket to the USA."

"The gutters are flooding," said Ben, looking out of the window. "We'll need a tractor to pull the cars out of the field. We'll have to find one, Harriet."

I nodded. I wanted to go back to sleep. I wanted to wake up and find that the fête was over. I didn't want the day to happen.

Ben went away and I dressed and went downstairs to find nearly everyone in the kitchen.

"For goodness sake, it's not the end of the world. We won't be washed away," Mum was saying. "The dogs can still jump and do their tricks." But the tone of her voice belied her words.

"And the jumble's waterproof," said Ben. "And the fire in the trench will burn in spite of the rain, and people will turn up in hundreds in wellies and mackintoshes. What optimism, Mum!"

"It's only half past seven, for goodness sake. Eat a good breakfast now, because there isn't going to be time for lunch," Mum replied.

After breakfast I put the props for my display ready outside the main ring – plastic bags stuffed with straw, three cavaletti which would have no space for a stride between them, an old door painted red, white and blue, a clothes-line with dusters on it and funny long pants picked out of the jumble. I would jump these obstacles each way before swinging round in the middle, turning Prince on his haunches. I was praying now that Prince would be in a good mood. Then I looked at the sky and saw that there was a blue streak in the midst of the clouds and I started shouting, "It's clearing up, it's going to be a fine day." And a wild cheer went up.

Then James rushed outside and started up the Land Rover, crying, " Will you help me fetch the tables from the village hall, Harriet? Hurry."

Ben started to fence off the car park with binder twine, while Dad disappeared in the car to fetch the double-glazing display.

"So God did listen after all," cried Lisa as the clouds slowly parted, revealing a blue underneath which spread and spread until it engulfed the whole sky.

Next Miss Steele appeared, crying imperiously, "Where's my table, Harriet? I want to set it up at once. I haven't got all day."

"It's only eight-thirty, we're fetching it now," said James from the Land Rover, while I jumped in beside him, my spirits soaring.

We had difficulty in collecting the key to the village hall. The old lady who kept it peered at us through a keyhole, saying, "You're muggers, I can see that," in an ancient voice which crackled like an old record on an even older record player.

"We aren't muggers, we're the Pembertons," cried James.

"Well, I don't know you," she replied obstinately.

"You try, Harriet," James said. "And hurry, for God's sake."

The cottage door was on a chain now. The old lady inside wore a pinny and bedroom slippers.

"No one said anything about you fetching the key. I can't give it to just anyone and I don't know you," she said again in a querulous voice.

"We're running a fête. We're trying to make enough money to send Gillian Ross to hospital in America. Haven't you heard about it?" I asked in the kindest voice I could muster. "The rector's helping and his wife and Mrs Eastman, and the WI. It's all right, I promise, and we have permission to hire six large tables and forty chairs and the Brownies are going to borrow the tea urn." I surprised myself by knowing so much, I must have heard it said and automatically assimilated it and now it was pouring out of me like tea from a teapot. The old lady undid the chain slowly. She was absolutely tiny with a mass of wild grey hair. She slowly handed me an enormous key.

"I want it back," she said. "Don't forget now. I'm responsible for it. I want it back this evening."

James stood looking at his watch.

"Thank you. We'll bring it back as soon as possible. I promise we won't lose it," I answered.

We drove to the hall and started loading the tables and chairs into the Land Rover. "We'll have to make at least three journeys," James said.

How can I describe that morning? We seemed never to stop running. Lunch was forgotten. Sweat ran off our faces. Prince stood on my foot. Solitaire escaped from his box and belted round the garden, churning up the gravel, then tore among the tables leaving devastation behind him, while people screamed and Ben stood helplessly laughing. Jigsaw had rolled and was covered with mud, while Limpet had rubbed his mane.

Soon James had set up his public address system and kept repeating, "One, two, three, four, testing," instead of helping with the tables. Then the Brownies arrived and took over the kitchen. Peter patched up the lawn once again and rolled the gravel. Mum set up a small tent she had found somewhere and put a notice outside, which read DOG GYMKHANA: Secretary's Tent. And all the time the sun shone, seeming like a miracle.

Richard arrived with his friend. I found them chairs to sit on and promised them that Dad would provide them with change. James had stuck up the notices which read CAR PARK, LOOS and another one which pointed to the house and said TEAS.

It was eleven-thirty now and I hadn't even combed my hair. Miss Steele and Mrs Tomson were pricing things, while the nearly new clothes were being put on hangers by Gloria and the cakes were arriving in tins and carrier bags, and more and more arts and crafts. And now it really did seem like a dream come true.

310

"Hello, Harriet, where am I to be?" called Leonard, arriving in his car. We had put his table in front of the house. Nearby a Union Jack was flying and there was a simply enormous notice saying: GILLIAN ROSS FUND – *Please give all you can.* And a blown-up photograph of Gillian looking ill and rather pathetic.

Walking over, Leonard said, "Well done, well done, Harriet, it's marvellous, truly marvellous."

"I didn't arrange your stand, James did," I answered. "And you've got to keep an eye on the raffle prizes as well, if you don't mind, that is."

"No problems. What a lovely day," he said next, looking round. "And everybody's here, Harriet, practically the whole village is helping. What a triumph."

Mrs Cooke appeared next. "They won't let me have my boot sale outside, they say it's common land," she wailed. "What am I to do? I asked the parish council and the rector, but apparently it isn't enough."

"Who are 'they'?" asked Leonard.

"The Meachers. They bought the Lordship last year at an auction," said Mrs Cooke. "They are upstarts, just wanting to throw their weight about."

"Come on, Harriet. Hop in my car and we'll go and see them," cried Leonard.

"But . . ." I cried.

"No buts, this is urgent," replied Leonard, propelling me towards his car.

The Meachers lived in a new house without a fence round it. Leonard went straight to the point. "These marvellous children at Black Pony Inn are running a fête to raise money to save a girl called Gillian Ross who needs specialist treatment in the USA if she is to survive," he said while Mr and Mrs Meacher stood before us wearing the sort of clothes one wears in the country if one's not country but wants to be.

"What's the problem?" asked Mr Meacher, who sported a large black moustache.

"You won't let Mrs Cooke hold her boot sale on the common, that's the problem," replied Leonard.

"What is a boot sale?" asked Mrs Meacher, smiling.

I explained briefly about a boot sale.

"Just half a dozen cars whose owners pay five pounds to sell unwanted goods from their boots. Nothing sinful, and all in aid of a poor little girl," added Leonard, smiling. "You can't say no in the circumstances, can you?"

"We only wanted to be asked. We are the Lords of the Manor and it is our common; but okay, hold it and we'll be there. When does the fête begin?" asked Mrs Meacher, fluttering her long, probably false, eyelashes at Leonard.

"One o'clock," I cried.

When I was home again, I combed my hair and washed my face and put on my best jeans and my favourite checked shirt. It was nearly half past twelve now and James was still saying, "One, two, three, four, testing."

Three dogs had arrived and Mum was sitting outside

her tent waiting for entries while Peter was walking about with stop-watch and measuring stick, trying to look like a judge.

Presently Mrs Cooke erected a large notice outside on the common saying, BOOT SALE. PARK HERE. And the first cars started arriving.

I found Lisa grooming Jigsaw. Mrs Eastman's niece had arrived and was watching her in tight jeans, high boots and striped shirt. She wore her hair in a ponytail and had a short, upturned nose and grey-green eyes.

I groomed Limpet. Then I helped Lisa harness Jigsaw to the governess cart.

"My legs are aching already," said Mrs Eastman's niece. "I don't know how I'll keep going for the rest of the day, I really don't."

"What's her name, Lisa?" I hissed.

"Sharon."

"Well, Sharon, do you think you can manage the pony rides? Limpet's very quiet and sensible. But whoever rides must wear a hard hat. I'll get you a collection from the tack room," I told Sharon.

Riders had started to arrive already for the clear round jumping. I looked round for Ben.

"Here's Rosie, down from London specially," cried Lisa. "Hello, Rosie, how lovely to see you. How are you?" They threw their arms round each other's necks.

"Okay, we'll do the pony cart rides, won't we, Rosie?" cried Lisa a second later. "Ben can manage the clear round jumping and Harriet and Sharon the pony rides. Oh, Rosie, I'm so pleased to see you, I really am."

"I'll show you what to do," I told Sharon. "I'll mark out how far to go, just there and back and not over and over again with the same tot. And no one older than ten, because Limpet's only a little pony."

"I can't stay long, I've got friends here," Sharon said,

looking round the yard. Looking for Ben I thought, because everyone fancies Ben.

People were pouring into Black Pony Inn now, like swarming bees. Over the address system, James announced the fête open. Next Leonard spoke, wishing everyone a nice day, then begging them to be generous for the sake of Gillian Ross.

Lisa stared at me with triumph in her eyes. "It's going to be all right. It's happening, Harriet," she cried. "It's really happening. We're going to make thousands and thousands of pounds. Just look at the people arriving. I just can't believe it."

A father approached us now, clutching two little girls by the hand. "They want a ride," he said, holding out a fiver.

Then Lisa remembered Bob and the dog gymkhana. "I've got to go now. Ask Harriet if you need any help, Rosie," she cried, vanishing into the crowd calling, "Bob, Bob, come here at once, Bob," while I stood looking for Dad because I hadn't change for a fiver.

Six

Fetch the ambulance

The Stamps stood watching me.

"You can pay later," I said after a moment, picking up the smallest of the girls and putting her on to Limpet, then putting a hat on her head which was far too big, her feet into stirrups which wouldn't go high enough for her short, pudgy legs which had white ankle socks on them and white sandals on tiny feet. Limpet put his ears back. He had given pony rides before and hated it. I gave the girl the reins to hold. She looked at her dad and smiled. Sharon watched me before turning to grin at Ben who was collecting money for the clear round jumping. It's going to be like this all day, I thought, leading Limpet across the paddock. Sharon isn't going to help. She's going to be ogling Ben the entire afternoon. Rosie was pushing children into the governess cart. She looked hot and flustered and had tied Jigsaw to the fence. It was obvious that she needed help. I lifted the girl, who was called Natalie, off Limpet and put her down. I gave Limpet to Sharon to hold and went to help Rosie. And now there was a restless queue forming for pony rides.

Children shoved one another and complained. They tried to stroke Limpet, who put his ears back and bared his teeth. I went back to help Sharon and up and down we went. For the next half hour I spent most of my time rushing from Jigsaw to Limpet and back again. I took money too and twice I gave the wrong change. The hats were all too big, so after a time we stopped using them. Stirrup lengths became erratic, and all the time I could feel the pressure building up. The children waited impatiently for their turn, dripping ice cream down their fronts; their parents waited with cameras to take pictures. The ponies became more and more stubborn, silently sweating in the heat. Then over the loudspeaker came the announcement: "First prize open jumping –

Bob Pemberton with a time of 33 seconds, second prize – Patch Saunders with a time of 35 seconds, third prize – Tatty Smith with a time of 40 seconds." And suddenly I knew that Bob was going to win nearly all the classes, because he's that sort of dog, the sort which loves to win and loves a crowd cheering him on. How embarrassing, I thought gloomily. And Lisa will let him win and Mum won't stop him, nobody will.

Our bowls of money were filling up. A large lady said, "You're charging far too much, dear. It should be ten pence a ride, not fifty."

"It's all in a good cause, and we've got plenty of customers, madam," I snapped back.

"They'll go somewhere else next year, I'm warning you," she replied.

"We won't be doing this next year, because by then Gillian Ross will be well," I replied.

Ben was mending one of the clear round fences with a hammer. The sun was growing hotter, the queue for pony rides longer. Rosie looked exhausted. A father was complaining. A child was crying. Never again, I thought. Soon the loudspeaker announced that Bob Pemberton had won the Best Trained Dog competition, with Sooty Ambrose second, and Pippa Davis third. After that there was a lull in the clear round jumping and Ben joined me.

"How's it going, Harriet?" he asked.

Answering for me, Sharon said, "It's chaotic, Ben. It needs reorganising."

"Rosie needs a rest. She hasn't stopped once, and she's only ten," I said. Ben took over the governess cart rides. Sharon took on the pony rides.

"We'll make a good team," she said, smiling at Ben.

I hurried to the main ring and found Lisa redfaced and triumphant. "Bob's winning nearly everything. I just can't believe it. He's absolutely fantastic. He's won both jumping classes. He cleared four foot in the high jump – four foot, Harriet!" she cried.

Grabbing her by the shoulder I shouted, "Everyone will accuse us of practising over the course beforehand. And don't you know it's bad manners to win everything at your own show?"

"It's not a show. It's a dog gymkhana," retorted Lisa. "Anyway, he hasn't won everything, only nearly, so that's all right. And he's not in the dog most like the owner competition, because he isn't like anyone. He's himself. And he won't be in the consolation race either, so shut up, Harriet, don't spoil everything."

Bob looked at me and wagged his tail. His collar was sagging under the weight of the rosettes he had won, his eyes were shining with satisfaction. "He's been wandering round bowing to people," Lisa said, laughing.

"In a minute you'll have to take over the pony rides. I've got to help Ben," I said.

"But I'm absolutely knackered," cried Lisa.

"So is Rosie, and so am I," I replied.

Drowning our voices, the loudspeaker announced that the Brownies were serving teas on the front lawn. "Why not the Cubs?" asked Lisa.

"Why not both?" I suggested.

"Actually Brownies do ride and do other things," Lisa said.

On my way back to the stable-yard I ran into Dad selling raffle tickets. "It's going like a bomb. I've sold two books already," he said.

"But, Dad, a bomb is the last thing we need," I replied.

"And Leonard keeps getting handed cheques," Dad continued. "I do like him, I really do."

Ben had stopped the governess cart rides and was changing into his clown's costume in one of the loose boxes. Rosie was back giving pony rides. Sharon had vanished.

"Lisa will be here in a minute to help you," I told Rosie.

"Lisa's got to light the fire in the trench," shouted Ben from the loose box, "so she can't give pony rides, okay?"

"I don't mind. I like giving pony rides, and Gillian was my best friend," Rosie said.

Children were still queuing. Limpet was walking slower and slower and making ugly faces at them. Soon he started stopping, saying plainly, "I've done enough, I want my tea."

"Only ten more minutes," I shouted to the waiting children. "No more rides after you've all had one, no second rides, okay?"

A small girl started to scream, "It isn't fair. I've only had one ride and Fergy's had two," she shrieked.

A boy shouted, "I didn't want a ride anyway. I would much rather ride a bike. I want an ice cream, Dad, now. Do you hear? A whopper, Dad. The biggest they've got."

The sun was hot on our backs. It seemed impossible now that we had ever feared rain.

The loudspeaker announced that Bob Pemberton had won the cup for the dog with the most points. Someone booed.

Then Richard appeared saying, "The cars are all parked, Harriet. Can I help with anything else?"

Suddenly I wanted to throw my arms round his neck and cry, "Thank you, oh thank you." Instead I asked, "Can you possibly take the money for pony rides and lift the children on to Limpet, because Rosie's only ten and she's exhausted."

"No problem, no hassle," replied Richard.

He had taken off his jacket and tie and his hair was rumpled. He looked quite different, not half as proper and much more fun.

"Fantastic," I said.

The dog gymkhana was over. I ran towards the ring in search of Lisa. Eventually I found her on the front lawn enjoying tea served by the Brownies.

"Ben wants you to light the fire in the trench, for goodness sake, didn't he tell you?" I shouted.

"No one told me. How was I to know if no one told me?" cried Lisa, rushing towards the house in search of paper and matches.

I found Ben leading Solitaire out of his loose box. A military march was playing. I don't know what it was, but then I'm not very good on marches, or any music come to that. Ben started to attach his false nose. It was held on by a rubber band and was pink and it changed his face completely. He had painted purple spots on his cheeks and on his hands.

I had a funny feeling in my stomach now. "Okay. Are you all right?" I asked.

"Of course, what do you think?"

I looked at Prince. He pushed me with his nose. Patting his neck I thought: Supposing he's frightened by the crowd, the loudspeaker or by a landscape suddenly so changed? Then James announced that the raffle would be drawn at four-thirty; and the result of the croquet tournament and the winners of the competitions.

"It's four o'clock. I'm on. Are you ready, Harriet?" Ben shouted. "Oh God, what's the matter with you? You've got to help me. Remember?"

I took a last look at Prince who was now wildly digging up the straw in his box. It was obvious he didn't want Solitaire to go and leave him. I said to him, "It's all right, take it easy," while the loudspeaker announced: "And now we have a display by that well-known clown, Ben Pemberton."

I ran ahead of Ben, who was riding bareback, his face tense and strange beneath his clown's hat. Lisa was blowing at the fire in the trench with a pair of ancient bellows. She had put on a cap which was half over her eyes, so that people thought she was part of the act and were laughing already. They were crowding round the ring ropes, small children astride their parents' shoulders. Virginia was sitting beside James in the Land Rover, Mum was selling raffle tickets, and Peter was going round the stalls with his aunt in tow. At that moment everything seemed set fair. And there still wasn't a cloud in the sky.

Saying, "Walk on, Solitaire," Ben rode into the ring sitting back to front, and that wasn't part of the act, we all knew that. And as I ran for the tennis balls he would soon need, my heart was pounding. Mum had stopped selling raffle tickets and was standing on tiptoe, trying to see over the heads of other spectators.

"What's he doing Harriet? I didn't know he was going to ride back to front. He is wearing a crash-helmet, isn't he?" she called, her face alarmed, her hands clasped together as though in prayer.

"Yes," I yelled, though I wasn't sure, because suddenly I wasn't sure of anything any more.

The fire was burning fiercely in the trench now, while Lisa stood triumphantly waving the bellows, her face covered with smuts.

Ben leaped off Solitaire and bowed to the crowd. There was a burst of clapping before he vaulted on again over Solitaire's tail and started to canter round the ring. Next he jumped the fire both ways. Then still mounted, he bowed to the crowd again before holding out his hands for the tennis balls.

Handing them to him I muttered, "Be careful, for heaven's sake be careful."

Ben cantered round the ring juggling with the balls, his hat slipping over his eyes. As he handed them back to me he said, "Damn this hat. It's far too big."

Then he halted by a chair and, lifting a pail of water, poured it over his head. Now it was plain that he wasn't wearing a helmet because the clown's hat clung to his hair. The crowd were cheering again. Children were laughing, grown-ups clapping. Ben's act was almost over. He bowed again. Mum unclasped her hands. Ben swung round on Solitaire's back and started to ride out, sitting back to front again. It wasn't part of his act either, because no one would have agreed to it. I ran after him as alarm spread across Mum's face. Perhaps I shouldn't have run, perhaps what happened next was all my fault. I'll never know. Some moments seem to last for ever. This was one of them. Leaving the ring Solitaire started to trot. The crowd scattered. "Steady, whoa, walk," Ben's voice sounded scared now.

I wanted to shout, "Jump off, Ben," but the words died in my throat. Solitaire broke into a canter and I knew now with dreadful certainty that he was making for the stable-yard.

Mum was running, her face twisted with fear. "Hang on, Ben. Don't let go," she cried.

But there was nothing to hang on to, not even Solitaire's mane, because Ben was still sitting back to front. I stifled a scream which rose in my throat and ran too. Solitaire was galloping now. He gave a triumphant buck as he reached the yard. Ben's arms seemed to clutch wildly at nothing then he lay still on the cobbles, still, oh so still, while Mum screamed, "He isn't wearing a hat. I told him to wear a hard hat or a helmet. Don't you notice anything, Harriet? Why are you so blind?" as if I was responsible. As if I was the eldest.

Then she was kneeling beside Ben while I caught Solitaire and with shaking hands put him in his loose box. Then the loudspeaker announced: "And now we have a display by that well known local rider, Harriet Pemberton, on her Wild West bucking bronco, Prince!"

"Fetch the ambulance. You're not riding, Harriet," Mum shouted.

I ran to the first-aid tent. Two nurses and a man were drinking tea.

"You're needed in the stable-yard, my brother's had an accident," I said, trying to keep my voice steady.

They leaped into the ambulance and drove through the crowd and then all sorts of people seemed to be running towards the stable-yard – Dad, a large woman I didn't know, the Stamps and a man crying, "I'm a doctor. I'll deal with this."

When I reached the yard again Ben was sitting up and saying, "What happened? Where am I? Where's

Solitaire?" He was soaking wet and his face was the colour of putty. Mum was crying.

"I told him to wear a hat," she sobbed.

"I thought he was, and why did he ride back to front?" I asked.

The loudspeaker was calling again. "Harriet Pemberton on Prince will now perform for your pleasure. Where are you, Harriet? We're waiting."

"You're not going, Harriet," cried Mum.

"But they are waiting for me," I answered. "I can't let them down, Mum. They've paid to see me. I'll be careful, I promise."

"You're all the same. You never listen to me," she complained. "You all go your own way. And I have to pick up the bits."

Prince was already wearing a headcollar. I added a rope, knotting it round his neck.

"I promise I'll be careful," I repeated.

Not everyone knew that Ben had fallen off. Some people were still talking about his performance as I rode towards the ring with Prince keyed up beneath me, with a spring in his back which wouldn't go away, his head high, his ears pricked. Cameras flashed. I didn't really want to perform now. I was too worried about Ben.

"Do you want me to lead him?" asked a tall man in jeans. I shook my head.

"He's over the top. You've just fed him oats," hissed Lisa suddenly.

The Stamps were watching. The children standing by their parents. Linda was smoking. What were they thinking? I wondered. Why didn't they ever smile?

"I haven't fed Prince a grain of oats," I said, turning to Lisa. Then I was talking to Prince, telling him everything was all right, trying to still the wild beating of my heart, which he could feel as surely as I could feel his.

I heard Richard call, "Good luck, Harriet. Don't rush it. Take your time." He sounded years older than me – almost grown up. I went into the ring and my whole performance seemed an anti-climax, for Prince behaved perfectly. He knew the act better than I did. I even had time to notice Dad watching and Peter talking to his aunt and Leonard laughing. Prince cantered and changed legs, jumped everything, even the fire now burning again, turned on his haunches and repeated the same performance the other way, then halted in the centre of the ring while I bowed, and then it was over and I hadn't touched the headcollar rope once, Prince had done it all himself. It seemed to me that the whole act had taken only seconds as I rode out of the ring to the cheers of the crowd.

The stable-yard was empty. The ambulance gone, the sun setting, the fête almost over. I dismounted and Lisa appeared and said, "Ben's only concussed. I'm going to jump the cross-country course on Lorraine. Rosie's jumping Jigsaw. I've turned Limpet out. I need your hat for Rosie."

I handed Lisa my hat and turned Prince out and went indoors on legs which suddenly felt weak. Richard followed me.

"Was it a success? Did you make enough?" he asked.

"I've no idea," I answered.

"You were tremendous. What a performance," he said.

"It was Prince. He's a wonder horse," I answered. "He did it all himself."

The Stamps were making tea. They handed us each a mugful. "Ben's not in hospital then? And you seem to have done all right," Tony said.

"But it won't be enough money," I answered. "We won't have made enough. And Ben *should* be in hospital."

"You may be surprised," said Linda, opening a packet of biscuits and offering them round, just as though the house was hers. "As for Ben, he will be right as rain by morning. He doesn't need to be in hospital, love. No way! They only take them in to safeguard themselves."

Drinking my tea I wondered who "they" were. After that Richard followed me round the stalls. Half the jumble was still there; but all the nearly new clothes had gone. The boot sale was over. James announced the number of the winning raffle ticket.

Finally Colonel Hunter appeared and was wildly cheered. Pointing to the television, Dad said, "I'll deliver it to your room, Colonel. Well done!"

Rosie won a box of chocolates. Mrs Eastman a bottle
of whisky. Otherwise the prizes went to strangers.

"Thank you very much, Richard, you've been wonderful. I don't know how we would have managed without you," I said.

Richard looked at me. "I'll be seeing you then. Don't
work too hard," he replied and sounded disappointed.

Then I dashed upstairs and found Ben in his room
with the curtains drawn. He was sitting up. "What happened? I can't remember a thing after I jumped the fire.
Did I finish my act?" he asked. Tears were running
down his face.

"Yes, it was a triumph. But you should have worn a
hat," I told him. "You could have been killed, Ben. Why
did you do it?"

"I don't know. I think I thought the crash-helmet
would spoil the look of the act," he replied after a time,
wiping his eyes.

"I expect you're meant to stay quiet for twenty-four hours," I said, moving towards the door.

"Did you fall off? How did your act go?" he asked grabbing me by the arm. "And is it over? Has everyone gone?"

He didn't want me to leave. He wanted me to stay and talk. He didn't want to be left alone. "Yes, and it's your fault you've missed the end. You should have worn a helmet," I said ruthlessly. "And I can't leave all the clearing up to Lisa and James, and Mum and Dad, we're all exhausted and it wouldn't be fair."

"Mum was crying," Ben said, letting go of my arm. "She was sitting on the concrete. I can remember that quite clearly, sitting on the concrete and crying. I feel I've let everyone down and I should be helping clear up," he said, pushing back the bedclothes.

"Stay where you are. You can't get up for hours, you've been concussed, Ben. And you know what that means, don't you?" I asked. "Someone will bring you supper, but I don't know when. I'm sorry." I edged out of the room guiltily.

The sun was going down beyond the stables. I was aching with hunger – the day seemed to have lasted for ever. Bob was waiting for me, his tail wagging slowly. He knew that Ben was hurt; he always knew when things went wrong. I kneeled down in front of him saying, "It isn't your fault. You've been wonderful. You always are."

Then I heard Lisa calling, "Harriet, where are you? They're counting the money."

Mum was saying, "I've called another doctor. I thought it best. I don't want anything to go wrong with Ben. It's better to be safe than sorry." But she didn't sound certain. At that moment, like me, I don't think she was certain of anything any more.

Before I went into the kitchen, I went outside. The garden smelled of roses. The blue sky was clouding over. Mrs Eastman and Gloria were pushing unwanted jumble into black plastic bags. Colonel Hunter was sitting on the lawn looking incredibly old.

"A young whippersnapper named Richard Catson won the tournament. Do you know him, Harriet?" he asked.

I nodded slowly. "He was a helper. He deserved to win. What was the prize?" I said.

"Twenty-five pounds. A man called Meacher was second. He's not my sort, too showy," Colonel Hunter continued.

"I agree with you there. Would you like me to help you indoors?" I asked.

I found his stick. We slowly went indoors together. The television he had won in the raffle was waiting in his room. I found a cricket match on BBC 2 and left him watching it. Everyone had left now except for a few staunch helpers. Virginia was listening to music with James in his room. Miss Steele and Mrs Tomson were lying down in theirs. The Stamps were watching television in the sitting-room. Like housewives of the future, the Brownies were still washing up in the scullery, which some people call the utility room.

In our house the boys help with everything, there are no divisions of labour. James lays the tables every day for the guests. Dad can make a good lasagne. I offered help but the Brownies didn't need any. They were giggling and humming and pushing each other. Next I found a man standing in the hall holding a black bag.

"Black Pony Inn?" he asked uncertainly. "I'm Doctor Bandhi." He wasn't our usual doctor. He came from a faraway land and his English wasn't very good. I led the way upstairs. Ben was sitting up in bed.

331

"I'm perfectly all right. I don't need looking at. Everyone's making a fuss about nothing," he said crossly. He still had paint on his face and hands.

A minute later Mum appeared saying, "He was concussed. He's better now. He won't have to go to hospital will he?"

Lisa was calling to me again. "They're counting the money, Harriet. Hurry," she shouted.

Seven

We start to crack up

I found Leonard counting money in the kitchen. He looked at home there, though the sink was full of mugs and the dishwasher full of unwashed crockery. He had been given nearly a thousand pounds in donations. The cheques were written to THE GILLIAN ROSS FUND though we hadn't yet opened an account in that name. The jumble sale had made ninety-nine pounds and three pence. The nearly new stall one hundred and six pounds and nine pence. The competitions forty pounds, the raffle two hundred and fifteen pounds and ten pence, the boot sale twenty pounds and the croquet tournament fifteen pounds, after the prize money had been deducted. The arts and crafts stall had made one hundred pounds exactly. Leonard was writing it all down neatly, in a red exercise book, his dog-collar slightly askew. Lisa was sobbing. Her sobs rocked her entire body. Bob licked her hand. "It isn't thousands of pounds. It isn't even two thousand," sobbed Lisa, looking at me with tear-filled eyes.

"It's a wonderful result," said Leonard. "It really is. You must be proud of your children, Mr Pemberton."

Mum appeared as Dad started to wash mugs. "It's a start. But I wish it were more," Dad said. "How is Ben, by the way?"

"All right, thank God. But he's got to rest, of course,"

333

Mum replied. "But you do realise that so much money has never been made before, Lisa, not even at the Church Fête."

"But it isn't enough," cried Lisa. "Can't you understand? We need thousands of pounds. Anything else is chicken-feed."

"But it will buy the poor girl a ticket to the USA," replied Mum. "Surely they have charities there which will help."

"Sick joke," sobbed Lisa.

Leonard put the money in a tin and stood up. "I've itemised everything. The next collection in church will be for Gillian. I've made up my mind," he said.

"It'll be too late. Time has run out," cried Lisa.

Dad saw Leonard out while Mum said, "We can

make some more. We can hold something else."

"But there isn't time," replied Lisa. "I keep telling you that, why don't you listen? She needs treatment now. I shall sell Lorraine. I've made up my mind. She'll fetch two thousand. And we can sell Jigsaw and the governess cart, because we never have time to drive him, and the antique chest in the hall and what about the tall-boy in your bedroom, Mum? What is furniture, after all?"

"But none of the furniture is worth thousands, Lisa. And if we got rid of it, we'd have to buy something new, and that isn't cheap either," Mum said.

"No, you wouldn't have to. You could keep your clothes in cardboard boxes under your bed. The Rosses do," replied Lisa.

"You can't sell Lorraine. She was mine first," I shouted, "and she's too old to sell. And Jigsaw is old too. You're not selling them, Lisa, because they're not yours to sell. So just shut up, will you?"

"I owned Jigsaw and then you gave me Lorraine. I shall ring *Horse and Hound* tonight. I bet they have an answerphone," shouted Lisa. "Gillian matters. She's my best friend. Lorraine can have a nice home somewhere, she can go on living, can't you see? She won't die if she's sold. But if we don't do something, Gillian will. It's as simple as that, Harriet."

I wished that Ben was with us, Ben who has an answer to everything. The sun was going down above the trees. The day was over. Mrs Tomson and Miss Steele joined us, carrying more dirty teacups. "What a day! And you were marvellous, Harriet, and so was Ben until he had his accident," Miss Steele said, smiling brightly. "And we sold all our arts and crafts; there's not a thing left. Not even a needlecase. You must all be so happy."

"You were wonderful, both of you, real troupers," Mum said.

"But we didn't make enough. We've got to sell a lot more to raise enough, jewellery and things. I'm selling my horse," said Lisa grandly. "She's worth at least two thousand pounds."

"How noble of you," replied Miss Steele. "Won't you miss it?"

"All the time, but that's not the point, is it? I have to sell her to save Gillian. That's all that matters – Gillian," Lisa replied.

I imagined Lorraine being sold. I imagined her loose box empty. She had been mine for three wonderful years. "She isn't yours. There's nothing in writing, Lisa," I said. "You didn't buy her, you just appropriated her. She's still mine. I only lent her to you."

"That's a lie, a downright lie," shouted Lisa. "She's mine. You said so. You gave her to me."

Fortunately James put his head round the door just then. "Virginia's left. Can you help me take the chairs and tables back to the village hall, Harriet?" he asked.

I was glad to leave the kitchen. We loaded the tables and chairs into the Land Rover. "What about Ben?" asked James.

"Still concussed," I answered.

"He's mad, Lisa's mad. Sometimes I think our whole family is mad," James said, starting the Land Rover, which is old and battered. "I mean Dad goes on and on making a pittance selling double-glazing, and Mum doesn't charge the guests enough to make a decent profit. She should have the whole place done up and charge double. Neither of them have an ounce of business sense. And now it's too late, any fool can see that."

"Have you any business sense?" I asked, climbing into the Land Rover.

"More than they have," replied James.

"I don't think they care much about money. They think happiness is more important," I answered. "Mum doesn't notice cobwebs, or chipped skirting-boards, she doesn't want lots of money. She's not made that way."

"And now they haven't any," said James bitterly.

We loaded the chairs and tables into the Land Rover and returned them to the hall. We made two more journeys, and then gave the key back to the old lady, who smiled at us this time and said, "You're welcome."

"I wish you would speak to Lisa," said James as we drove homewards in the gathering darkness. "She's going on and on, and there's nothing more we can do. She'll take it better from you, Harriet. She's becoming a bore. She's making us all miserable. It's bad enough having the Stamps without Lisa going on and on about Gillian; we've done our best. We didn't make Gillian ill, and we're not responsible for her. Her mother is."

"I can't influence Lisa. She wants to sell Lorraine. She wants us to sell all our valuables," I answered. "She wants to be a martyr."

"I suppose I can see her point," James replied slowly, "but by the time we've done it, Gillian could be dead."

I was so tired now that my eyes would hardly stay open any more. We parked the Land Rover in the yard. There was paper scattered everywhere. It didn't look like our yard any more. It looked like the beginning of a garbage heap.

"We can clear up tomorrow," James said, switching off the engine. "God, what a day! I shall be glad to get away from here. It's getting me down. I'm sick of waiting on everyone. I'm sick of being the guests' 'dear boy'. I want to be free."

We walked indoors together. Lisa was talking into the telephone. She was saying, "This is Lisa Pemberton speaking. I want to put in an advertisement. It is: Grey mare, 14.1, 12 years old. Excellent jumper. Ideal for Pony Club events. £2,000 to good home only." Then she turned to me and said, "I'm putting it on *Horse and Hound*'s answering service. I've said good home only."

Suddenly, I wanted to scream. Everything seemed to be falling apart. Lisa was selling Lorraine and James wanted to be free. I sat down in the hall and burst into tears. James made me a cup of tea. Mum put her arms round me. "You're exhausted, darling, that's what it is. It's been a long day. You'll feel better in the morning," she said.

"No, I won't. I'll be worse. Lisa's selling Lorraine. Can't you see, Mum, everyone's going mad?" I cried. "We all are. There's Ben talking gibberish upstairs and you absolutely exhausted, looking like a zombie, and the guests getting more peculiar every day. What's happening to us, Mum? That's what I want to know."

"You're tired," Mum repeated.

"And if Gillian dies, Lisa will never get over it," I continued remembering her organising funerals for small birds which had fallen out of nests. The weeping and the wailing when anything died. "And if she sells Lorraine, I'll never forgive her, not as long as I live. And what about Black Pony Inn? Are you selling it?"

"I don't know where to hide the money. Any suggestions?" asked Dad, appearing with a tin full of money in his hand.

"Put it under the sofa cushions," James answered.

"In our bedroom where we can guard it," suggested Mum.

"We'll have to go to church tomorrow because Leonard helped. We can't let Leonard down," said Lisa, joining us, looking smug because she felt that she alone was doing the right thing.

338

"I'll never speak to you again if you sell Lorraine," I shouted, glaring at her.

"Please don't quarrel," begged Mum. "We're all so tired; everything will look different in the morning."

I was crying again now. Dad was laying the table for the guests sitting in their places already in the dining-room, waiting for a meal. Mum looked absolutely worn out. We had been on our feet for thirteen hours and were all exhausted. And dinner was two hours late, though no one had complained.

Later, sitting down at the kitchen table, I said, "I don't want to go to church tomorrow, because I always lose my way in the service. Do you mind if I stay at home? God doesn't seem to be helping much, does he?"

"I lose my way too. They keep changing the order. It doesn't matter. The thing is to go," Mum answered. "And God doesn't help you just like that."

Next door Miss Steele was humming a hymn. James made a face in her direction and said, "Silly old fool."

"Don't say that. Just don't, that's all," Mum told him.

"Virginia says this is an old people's home," retorted James.

"It's kept you," Dad replied.

"Virginia's father's a solicitor. They have plenty of money," James answered smugly. "And a big house."

"Not as big as ours, and they don't have horses," I said.

"I don't ride anyway," James replied.

We seemed to be cracking up. We seemed to have reached what people call a watershed in our lives. We were beginning to break up like ice breaks, starting at the edges. If Ben had been there he would have diffused the situation. But Ben wasn't there. He was upstairs in a darkened room. And now like dogs, when one snarls, another snarls and another and another, I turned to Lisa and cried, "I mean what I say! If you sell Lorraine, I'll never speak to you again. I'll never help you with your homework or discuss anything with you. I won't lend you dresses either or make-up, or anything."

"Your dresses aren't worth borrowing, and you haven't any make-up," Lisa answered, smiling. "Besides, I'm doing it for Gillian, not for myself. I'm selling Lorraine for Gillian. What's wrong with that, for heaven's sake? Doesn't her life matter? Don't any of you care?"

Mum went to shut the door between the kitchen and the dining-room.

James said, "Here we go again."

I started to eat and all I could taste were my tears falling into the food. The guests were silent in the dining-room. I guessed that they were trying to hear our words and then, except for the Stamps, they would shake their old heads and say, "Listen to the young. They haven't any manners nowadays. If they had grown up in the war like we did, they would be different." Peter had gone out to dinner, so it *did* seem like an old people's home and suddenly I could see James' point of view. But I hated it coming second-hand from Virginia; somehow that made it seem like poison.

Later Mum said, "Lisa's asleep upstairs fully dressed. I don't think she will wake up for hours."

Dad was still worrying about the money. We should have had a safe but because our permanent guests always paid by cheque, we had never needed one until now.

"People will know we have it here. So we've got to be vigilant," Dad insisted.

We all made suggestions. I said, "Put it under your pillow, Dad, and have Bob in your room for the night and lock the door."

James suggested the cellar. Mum suggested he put it under some loose floorboards. But in the end I didn't know where he put it. I was just glad that Lisa wasn't there to insist that we pay Mrs Ross first thing in the morning because with so much of the money in cheques and everything having to be accounted for, it might be days before we could give her anything at all. Later I went outside to say goodnight to the horses. Everything was marvellously still now with a dark sky full of stars. The scattered paper lying everywhere looked like flakes of snow. Success seemed so near and yet so far. It seemed near because the fête had been a tremendous success, but far because we still needed thousands of pounds. I imagined Gillian lying in a hospital bed. She was the same age as Lisa and always ill. It seemed so unfair.

Dad was locking up. "You were wonderful, Harriet. You all were. I feel so proud of you," he said, putting an arm round my shoulders.

"But we didn't make enough and it will haunt me for ever," I replied.

I lay in bed and everything was quiet and empty and sad, because we had failed. My mind went backwards and forwards over the day's events. I kept seeing Richard tousled and helpful. He had been so nice. I would ask him round, I thought. Lisa was right. I was growing older and older; it was time I had a boyfriend. I would enter Prince for the cross-country next weekend in Lord Lester's park. I would put Gillian out of my mind. But what would we do with all the money, I wondered. Surely donations would have to go back if Gillian died? And then I slept at last.

Next morning I rose early and fed our horses. A mist lay over the yard. Bob followed me. There was no sign of anyone else. I made tea for Mum and Dad and took it upstairs. Miss Steele was in the bathroom. Ben was recovered and shouted, "What about me? Where's my tea?" so I went downstairs and fetched him tea in his favourite mug, and went upstairs with it, and sat on his bed.

"Sunday, church," he said. "I suppose I'll have to wear a tie."

"I'm going riding after lunch. I'm going to enter Prince in the cross-country next weekend. It's only two foot nine," I told him. I wanted to forget the fête and Gillian. I wanted to forget all about money and the future.

"You'll have to wear a dress," said Ben, smiling.

"What for?"

"Church, of course."

The service was at ten o'clock. We filed in all together, Lisa wearing an absurd hat and gloves. "Because God would like me to," she said.

Miss Steele and Mrs Tomson came with us, but not Ben. The congregation, already assembled, stared as we entered. We filled three pews in the old grey church. Leonard said prayers for Gillian. Lisa sobbed and I could hear Bob barking outside the church door. I was wearing a dress I had had for two years. It was too short and too tight.

We shook Leonard's hand as we left. He held mine for ages murmuring, "Well done, Harriet, well done." Then we hurried home to the Sunday papers and mugs of tea.

"What are we going to do with the money we've got? Are we taking it to Mrs Ross now?" asked Lisa, blowing her nose.

"Not just like that. We have to pay it in and account for it properly," Dad said.

"Can't I even take them a hundred pounds, just to cheer them up, to give them hope?" demanded Lisa.

"Not yet. We must do it legally," replied Dad.

In the afternoon Lisa and I rode through the woods; then across a field just cleared of hay. Lisa said that she would compete in the cross-country event before she finally sold Lorraine. "Then if I win some money, I'll give it to the Rosses," she said.

I wanted to say, "Supposing Gillian doesn't live that long," but I didn't. People waved to us now as we crossed the common. Even Mr Meacher shouted, "Hi there!" and then something silly about fair girls on grey horses. We seemed to have made a great many friends in a very short time.

Then we heard Ben calling, "Harriet, Lisa, where are you? There's good news. Really good news. Hurry."

I pushed Prince into a canter while Lisa shouted, "What's happened? What is it? Is it about Gillian?"

"Yes, hurry. Gallop," yelled Ben. "It's great, terrific."

As I galloped I remembered that Ben was supposed to be keeping quiet for another twenty-four hours and I yelled, "Go back to bed. You're supposed to be resting."

Eight

Too late!

Everybody seemed to be waiting for us in the yard.

"The *Echo* rang," Ben said.

"The *Echo*? What's that?" cried Lisa, dismounting, her face suddenly scarlet with hope.

"The newspaper, of course," Ben said.

"They are going to take over the appeal," James added quickly.

"They are arriving to interview us tomorrow morning," Ben continued as though James had never spoken. "They are going to make a feature of it."

"The awful Mr Meacher put them up to it. Apparently he owns it," James said.

For a moment everything seemed to be going round and round. I leaned against Prince. "I just can't believe it," I said.

"Nor can I," said Ben.

We turned our horses out in a daze. I imagined Gillian catching a plane. I imagined her returning cured.

"I hated Mr Meacher. I feel awful about it now," I said.

"It will increase his sales, so you don't need to. It's an emotive story, which is just what he wants," replied James.

"Exactly," agreed Ben.

I watched Prince roll. So the fête hadn't been in vain

after all. It was like a snowball which started rolling, and gradually grew bigger and bigger, gathering more and more money as it rolled along. And we had given it the first push.

When we rushed indoors Mum was singing in the kitchen. "Isn't it wonderful? I'm so happy," she cried.

"I want to tell Gillian's mum, right away," Lisa said.

"We'll drive round to her place. It will do Jigsaw good to have some exercise," suggested Ben.

We harnessed Jigsaw, who was glad to be working and pushed his head into the collar. Lisa was singing, Ben was whistling. Bob followed us out on to the common. James had already gone to tell Virginia the good news.

"She will be so thrilled," he had shouted, leaping on to his bike, then pedalling away like a madman.

"I can't wait to see Mrs Ross's face," cried Lisa as we bowled along in the governess cart, feeling like people of long ago. All around us the gardens smelled of new-mown grass. The sky was blue and everything seemed lit with hope.

"It's our prayers, our prayers have been answered," Lisa cried dramatically a minute later. "And I'm so happy."

Jigsaw's ears were pricked in front of us. The harness gleamed, his hoofs were quick and cheerful on the road, while on the common people were walking their dogs gleefully, because of the sunshine.

"I hope we can settle down after this. I'm sick of constant pressure," said Ben.

"You sound like an old man already," complained Lisa.

I looked at Ben's sore hands and knew what he meant, and thought he should still be resting.

Gillian and her mother live in the last house in a row

of council cottages built at the beginning of the fifties. When we reached them, Lisa, who was driving, threw the reins at me and, leaping to the ground, cried, "Bags tell her the good news."

"Lisa gets madder every day," complained Ben.

"She cares desperately," I answered.

"Perhaps she'll become a social worker," suggested Ben. "She can drive other people mad then."

The Rosses' house was the shabbiest in the row. Everything needed painting. There was a broken window stuffed with cardboard and the tiny front garden was full of weeds. The front door was scratched and battered and the chimney stack askew. Then I saw that the curtains were drawn across all the windows. Lisa banged on the door while Bob barked, and a cat retreated to the top of a tree in the next garden.

"She isn't there. Look, the curtains are drawn, that means Gillian's dead, doesn't it?" shrieked Lisa. "People draw curtains when there's a death in the house, don't they?"

"They did years ago, but not now. You got that out of a book," replied Ben in a practical voice, though I knew that he was worried too.

Ben and Lisa walked round the house and banged on the kitchen door. Bob barked. They banged again and again until Ben said, "There's no one here. They're out."

"What are we going to do then?" asked Lisa in a frantic voice.

"Go home," said Ben. "And just remember, 'Too late' are the saddest words in the English language," he added bitterly.

"But we've got to find them," cried Lisa. "They can't both be dead. We've got to know the truth."

"But not here, they're not here," replied Ben, getting into the governess cart.

"So we're too late. I feel it in my bones," said Lisa. "I feel death all about me. It's the end, isn't it?"

"Oh, do shut up," I said. "Nothing is certain. We don't have to give up just like that. Mrs Ross may be out shopping. She may have forgotten about the curtains. She may be like James and not notice such things."

"But it's Sunday," cried Lisa.

Then a voice called, "Are you looking for Mrs Ross?" and we saw a tall, thin woman with tangled hair which reached to her shoulders.

"That's right," said Ben. "We have some good news for her."

"Well, her little girl took a turn for the worse last night. She's in intensive care. Her mum's in the hospital with her. I can't tell you any more," the woman said.

"What time was that?" I asked because suddenly it seemed important to know.

"Yesterday about ten o'clock. She called a taxi. She looked terrible. So distressed. I'm feeding their cat," the woman said.

"Thank you for telling us," said Ben glumly.

We turned Jigsaw round and drove home.

"So we are too late," cried Lisa with awful certainty in her voice.

"All that for nothing. What will we do with the money if they've flitted?" asked Ben.

"You're both crazy. Why should she be dead, for goodness sake?" I asked, taking the harness off Jigsaw.

"She may be recovering. There *are* miracles, you know."

"But not enough to fly to America. You have to be well to fly to America," insisted Lisa.

"Not that well," said Ben.

We left Lisa with her arms round Lorraine, crying into her mane. Mum rang the hospital but no one would

tell her anything. "Apparently they'll only talk to close relatives," she said gloomily. Then she rang Mr Meacher.

"Everything is in hand. We have a reporter at the hospital. If she dies we will still run the story – rather differently, of course," he said. We were all listening and he sounded unconcerned, as though whether Gillian died or not was immaterial. It was the story which mattered.

"Is she dying then?" Mum asked.

"No, she's in intensive care, that's all I can say," replied Mr Meacher.

I don't think any of us slept much that night. Ben and I met in the kitchen at two o'clock in the morning and made ourselves cucumber sandwiches.

"I'll look a wreck for the press," I said.

"It doesn't matter, nothing really matters compared to death," replied Ben.

"What's actually wrong with Gillian?" I asked next.

"Something with a long name; something so rare that no one has ever done the operation before," Ben replied.

Soon dawn was breaking, heralding another day. But would Gillian ever be better, I wondered, creeping back to bed. And as I crept, I saw that Mrs Tomson's light was on and wondered whether she too was worrying. I could hear Mum and Dad talking. I longed for morning then, and news, as you long for water when you're thirsty. I wanted everything settled one way or the other. Then Lisa appeared and sitting on the end of my bed said, "I can't sleep."

"I can see that," I answered.

"There's no need to be horrible," Lisa retorted. "We are living through a terrible time, when someone may be hovering between life and death at this very minute. It's awful. And what about Black Pony Inn?"

"Whatever happens we'll have to go on," I said.

"Right to the end," said Lisa. "But to what end? We've been so lucky, we have had so much and she's never had anything. I mean we've had a lovely house and horses and a mum and dad, and plenty to eat; poor Gillian had free school lunches and everyone knew and sneered at her. She had clothes from Oxfam too. And her satchel was held together by safety pins."

Outside the birds were singing fit to burst their lungs. Then the milk float arrived and there was a rattling of milk bottles below my window and Bob barked. It was all wonderfully normal. "I want to stay like this for ever, in this house, with Mum and Dad and you and Ben and James. I don't want things to change," I cried.

"You're mad," cried Lisa. "You can't stop progress. You can't stop growing. Do you want to be a dwarf?"

"I can't be a dwarf because I'm five foot already," I said. "And another thing," I added, "I don't want Lorraine to go, not ever."

"But an advertisement will be out tomorrow. I telephoned the *Echo*. They had an answerphone too," Lisa said, not looking at me. "So we may get some calls quite soon."

"I shall slam down the receiver then; and I don't want you on my bed a minute longer, because I hate you," I shouted. "Go away, go on, go, because you know we can't sell Lorraine. She's too old to start a new life. It isn't fair."

"She's only twelve. That isn't old. I'm being unselfish, that's all," replied Lisa, bursting into tears.

Nine
Please go away

So next day Lisa and I were not on speaking terms. She rose early and at eight o'clock went in search of Gillian's mother. At ten minutes past eight the telephone rang. I picked up the receiver, my heart hammering. "I've rung up about the advertisement in the *Echo*," a voice said.

I hesitated, then I said, "I'm sorry, the mare's sold," and put down the receiver.

"Who was that?" Mum called from the kitchen.

"Nothing. Wrong number," I lied.

Two minutes later it rang again. "This is Mrs Carr," a voice said. "I saw your advertisement. Can we see Lorraine this morning?"

"Sorry, she's sold," I answered, putting down the receiver once more.

"Another wrong number," I said.

"Perhaps we should complain; there must be a fault somewhere," Dad said, scrambling eggs. "But why don't you have breakfast instead standing near the telephone like a lost soul."

"I *am* a lost soul," I answered. "And I can't leave the telephone because Lisa's selling Lorraine."

"Already?" asked Mum.

"Yes, already."

"I'll speak to her," Mum said without enthusiasm.

"It's too late. Lorraine's advertised in the *Echo*. Life's

a nightmare; but Lisa's not selling Lorraine because I love her just as much as I love Prince. I shan't let her," I shouted.

"Well, we can't keep all the ponies for ever. It isn't fair on them," Mum said, trying to be neutral. "Besides, the future is rather bleak just now."

I took the receiver off the hook and went outside. Lorraine and Prince were waiting at the gate to be let in. Flies hovered round their eyes. A breeze stirred the trees.

I counted the years we had had Lorraine. It came to five. I saw her going away and never returning. I saw her growing old. I saw her tethered on waste land, neglected, unloved, for once you've sold a horse anything can happen. All sane people know that. And even if Lorraine was sold, two thousand pounds might not be needed, because the readers of the *Echo* might donate enough. So it's all mights, I thought. Life seems made up of them, and if onlys. And I wished that Dad was a solicitor or a doctor. Just someone with a large safe income coming in every year.

Then a lady appeared with three children, and waving madly ran across the yard towards me crying, "We've parked outside. I hope that's all right. You see, I'm not much good at turning with a trailer hitched on the back. My husband can manage, but I can't. We saw your mare advertised. We've seen her at Pony Club rallies. We rushed straight here because we wanted to be first. You see, we know we want her. She's still here, isn't she? She hasn't been sold yet, has she?"

I looked at them while my heart sank down as far as a heart can go. I said, "Yes, well," to gain time. But they were already leaning over Lorraine's door, talking to her, their pockets bulging with titbits. Dressed in riding-clothes, the lady was slim with long hair, and the three children looked as though they were roughly nine,

eleven and twelve years old – just right for Lorraine.
"Will she have to live alone?" I asked to gain time to
think.

"Goodness no. We would never keep an animal on its
own. By the way, the name's Wallace. You must have
seen us at rallies. I'm Trudy and the kids are Lucy,
Emma and Giles."

It was a perfect home, anyone could see that.

"Can we try her?" she asked next, obviously puzzled
by my lack of enthusiasm. Like a sleepwalker I fetched
Lorraine's tack and watched them put it on.

"I'll ride her first," said Trudy, mounting easily before riding into the nearest paddock.

"She's lovely, I do love greys, don't you?" exclaimed Lucy.

"We've always wanted her," said Emma.

Giles was playing with Bob, throwing a stick for him to fetch.

It was eight forty-five now. Soon Ben must appear, I decided, and wished he would hurry. Trudy dismounted and helped Lucy on to Lorraine. I started to cry and, because of that, I rushed into the tack room and shut the door after me, and all around me was the wonderful smell of saddle soap. I said to myself, "Think of something, Harriet, you fool, go on, think. Don't give up without a fight."

Then I thought of Gillian and I didn't know what to do. I thought that life was full of choices and whichever one chose one would be filled with remorse afterwards. I thought: If I turn the Wallaces away, Lisa may sell Lorraine to someone ten times worse; and what if Black Pony Inn is sold? Doesn't that make a difference?

At last Ben appeared. "So there you are," he said, opening the tack-room door. "What's going on?"

"They want to buy Lorraine," I told him. "They've always wanted her. They're terribly nice, and I don't know what to do."

"We must stall," said Ben. "We must say we have ten other prospective buyers lined up. We must play for time."

"But that's a lie about the buyers."

"Sometimes one has to lie," Ben said.

"I feel so guilty," I said. "They're so nice. I don't want to let them down."

"It's Lisa's fault, not yours," Ben replied. "By the way, did you take the telephone off the hook?"

I nodded miserably.

"You are a fool. Someone might ring to say that Gillian's better, which would solve everything," he told me.

"Oh Ben, what a hope," I answered.

"While there's life there's hope, and for goodness sake wipe your eyes and stop being an idiot. All is not lost," Ben said.

"But even if the Wallaces don't buy Lorraine, people will go on ringing up. Lorraine is so well-known, there will be dozens of them," I moaned, wiping my eyes with a stable rubber.

There was a knock on the tack-room door. Ben opened it. Trudy Wallace stood outside smiling.

"We love her. We want to buy her. We don't even want her vetted," she said, as though she was doing us a favour, almost as though we should be grateful that she was offering to buy Lorraine. I stifled a sob, which I tried to make sound like a hiccup. She took a cheque book out of an expensive handbag. "It's two thousand pounds, isn't it?" she asked.

"Thank you very much, but we have many other prospective buyers arriving throughout the day," said Ben, sounding rather pompous. "So we can't say yes until this evening; but if we do sell her, we promise that she will go to you."

"What do you mean, if?" said Trudy Wallace.

"That nothing is final."

"But she was advertised. And who are the prospective buyers? I'm ready to write out a cheque this minute."

"I know. My sister Lisa wants to sell her and give the money to the Gillian Ross appeal," explained Ben.

"The Gillian Ross appeal?"

"It'll be in the *Echo* tomorrow morning. You'll know all about it soon enough," replied Ben wearily.

"I still don't understand."

I was crying now; the tears cascading down my cheeks in an unstoppable flood. "Please go away," I sobbed. "I'll write to you. I'll explain everything in a letter. I'm just terribly sorry."

"The kids will be broken-hearted. They had set their hearts on the mare. They'll be crying all the way home," Trudy replied crossly. "You can't do this to people, it isn't fair and it's dishonest, totally dishonest."

"But not illegal. It happens with houses all the time. You think you can buy one and then you can't," replied Ben.

Trudy Wallace called to her children, "Come on. They seem to be crazy here. I don't know what's going on," she said. Then they all walked out of the yard without another word.

"Damn everything," I said. Then, "Why do these

things happen to us, Ben? It's so horrible, I can't bear it and I hate letting people down."

Lisa appeared then, whistling, with Bob at her heels.

"I've been to see Mrs Ross. Gillian is out of intensive care. She's very grateful. I told her I was selling Lorraine," she said. "Who were those people here, by the way, Harriet?" she added.

"They were looking for somewhere else. They thought we were a riding-school," I lied.

"That's right, and super, great, well done, Lisa," Ben told her, his voice full of bitter sarcasm. "You must be feeling terrific, a real martyr. Girl sells horse to save friend – what a headline! Just right for the *Echo*. Perhaps it'll even make the national press, think of that Lisa, your photo in *The Times*."

"Don't be so beastly, Ben. You know I'm not doing it for fame," Lisa replied calmly. "I'm doing it for Gillian, that's all. I shall miss Lorraine all the time. I shall miss her for ever and ever. I shall cry myself to sleep."

I went indoors and ate breakfast. I didn't taste it. Mum looked distraught. Colonel Hunter was feeling ill. The toast was burnt and the scrambled eggs had stuck to the pan. Worse, our help Peggy had failed to show up, and Twinkle, Lisa's cat, had stolen the bacon. It wasn't Mum's morning, anyone could see that.

"Peter's leaving today; and Miss Steele and Mrs Tomson were talking about moving to Oxford soon. I think they're tired of burnt toast and late meals. And we haven't anyone else booked in," Mum said.

"You can enjoy a well-earned rest, then, Mum. People will turn up, they always do," Ben said.

"More oldies, or problem children, or the dregs of broken marriages, or people like the Stamps to drive us mad," Mum replied. "We can't go on like this. We'll have to have fewer horses. They're not earning their keep. Perhaps it's a good thing Lisa's selling Lorraine, because we'll have to cut down sooner or later. It's inevitable."

I knew then that we should have let Lorraine be sold, because it would have been one less horse to feed through another winter, and one fewer set of shoes every six weeks. Silently I made some more toast. Then I took a breakfast tray up to Colonel Hunter. The sun was shining again. We should have been happy. Why weren't we, I wondered? Why were we always quarrelling? What was happening to us? I helped Mum clean the house while Ben shook the mats and went round with a cobweb brush, removing spiders. We were sitting in the kitchen enjoying mugs of tea when the press arrived in the shape of one girl and a photographer. They introduced themselves as Paul and Caroline. Caroline was wearing a checked shirt and jeans.

"We're from the *Echo*. We want to make the Gillian Ross appeal a big splash. It's going to be our lead story," she said. Paul wore jeans too and a tee-shirt.

Ben fetched Lisa and James. I should have felt excited, but I didn't. Too much had happened. Too much seemed to have been said already. I felt like someone who has tried to climb a mountain, and returned without reaching the summit. I wished I had not cried in front of Trudy Wallace. I felt a failure with a capital F. And I couldn't think of anything to say to the press. Anyway, Lisa did most of the talking, which was only fair because Gillian was her friend. Unfortunately we failed to stop her saying that she was selling Lorraine to raise more money for the fund. I made a face at her, and Ben kicked her foot but she just continued talking and we could all see that she was enjoying being the centre of attention, and for some reason that made it seem much worse.

But at last the talking was over and the photography began, the main picture being of Lisa with her arms round Lorraine; and we all knew what the caption would be for that one: FOR SALE TO SAVE A FRIEND. I felt frozen inside now. Ben wouldn't look at me. James was in a hurry because he had arranged to spend the morning with Virginia and the morning was fast disappearing. Mum wanted to finish the cleaning. Finally Caroline asked us about Black Pony Inn.

"We may as well get you some more business. You certainly look as though you could do with it," she said.

So Mum told her about the set-up. She sounded tired and disheartened. Then Paul photographed the house. "A little free publicity," he said as though handing us a present. Then they both got into their car which had *Morning Echo* written across it in red, and drove away with Caroline waving out of a window.

"They were great, weren't they?" said Lisa. "And we won't have any trouble selling Lorraine now, will we?"

"I just thank God it's over because they're sure to misquote us," James said.

"The whole piece will be hotted up and emotive. It has to be."

"Will it be on the front page?" asked Lisa happily.

"More likely to be the middle spread," replied James, who has a friend on the local paper.

"I won't read it. I don't even want to see it. I hated them; they were so condescending. We don't look as though we need business, and it's an insult to suggest we do," I cried.

"But it's true," said Mum quietly. "We are not making money, anyone can see that. If things don't improve soon we'll have to sell up, lock, stock and barrel."

"Not yet," I cried. "Not until next year. Not now."

Mum nodded. "I keep telling you so. The bank won't lend us any more money, it's as simple as that," she said.

"But there must be something we can do . . ." my voice tailed off.

"Not the horses as well?" asked Ben.

"I don't know. We haven't decided anything yet. It's

362

still in the balance, but time is running out, because you can't run a guest house without guests and the place is getting shabby, or haven't you noticed?" asked Mum.

"Where will we go?" asked Lisa.

"Somewhere smaller," Mum said. "I'm sorry, but that's life. I kept warning you. We simply can't go on any longer with all the horses and the huge garden and no one to clean the windows or the gutters. I've reached the end of my tether."

Tethers again, I thought furiously. God how I hate tethers.

"We must go on fighting. We must never give up," insisted Ben, wiping tears from his eyes.

"We've lost the battle, can't you understand?" cried Mum. "Your dad and I have tried and tried to make things work. Do you think he likes selling double-glazing? Do you think I like having Linda Stamp dropping cigarette ash in the soup? We may be grown-ups, but we have feelings too, you know."

Only a year ago we had been in the same state. Then a film company had rescued us by using Black Pony Inn as a film set, paying us thousands of pounds. Now we were in the same state again and it was too awful to contemplate. But this time I had the feeling it really was going to happen and it seemed so unfair when we had spent so much time trying to save Gillian Ross and we were to lose Black Pony Inn. That was the cruellest blow of all.

Ten

A gift straight from heaven

I spent the afternoon trying to forget what Mum had said. I jumped our cross-country course on Prince and once again he went beautifully. Peter had checked out at mid-day saying, "Duty calls. It's been wonderful here. But now it's back to the regiment."

He had kissed Mum goodbye and shaken Dad's hand. Mum had turned away without a word, while Dad had stood in the drive waving him goodbye. In the evening I groomed Prince for ages and I couldn't help thinking that next year he could be gone, they could all be gone. We could be living in a small modern house with just Bob for company. And I wondered what I would do all day without any horses.

Later that evening Mr Meacher rang. I answered the telephone. "Is that Harriet?" he asked and without waiting for my reply said, "I thought you would like to know that the little girl is sitting up and taking food. The crisis seems over for the time being and the appeal opens tomorrow with a centre-page spread. There's a lot of local interest already and we hope to reach our target within forty-eight hours. I think it will make national news, so don't be surprised if radio and TV news contact you."

I tried to sound interested, but really at that moment I could only think of Black Pony Inn being put up for

364

sale. It had eclipsed everything else.

"So, Harriet, you're going to be news whether you like it or not, because it's a heart-warming story which shows the young in a new light, as carers rather than vandals. And that's what everybody likes to hear," Mr Meacher continued.

"I'm so glad, Mr Meacher. Thank you for calling," I replied slowly. "It's great, really great." I put down the receiver and rushed into the kitchen. "Mr Meacher thinks the appeal will raise enough money for Gillian to go to the USA in forty-eight hours. Aren't you going to cheer?" I cried.

"Terrific," said Mum.

"Another nightmare over," exclaimed James.

"I will bike into town first thing and get a copy," Ben said.

"It's like a dream come true," said Lisa. "Will Gillian see the paper?"

"I don't see why not," replied Mum.

"And I hated Mr Meacher. I thought he was a phoney," said James.

"Perhaps we can turn Black Pony Inn into a home for the elderly now," I suggested, looking at Mum. She was making a cup of Ovaltine for Colonel Hunter, who was already in bed. "I quite like elderly people."

"The wrinklies, you mean," said Ben.

"But we're not qualified. You need to be a nurse," Mum said.

"And I suppose you need fire escapes and wheelchairs and lifts," Ben added.

"We could hire a nurse and change the place," I suggested slowly. "It would be better than leaving, wouldn't it? I don't mind sleeping in the cellar, if only we can stay, Mum."

"Oh, Harriet," Mum cried, putting her arms round

me. "It may not happen, it's just a possibility. Anyway, life changes and one has to put up with it. Life was never meant to be a picnic. You may even like living somewhere else."

"Something will happen," Ben said. "Don't jump your fences until you come to them, Harriet. Something will turn up."

"I think I've heard that somewhere before," I said.

Bob followed me outside. The sun was setting above the common. Soon the summer would be over. I saw the leaves falling off the trees, the apples ripe in the orchard, the hedges festooned with blackberries. I saw Black Pony Inn with new people moving in. The old pump removed from the kitchen, the bread oven turned into an alcove with a light inside. I saw someone else sleeping in my bedroom and the fields sold one by one for development. I saw the trees in the orchard falling into the long grass, and the stables being converted into a house. I saw diggers and cranes and men with ladders. Then I saw us in a different house with a small garden and a front-door bell which went ding-dong. And I knew that I should be celebrating the money being raised for Gillian, but I couldn't. Bob licked my hand. I cleaned the loose boxes ready for the morning. I swept the yard and all the time I was thinking that in a moment we could be gone. Then I heard Dad calling, "Harriet. What are you doing out there? It's past your bedtime."

Bob ran ahead of me. The Stamps had gone out so Ben was watching show jumping on television. Mum was laying breakfast. I went up to bed and dreamed I was on a ship sailing to an unknown destination.

I was wakened next morning by Ben outside my room saying, "I've bought the *Echo*. They've got it all wrong, of course. And I look awful, really ugly."

I pulled on my dressing-gown and went downstairs and read the article with Ben, sitting by the Aga in the kitchen. It made Black Pony Inn sound like paradise and us like ministering angels. There was a photograph of the house in colour and one of us grouped around Lorraine with a caption which read: BELOVED PONY FOR SALE TO SAVE FRIEND, just as James had forecast. Lorraine had her ears back. I was scowling, but Lisa was smiling showing off her almost perfect teeth.

"They've done us proud," said Ben. "I didn't expect colour, did you? If only I looked better, but the house looks fantastic, doesn't it? You don't even notice the crooked chimney and you can't see the cracks in the walls. It looks so old, and smart as well. It looks worth half a million at least."

"Yes, it's as good as a house agent's advertisement," I said. "You know, unique property, grade 2 listed, that sort of thing."

We ate an early breakfast. Outside the flies were already buzzing, so I brought the horses in, or rather they rushed into their boxes and started munching feeds the moment I opened the gate.

It was like any other morning, except that our guests were soon leaving and the Gillian Ross Appeal in the *Morning Echo* had opened. And Lorraine was still for sale. But I couldn't object, because all our other horses might be going too. I'll ring up the Wallaces later, I thought. I'll apologise for our strange behaviour. I'll say, "Of course you can have Lorraine, you're a perfect home." And the money won't have to go to the Gillian Ross Appeal, it will go to placate the bank which won't lend us any more. It's all quite simple if you don't think too hard, I decided. If you keep your emotions out of it and don't look back at the wonderful days you've had riding your grey mare. We'll move, I thought, and Dad will go on selling double-glazing and Mum will get a part-time job, and they'll have the difference between Black Pony Inn and our new home stashed away in a building society.

I leaned over the loose-box doors and looked at Prince, who had arrived unrideable and untouchable. Now he was my best friend. I could hardly bear to look at Lorraine, because I had loved her so much and still did. She was part of my life, a whole chapter of it, a part

368

which would remain with me for ever. I spoke to dark brown Solitaire, who could out-walk all the others, and go all day without tiring. I spoke to the ponies and re-membered riding Limpet for the first time when I was six, just before Mum and Dad bought Black Pony Inn.

Presently Lisa appeared. "Mr Meacher's on the phone and there's been three other calls. Things are happening, Harriet. You're not crying, are you?" she asked.

I shook my head. "Nice things or nasty?" I asked.

"They sound nice," Lisa replied.

"Where's Dad?"

"Singing."

"I bet," I said. "Why do you lie, Lisa? You always do. It's a bad habit. And what about Lorraine? Is she still for sale?"

"I don't know, and don't you try that big sister act on me, Harriet," Lisa replied.

There was a feeling of autumn in the air already. A plane roared overhead. Soon Gillian might be on her way to the USA. We had started it all; so she would recover because one day a few weeks ago Lisa had arrived home from school crying. At that moment it should have been enough but it wasn't. I felt no triumph and my name in the *Echo* meant nothing to me. For none of it mattered compared with the possibility of losing Black Pony Inn.

"I suppose you're in one of your moods again, Harriet," Lisa said.

I didn't answer.

"Breakfast, Harriet," Dad called. "Hurry up, there's good news again. Run."

I walked. I still didn't believe it. I had given up believing anyone or anything. Dad was laying the table while Mum was cooking breakfast.

"Mr Meacher rang and talked for forty minutes. He's already had several thousand pounds donated, mostly from local companies. Isn't it fantastic?" she asked.

Colonel Hunter was still in bed. Recently he had seemed very old. He had stopped appearing for breakfast and now had it in his room every day. Miss Steele and Mrs Tomson were in the dining-room talking once again about Oxford. It seemed like the end of an era.

"I was going to several shows," I said. "But I suppose I had better not now."

"Why not, darling? What are you talking about?" asked Mum, unusually pretty in a flowered dress.

"Because if we've got no guests, we won't be able to afford anything, will we?" I asked. "We'll be back to square one, no money and no hope."

"But haven't you heard? Didn't Lisa tell you, darling? We've had three calls already about accommodation; and, even better, a woman who runs long-distance rides wants to put up here on a regular basis," Mum said.

I stared at Mum. "But will it be enough?" I asked.

"And Mr Meacher wants to help us to improve the place," Dad said. "We haven't worked out a deal yet. But we'll probably have a swimming-pool and tennis courts. We're going up in the world, Harriet, so don't look so glum. Of course we've got to work things out. Mr Meacher wants to put up his business associates here. He owns lots of companies as well as the *Echo*. I think we'll even have a chef, and a waitress," finished Dad, laughing.

"And so I'm not selling Lorraine after all, because they expect the fund for Gillian will be over-subscribed by lunch-time," cried Lisa.

"We're going to have a celebration tonight," Dad said. "Mr Meacher has invited us to dine with him. We deserve a good meal, don't we?"

"Definitely," replied Ben, appearing in the kitchen.

"I thought . . . I thought," I began but now I couldn't remember what I had thought, because a feeling of total happiness was stealing over me. Then I thought: We've won, we've won on both fronts. Maybe God has answered our prayers. Maybe it was going to happen anyway – who can tell? Only one thing is certain – if we had left Gillian to die we would have been selling Black Pony Inn by the end of the summer.

"An architect's calling later to see what we can do

about the old rooms above the stables," Dad said.

"But they aren't safe; the floors have holes in them," I replied.

"Exactly. He's going to make a plan. We want them as rooms for the long-distance riders, with a bathroom at one end. They'll eat in the house and sleep over the stables. They'll love it," Dad said.

"And if anyone rings up, Lorraine's no longer for sale," Ben added. "It's definite. We agreed to it five minutes ago."

In my imagination I saw everything done up; the window frames gleaming white, the old stairs to the rooms where grooms had once slept repaired. The sound of

many hoofs on the cobbles. A coming and a going which hadn't happened there for years.

"If it takes off, we'll get a girl groom to help, so you won't have to work so hard," Mum told me, her arm round my shoulders, her face against mine.

"Mr Meacher may buy a couple of horses and keep them here, so you see everything's going to be all right after all," Lisa said smugly.

"And Mr Meacher wants us to stay in his villa in Corfu," Dad continued. "It's off the beaten track, and it sounds beautiful."

"I just don't believe it," I said. "So many things can't happen all at once. It isn't real. There must be a catch somewhere."

"Black Pony Inn remains ours," said Dad firmly. "The agreement is only for ten years. After that we will review the situation. It's a godsend, Harriet, a gift straight from heaven. The solicitors are drawing up the details today. This means we're really safe at last. We needn't worry ever again."

I wasn't used to gifts straight from heaven. I couldn't believe it and still thought that there must be a catch somewhere.

"And now we have to go to hospital to see Gillian," Mum said.

"What, all of us?" I cried. She nodded.

"It's another publicity stunt, isn't it?" I asked.

"Yes, but in a good cause. Go and do your hair and put on tidy clothes. You smell of horse, Harriet. And hurry."

"But I haven't had any breakfast," I cried.

"It doesn't matter, eat something in the car," Mum said.

When we reached the hospital, we found Gillian sitting up in bed in a private room, surrounded by

flowers. There were reporters in the corridor and a flustered nurse who said, "You're late and this hospital is
no place for the press."

"Just look at the cards, there must be hundreds,"
Mum cried smiling brightly.

Lisa rushed straight into the room and, throwing her
arms round Gillian, cried, "Oh, it's so lovely to see you."

The nurse looked on disapprovingly. "You can't stay
long. She mustn't be tired out; she's got a long journey
ahead of her," she said.

We stood around Gillian's bed while lights flashed
and questions were asked and answered, written down,
recorded. There were tall men in sandals from television,
earnest young women from the *Echo*. Lisa talked and
talked. Ben smiled the polite smile which he keeps for
such occasions, a smile which never reaches his eyes,
which is really not a smile at all. I looked at the polished
floor and thought of Black Pony Inn done up, while
James picked at his fingernails and Mum and Dad stood
in the doorway holding hands. At last it was over.
Gillian lay back in bed, exhausted. The nurse ushered us
out while Lisa waved, calling, "See you, Gillian. Next
stop USA."

We hurried along hospital corridors to the car park
which was now jammed with cars.

"Well done, you were fine," Dad said.

"I don't want to be famous. I know that now. I hate
the press," I said.

"I don't. I think I want to be an actress," Lisa cried,
running ahead.

After lunch, which was cold meat and salad, Ben and
I rode through the woods talking about the future.

"It's going to be different, of course," Ben said.
"We're going to have more time and holidays abroad
like everyone else."

"Do you think the girl groom will look after our horses too?" I asked.

"I expect so. I expect Mr Meacher will pay a lot to keep his horses here. I think it's rather like winning the pools," Ben continued.

"I suppose we'll have to be a bit smarter," I said as we started to trot.

"Yes, we'll have new clothes for a start and new tack. Everything is going to be run on a different basis. I think Dad is going to be paid a huge salary to be manager. We'll probably have a licence too. We're going to be rich, Harriet," said Ben grandly.

I thought of new tack, of a navy-blue riding-coat with a red lining which I had wanted for years and years. I imagined a horse box with a wide ramp and room for five horses. I imagined going out for the day and knowing that there was someone to look after the horses, so that we needn't hurry back.

"We'll have to change our image. We must look successful. I expect we'll fly a flag, that sort of thing," Ben continued.

"What flag?"

"Our own flag," said Ben.

The horses caught our mood and tossed their heads and reached into their bits. The woods were cool and secret, the sun bright above us.

"You'll have to buy things for Corfu," said Ben as we turned homewards. "Suntan lotion, a bikini, dark glasses. You'll have to change a bit."

"I'm hoping to get out of going," I said. "It's not my sort of life. I'm not right for it."

But Ben just laughed and trotted on.

After that we dressed up to go out. It wasn't easy because we simply hadn't the right clothes, but we did our best.

There were cameras at the dinner too – Mr Meacher, self-made man, newspaper baron dining with the Pembertons; that would be the caption I decided.

There was selection of starters, followed by a huge choice of dishes, followed by something off the sweet trolley or cheese. None of us were used to eating so much and Lisa muddled up her knives. Mrs Meacher talked to me about school. She told me about her education which had been expensive and private. I tried to pay attention to what she was saying, but all the time I was imagining Black Pony Inn restored to its former glory with more rooms and bathrooms added, but carefully because Black Pony Inn is a listed building and cannot be spoilt. I saw new riding-clothes for me and new rugs for Prince, and Lorraine growing old in peace with us. I saw worry wiped from Mum's face for ever and Dad sitting in an office totting up the money coming in. I saw myself going out with Richard, wearing new shoes and a new dress. I saw Gillian returning cured.

Then I noticed Mum looking at me and saying, "You'll never have to give up your room again for guests, Harriet, because we're keeping the old bit of the house separate."

Everyone was standing up now because the dinner was over. Mr Meacher kissed me and Mum goodbye. Except for the moustache, his face was smooth and smelled of aftershave lotion. Dad kissed Mrs Meacher and so did James. Ben avoided kissing anyone and so did Lisa. Outside the sky was full of stars.

"What a dinner," said Ben, smiling his true smile as we walked towards the car park.

"I ate too much. I had two helpings of nearly everything and now I feel sick," complained Lisa.

"We must get a better car," said Mum, getting into the driving seat of our old estate car. "We must cultivate a new image. You know the saying, success breeds success. Well, we must look successful from now on, all of us. No more old clothes and elbows out of sweaters. If you need something new, say so. All right?"

"Okay," I said. "But I hate being smart."

Bob welcomed us home. The horses whinnied from the paddocks. It was difficult to accept that Gillian was actually going to the USA. It just seemed too good to be true. Suddenly I seemed to have everything I had ever wanted. But then, as I climbed into bed, I heard Mum say to Dad, "Sally has left a message saying the Stamps have left. Apparently they packed their bags in a great hurry after a phone call. It sounds fishy to me." Sally had come in to see to the guests while we were out. She's young and cheerful and very efficient, unlike Peggy, our more regular help.

"Well, at least they had paid up," replied Dad. "So that's all right. We needn't worry, darling, even if they didn't say goodbye."

But of course nothing is as simple as that, and the next morning we were woken by policemen hammering on the front door. There were three of them and they flashed cards at Dad, muttering "Police", and rushed into the house with Dad in hot pursuit, still in his pyjamas, crying, "What do you want? This is private property. Where's your search warrant?"

Mum followed barefoot, in her dressing gown, wringing her hands together, while Bob barked and Miss Steel appeared at the top of the stairs in her nightgown asking, "What is it? Is the house on fire?"

Only Ben remained calm. "If you're looking for the Stamps, they left yesterday evening while we were out. They cleared their room. I checked last night; there's not a thing left of theirs, not even a paper tissue," he told the police.

378

"How do you know that?" I asked a second later.

"Because I saw the note before Dad did. I always knew there was something wrong with them."

I sat on a chair in the kitchen wondering what it was

like to be the Stamps, forever on the run, while Dad showed the police out and Mum put the kettle on to boil. "We shouldn't have taken them. But they did pay in advance and we were so hard up I couldn't refuse," she said.

"But never again," I answered. "Never ever, please, Mum."

"I wonder whether they've taken anything," said Ben.

"The police say we're to check everything. Apparently Tony Stamp is well known to them under the name of Terry Blackstone," said Dad, returning to the kitchen. "He has been sent to prison three times for theft."

"Oh no," cried Mum. "And he's been staying here. How awful."

"I'm so sorry for the boys, no wonder they always seemed on their guard," I said. "They were probably expecting the police to turn up."

James and Lisa were still sleeping upstairs. The rest of us discussed the Stamps and drank tea in the kitchen, while day broke outside, all pink and yellow, with birds singing in the tall trees.

"People don't usually pay cash, that should have put me on my guard for a start," Mum said.

"We had better see what's gone," suggested Dad, sounding resigned. So we checked everything valuable; but miraculously nothing was missing.

"They must have liked us after all," said Ben, because some of our ornaments are quite valuable, and they would have been easy enough to steal.

"It's funny how we knew from the start they were wrong somewhere, at least I did," I cried.

"Has Dad checked the money from the fête? Oh my God, where did he hide it?" cried Ben suddenly. "I bet he's forgotten all about it, oh sugar, I bet it's gone and then we'll be in the soup."

380

We found Dad shaving and of course he had forgotten all about the money and now we were in turmoil with Bob running about barking madly, imagining some sort of game. Dad seemed very slow. I think he had drunk a little too much the night before, which was why Mum had driven home. After several seconds he shouted, "Oh good lord, where on earth did I put it? I can't remember."

Then he rushed to the chest in the hall with us following him at high speed and Bob in the rear still barking. Lisa and James were rushing about in their night things shouting, "Whatever is it now? What's all the fuss about?" But of course no one had time to tell them. Dad pulled a pile of cushions and old curtains out of the chest and there was the money still in the tin.

And this is really where my story ends. For the money

was banked and Gillian caught her flight to the USA in time and months later returned cured. And as we had the Meachers' house in Corfu to ourselves, Richard and Virginia joined us there, and Ben found himself his first girlfriend ever, and Mum and Dad walked about holding hands, saying that it was their second honeymoon. Poor Lisa looked rather left out. Sally, who turned out to have horsy qualifications, looked after Bob and the horses while we were away. And though I grew to like Richard more and more, we never got further than holding hands, perhaps because, as Lisa says, I'm very backward when it comes to boys.

When at last we returned home, the rooms above the stables had become bedrooms with marvellous beams and a bathroom and loo. But my room was just the same, and it was wonderful to know that it was mine as long as I wanted it, that I would never have to give it up for guests again.

The horses welcomed us home, and Bob ran round and round in circles barking with joy. There wasn't much of the summer left now, but somehow it didn't matter any more, because our worries seemed to have been swept away like autumn leaves. Soon Dad stopped selling double-glazing and became fully occupied supervising the additions to Black Pony Inn. Mr Meacher visited us in a chauffeur-driven car from time to time, his grey hair always immaculate. As for myself, I wandered about in a happy dream thinking how life might have been with no Lorraine and no more Black Pony Inn. Instead I seemed to be living in paradise, and all because we had decided one July day to help someone who was in the shadow of death. And, as Mum says, there must be a moral there somewhere.

We never saw the Stamps again. But Mum visits Colonel Hunter regularly in his new home. Miss Steele and Mrs Tomson write from time to time and seem to like living in Oxford. As for the rest of us, time moves on and we're all changing, but the summer when we held the fête will always remain a milestone in our lives, a time when great things were accomplished at Black Pony Inn. A summer when our fortunes changed for ever.